Garfield

BY JIM DAVIS ®

VOLUME 3

Garfield

BY JIM DAVIS

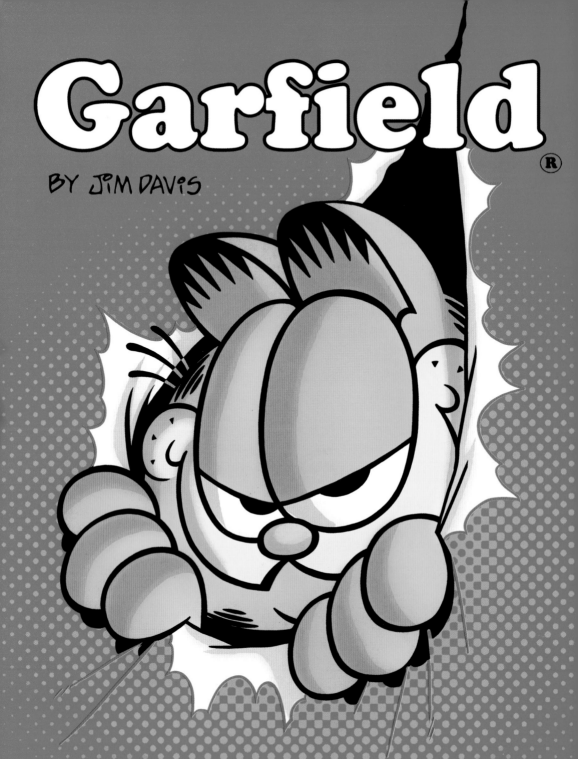

ROSS RICHIE CEO & Founder • **JACK CUMMINS** President • **MARK SMYLIE** Chief Creative Officer • **MATT GAGNON** Editor-in-Chief • **FILIP SABLIK** VP of Publishing & Marketing • **STEPHEN CHRISTY** VP of Development **LANCE KREITER** VP of Licensing & Merchandising • **PHIL BARBARO** VP of Finance • **BRYCE CARLSON** Managing Editor • **MEL CAYLO** Marketing Manager • **SCOTT NEWMAN** Production Design Manager • **DAFNA PLEBAN** Editor • **SHANNON WATTERS** Editor **ERIC HARBURN** Editor • **REBECCA TAYLOR** Editor • **CHRIS ROSA** Assistant Editor • **ALEX GALER** Assistant Editor • **WHITNEY LEOPARD** Assistant Editor • **JASMINE AMIRI** Assistant Editor • **STEPHANIE GONZAGA** Graphic Designer **MIKE LOPEZ** Production Designer • **HANNAH NANCE PARTLOW** Production Designer • **DEVIN FUNCHES** E-Commerce & Inventory Coordinator • **BRIANNA HART** Executive Assistant • **AARON FERRARA** Operations Assistant • **JOSE MEZA** Sales Assistant

kaboom!™

A catalog record of this book is available from OCLC and from the KaBOOM! website, www.kaboom-studios.com, on the Librarians Page.

BOOM! Studios, 5670 Wilshire Boulevard, Suite 450, Los Angeles, CA 90036-5679. Printed in China. First Printing. ISBN: 978-1-60886-348-8 eISBN: 9781613982020

CHAPTER ONE

"AN ODIE STORY"
WRITTEN BY
MARK EVANIER
ART BY
ANDY HIRSCH

"PET FORCE VS. THE FEARSOME FOUR!"
WRITTEN BY
SCOTT NICKEL
ART BY
GARY BARKER
WITH MARK & STEPHANIE HEIKE

CHAPTER TWO

"MONDAY MADNESS"
WRITTEN BY
MARK EVANIER
ART BY
MIKE DeCARLO

"THE LASAGNA MONSTER"
WRITTEN BY
SCOTT NICKEL
ART BY
DAVID DeGRAND

CHAPTER THREE

"THE NEW CUTE"
WRITTEN BY
MARK EVANIER
ART BY
ANDY HIRSCH

"PET FORCE TIME OUT"
WRITTEN BY
SCOTT NICKEL
ART BY
FRED HEMBECK

CHAPTER FOUR

"THE CATBIRD SEAT"
WRITTEN BY
MARK EVANIER
ART BY
ANDY HIRSCH

"RETURN OF THE LASAGNA MONSTER"
WRITTEN BY
SCOTT NICKEL
ART BY
DAVID DeGRAND

COLORS BY
LISA MOORE

LETTERS BY
STEVE WANDS

COVER BY
GARY BARKER & DAN DAVIS
COLORS BY LISA MOORE

TRADE DESIGNER
MIKE LOPEZ

ASSISTANT EDITOR
CHRIS ROSA

EDITOR
MATT GAGNON

GARFIELD CREATED BY
JIM DAVIS

SPECIAL THANKS TO SCOTT NICKEL, DAVID REDDICK, AND THE ENTIRE PAWS, INC. TEAM.

CHAPTER 1

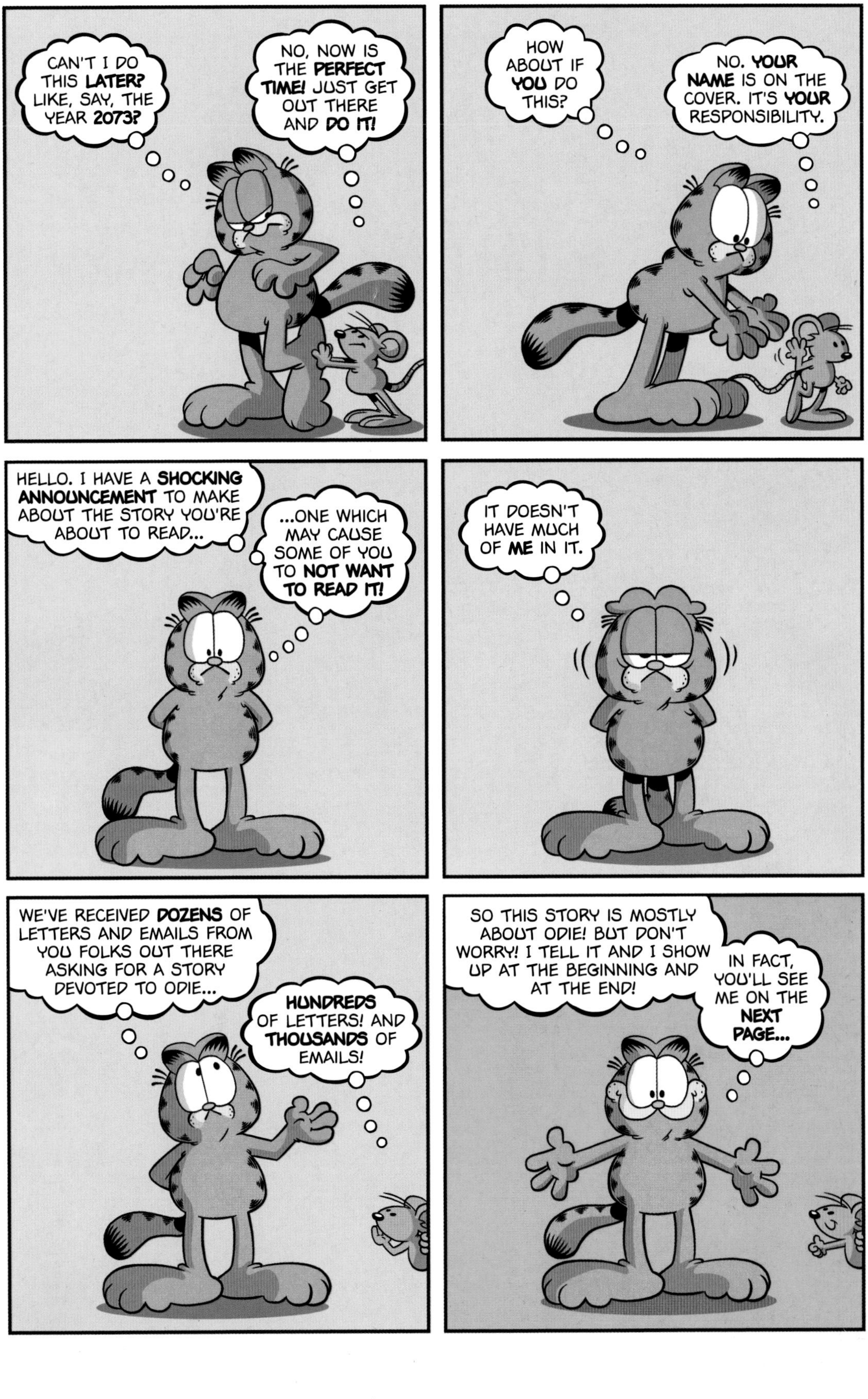

CAN'T I DO THIS LATER? LIKE, SAY, THE YEAR 2073?
NO, NOW IS THE PERFECT TIME! JUST GET OUT THERE AND DO IT!
HOW ABOUT IF YOU DO THIS?
NO. YOUR NAME IS ON THE COVER. IT'S YOUR RESPONSIBILITY.
HELLO. I HAVE A SHOCKING ANNOUNCEMENT TO MAKE ABOUT THE STORY YOU'RE ABOUT TO READ...
...ONE WHICH MAY CAUSE SOME OF YOU TO NOT WANT TO READ IT!
IT DOESN'T HAVE MUCH OF ME IN IT.
WE'VE RECEIVED DOZENS OF LETTERS AND EMAILS FROM YOU FOLKS OUT THERE ASKING FOR A STORY DEVOTED TO ODIE...
HUNDREDS OF LETTERS! AND THOUSANDS OF EMAILS!
SO THIS STORY IS MOSTLY ABOUT ODIE! BUT DON'T WORRY! I TELL IT AND I SHOW UP AT THE BEGINNING AND AT THE END!
IN FACT, YOU'LL SEE ME ON THE NEXT PAGE...

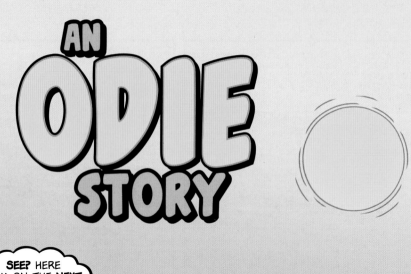

AN ODIE STORY

SEE? HERE I AM ON THE **NEXT PAGE!** I SEEM TO BE ON THE **NEXT ONE,** TOO!

THIS IS ME, JUST TRYING TO CATCH A LITTLE NAP ON THE FRONT LAWN, SO I'M NOT TOO TIRED TO GO INSIDE AND NAP **IN THERE!**

IT WOULD BE A PEACEFUL THING TO DO IF A CERTAIN "SOMEBODY" WHO **THIS STORY IS MAINLY ABOUT** DIDN'T WANT ME TO THROW THE STICK SO HE COULD FETCH IT!

ARF! ARF!

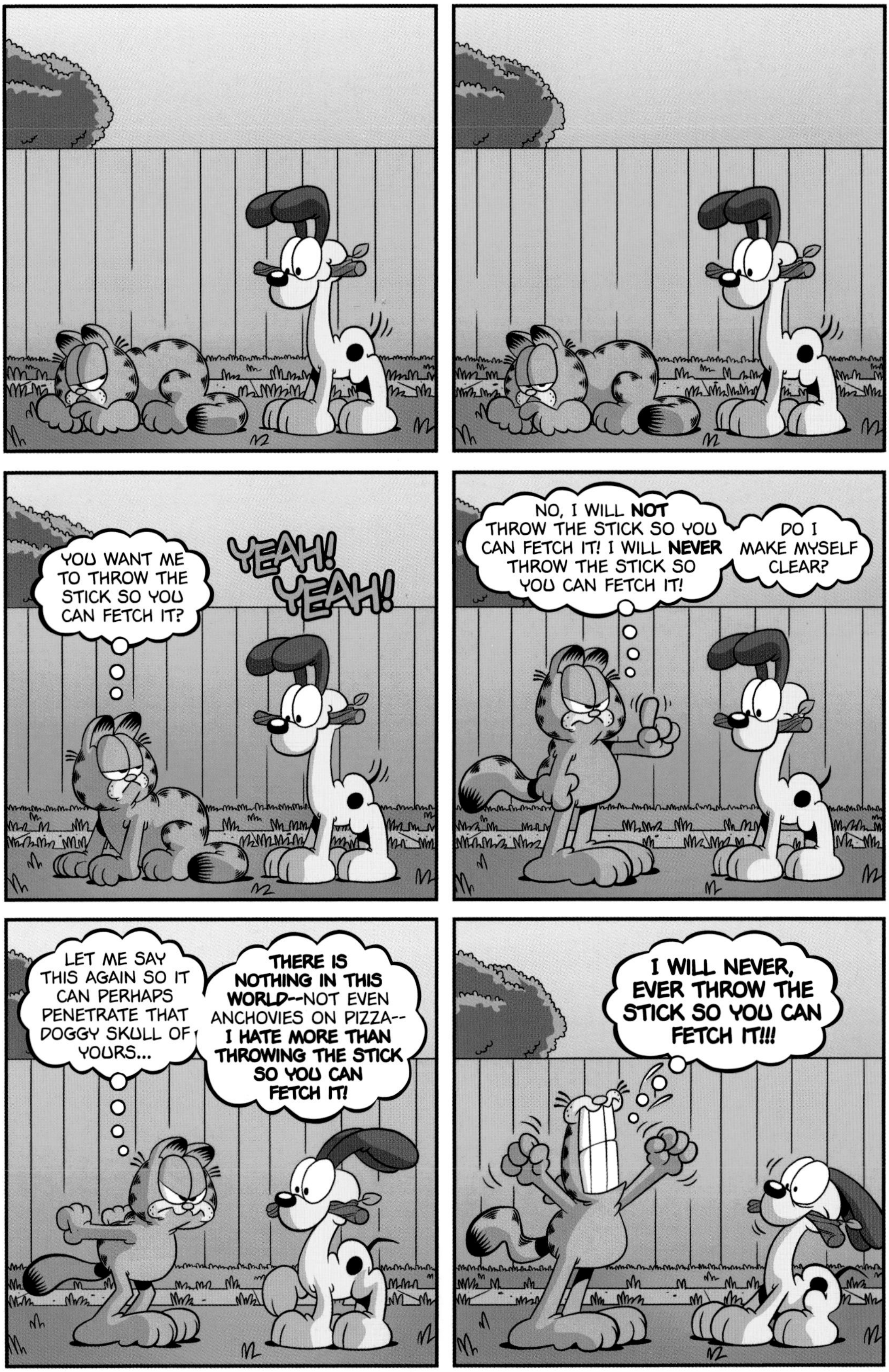
YOU WANT ME TO THROW THE STICK SO YOU CAN FETCH IT?
YEAH! YEAH!
NO, I WILL **NOT** THROW THE STICK SO YOU CAN FETCH IT! I WILL **NEVER** THROW THE STICK SO YOU CAN FETCH IT!
DO I MAKE MYSELF CLEAR?
LET ME SAY THIS AGAIN SO IT CAN PERHAPS PENETRATE THAT DOGGY SKULL OF YOURS...
THERE IS NOTHING IN THIS WORLD--NOT EVEN ANCHOVIES ON PIZZA--**I HATE MORE THAN THROWING THE STICK SO YOU CAN FETCH IT!**
I WILL NEVER, EVER THROW THE STICK SO YOU CAN FETCH IT!!!

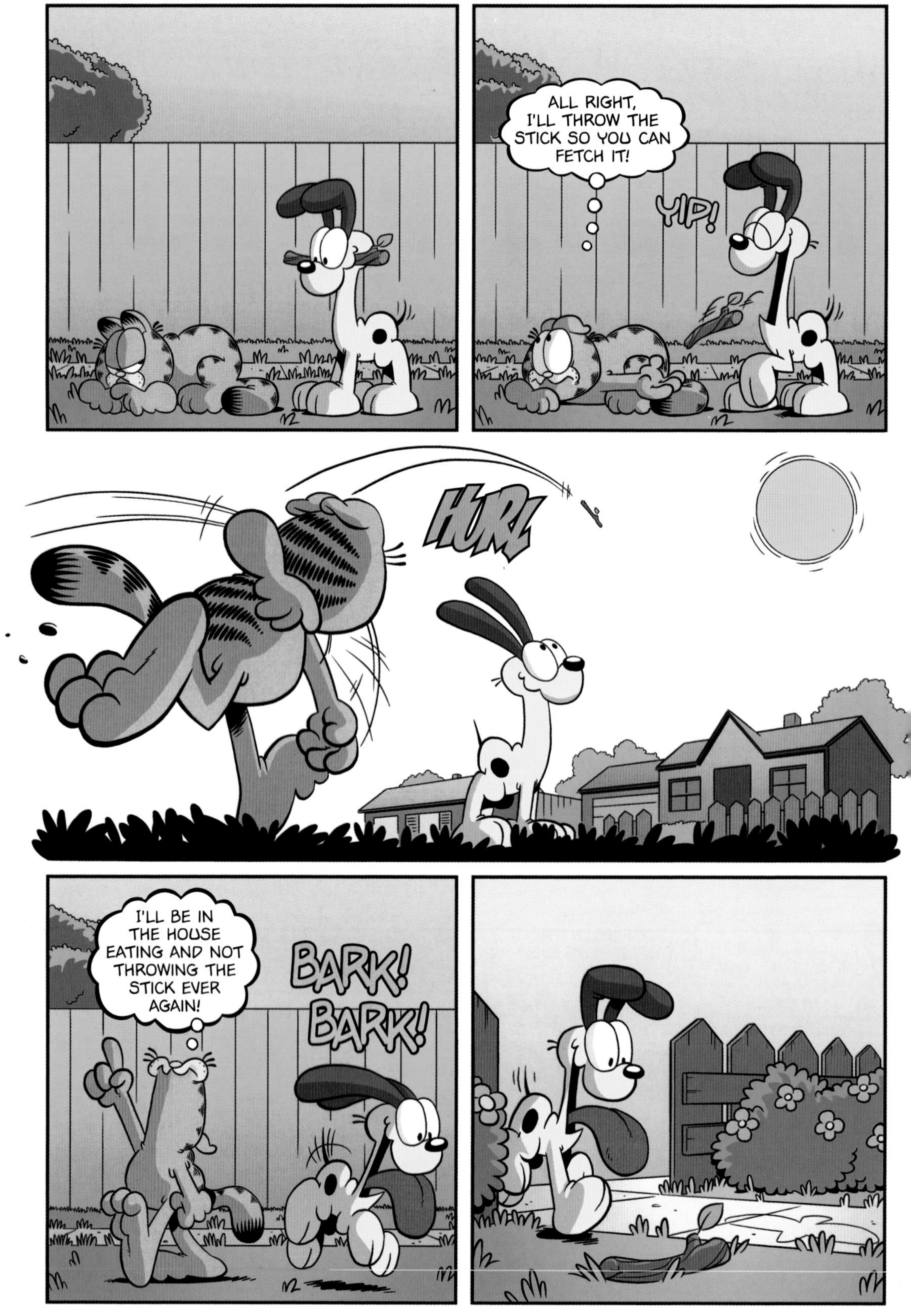
ALL RIGHT, I'LL THROW THE STICK SO YOU CAN FETCH IT!
YIP!
HURL
I'LL BE IN THE HOUSE EATING AND NOT THROWING THE STICK EVER AGAIN!
BARK! BARK!

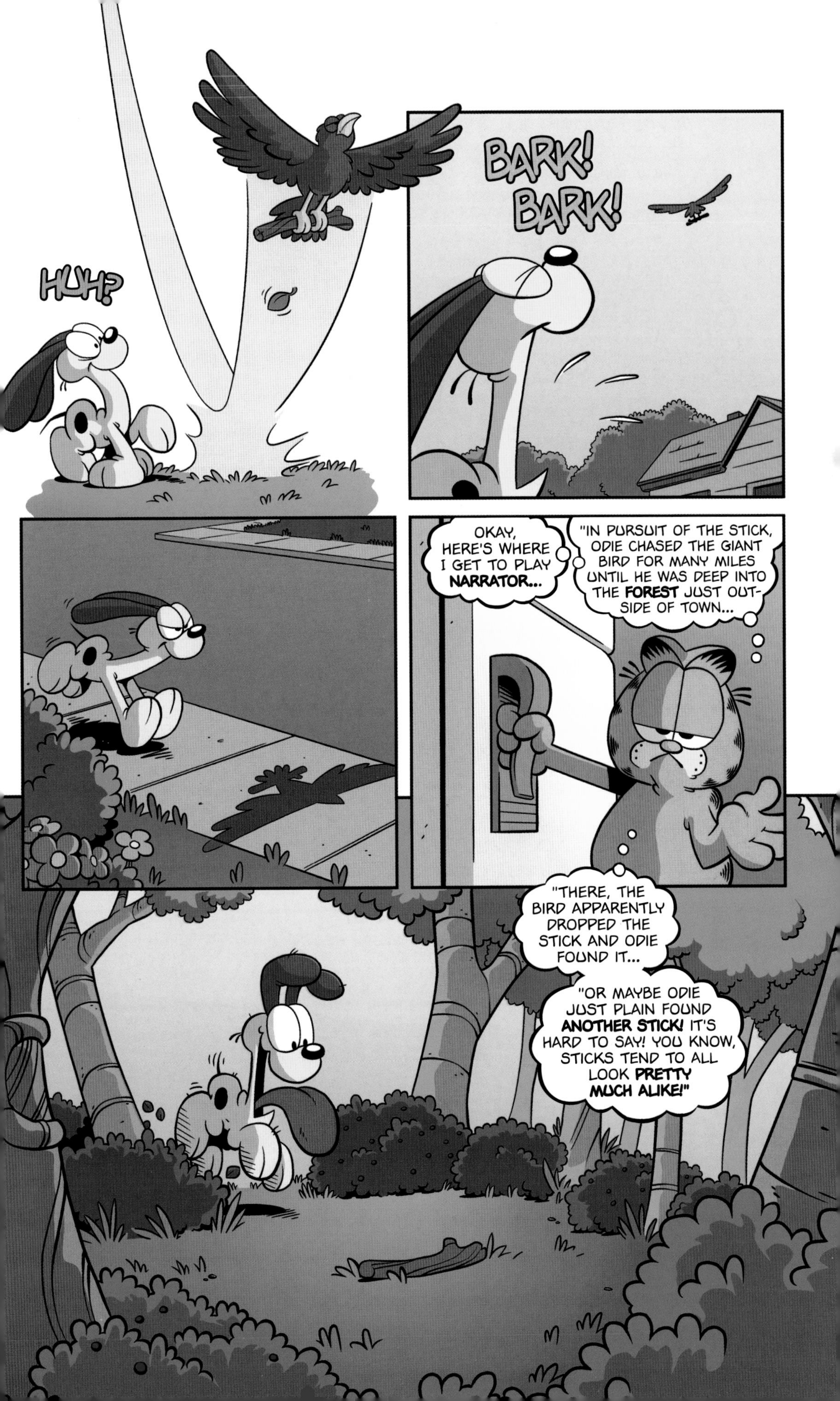
HUH?
BARK! BARK!
OKAY, HERE'S WHERE I GET TO PLAY NARRATOR...
"IN PURSUIT OF THE STICK, ODIE CHASED THE GIANT BIRD FOR MANY MILES UNTIL HE WAS DEEP INTO THE FOREST JUST OUT-SIDE OF TOWN...
"THERE, THE BIRD APPARENTLY DROPPED THE STICK AND ODIE FOUND IT...
"OR MAYBE ODIE JUST PLAIN FOUND ANOTHER STICK! IT'S HARD TO SAY! YOU KNOW, STICKS TEND TO ALL LOOK PRETTY MUCH ALIKE!"

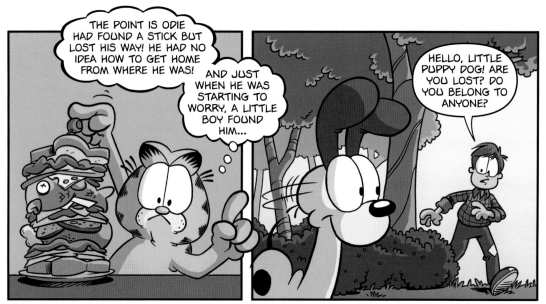

THE POINT IS ODIE HAD FOUND A STICK BUT LOST HIS WAY! HE HAD NO IDEA HOW TO GET HOME FROM WHERE HE WAS!

AND JUST WHEN HE WAS STARTING TO WORRY, A LITTLE BOY FOUND HIM...

HELLO, LITTLE PUPPY DOG! ARE YOU LOST? DO YOU BELONG TO ANYONE?

BOY, YOU'RE FRIENDLY! I WISH I HAD A DOG LIKE YOU BUT MY POP...HE WON'T LET ME HAVE A DOG.

HE SAYS THEY'RE TOO MUCH TROUBLE!

YOU LOOK HUNGRY, LITTLE PUPPY! COME HOME WITH ME AND I'LL FIND YOU SOMETHING TO EAT!

WE'LL JUST HAVE TO MAKE SURE MY POP DOESN'T SEE YOU!

THAT'S WHERE WE LIVE! IT'S JUST MY **POP AND ME!** HE WORKS DOWN AT THE MILL ALL DAY SO I'M ALONE A LOT!

SO THE BOY--WHOSE NAME WAS RONNIE--PLAYED ALL AFTERNOON WITH ODIE! HE THREW THE STICK AND ODIE FETCHED IT! THEN HE THREW THE STICK AND ODIE FETCHED IT! THEN HE THREW THE STICK AND ODIE FETCHED IT! THEN HE THREW THE STICK AND ODIE FETCHED IT! THEN HE THREW THE STICK AND ODIE FETCHED IT! THEN HE THREW THE STICK AND ODIE FETCHED IT! THEN HE THREW THE STICK AND ODIE FETCHED IT! THEN HE THREW THE STICK AND ODIE FETCHED IT! THEN HE THREW THE STICK AND ODIE FETCHED IT! THEN HE THREW THE STICK AND ODIE FETCHED IT! THEN HE THREW THE STICK AND ODIE FETCHED IT! THEN HE THREW THE STICK AND ODIE FETCHED IT! THEN HE THREW THE STICK AND ODIE FETCHED IT! THEN HE THREW THE

AND THEN DO YOU KNOW WHAT THEY DID **NEXT?**

HE THREW THE STICK AND ODIE FETCHED IT!

HA! BET YOU DIDN'T EXPECT **THAT!**

HERE--**THIS** IS WHAT IT LOOKED LIKE...

GOOD GOING, BOY!

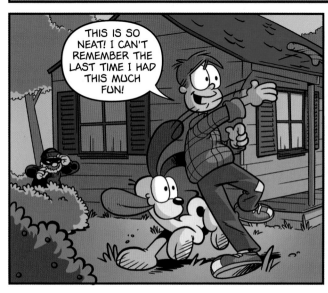

THIS IS SO NEAT! I CAN'T REMEMBER THE LAST TIME I HAD THIS MUCH FUN!

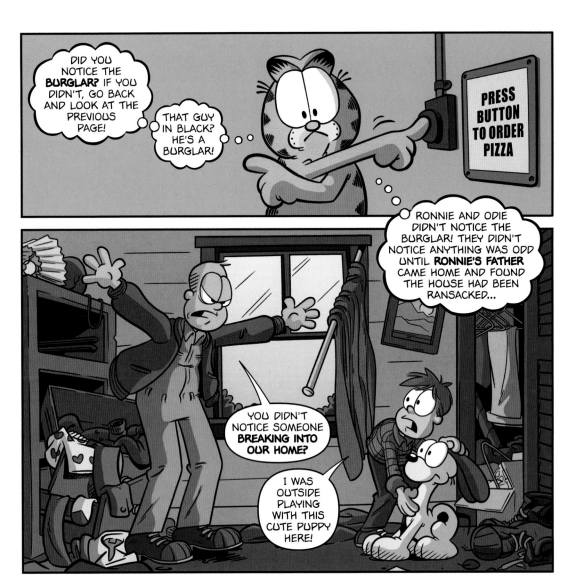

DID YOU NOTICE THE **BURGLAR?** IF YOU DIDN'T, GO BACK AND LOOK AT THE PREVIOUS PAGE!

THAT GUY IN BLACK? HE'S A BURGLAR!

PRESS BUTTON TO ORDER PIZZA

RONNIE AND ODIE DIDN'T NOTICE THE BURGLAR! THEY DIDN'T NOTICE ANYTHING WAS ODD UNTIL **RONNIE'S FATHER** CAME HOME AND FOUND THE HOUSE HAD BEEN RANSACKED...

YOU DIDN'T NOTICE SOMEONE **BREAKING INTO OUR HOME?**

I WAS OUTSIDE PLAYING WITH THIS CUTE PUPPY HERE!

THAT'S **ANOTHER THING!** I THOUGHT I TOLD YOU **NO DOGS!** DIDN'T I TELL YOU THAT?

YOU SAID I COULDN'T HAVE ONE BUT YOU DIDN'T SAY ANYTHING ABOUT NOT PLAYING WITH ANY THAT CAME AROUND!

SEE? THAT'S ONE REASON WHY I DIDN'T WANT **ANY DOGS AROUND!**

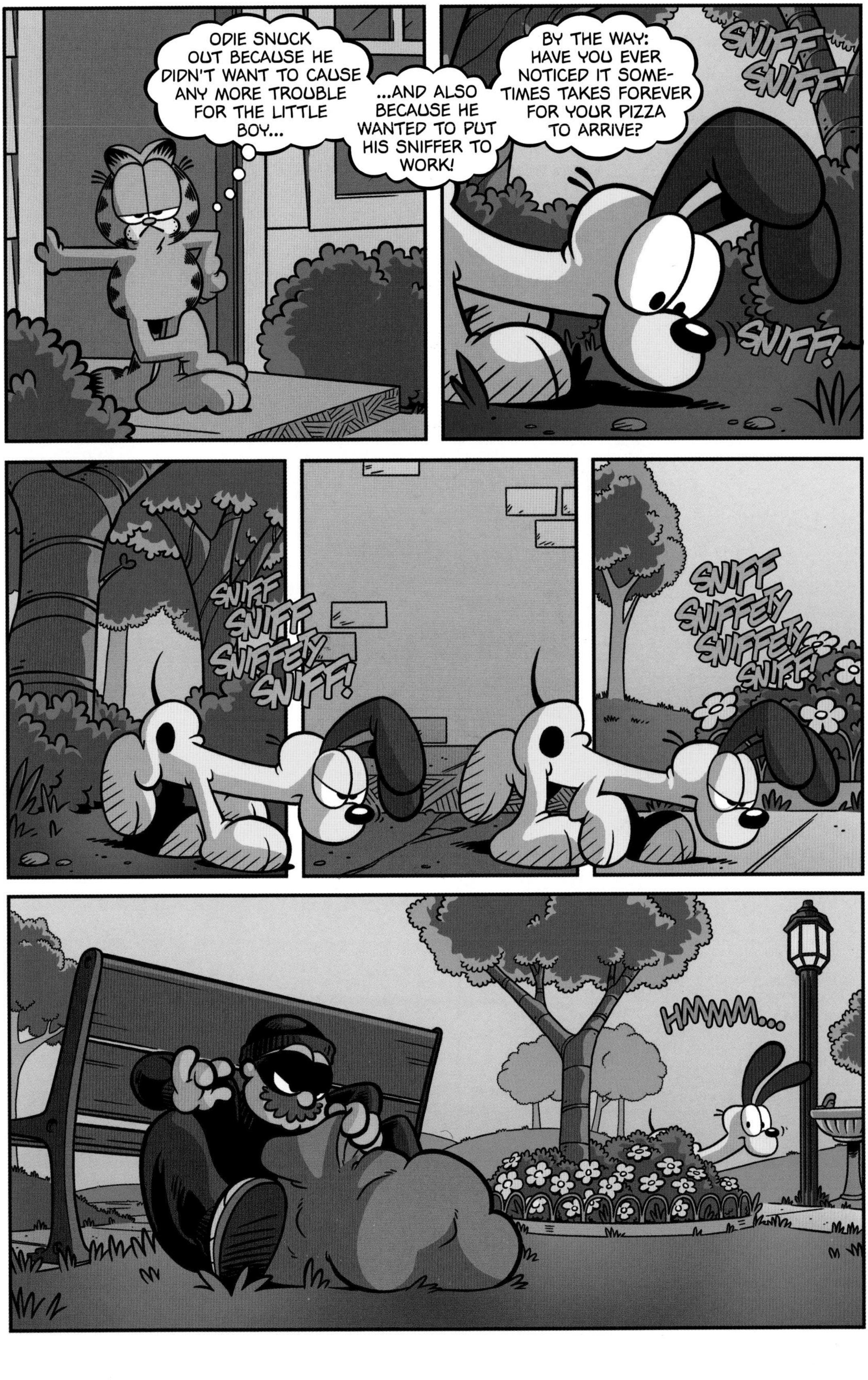
ODIE SNUCK OUT BECAUSE HE DIDN'T WANT TO CAUSE ANY MORE TROUBLE FOR THE LITTLE BOY...
...AND ALSO BECAUSE HE WANTED TO PUT HIS SNIFFER TO WORK!
BY THE WAY: HAVE YOU EVER NOTICED IT SOME-TIMES TAKES FOREVER FOR YOUR PIZZA TO ARRIVE?
SNIFF SNIFF
SNIFF!
SNIFF SNIFF SNIFFETY SNIFF!
SNIFF SNIFFETY SNIFFETY SNIFF!
HMMM...

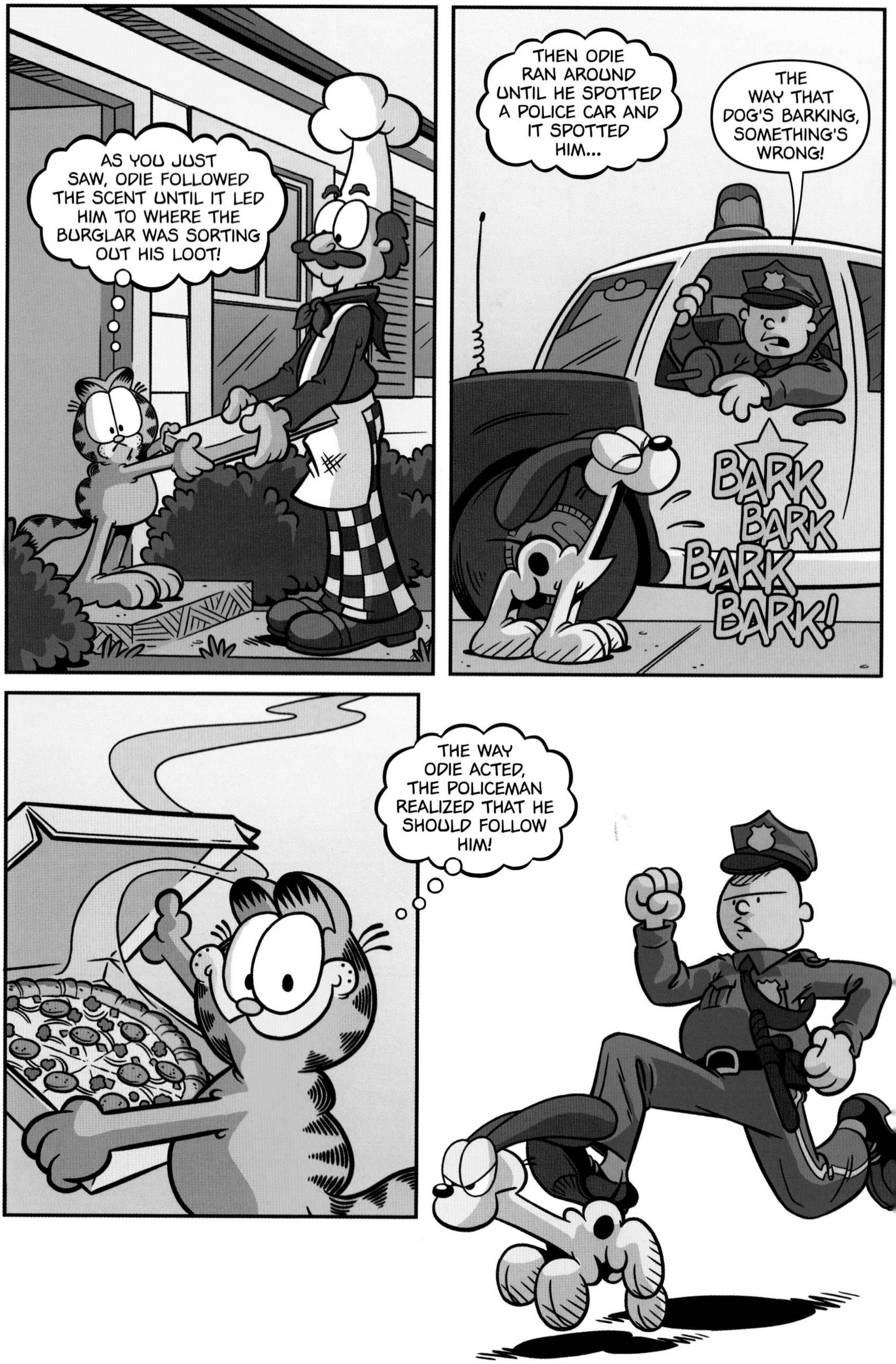
AS YOU JUST SAW, ODIE FOLLOWED THE SCENT UNTIL IT LED HIM TO WHERE THE BURGLAR WAS SORTING OUT HIS LOOT!
THEN ODIE RAN AROUND UNTIL HE SPOTTED A POLICE CAR AND IT SPOTTED HIM...
THE WAY THAT DOG'S BARKING, SOMETHING'S WRONG!
BARK BARK BARK BARK!
THE WAY ODIE ACTED, THE POLICEMAN REALIZED THAT HE SHOULD FOLLOW HIM!

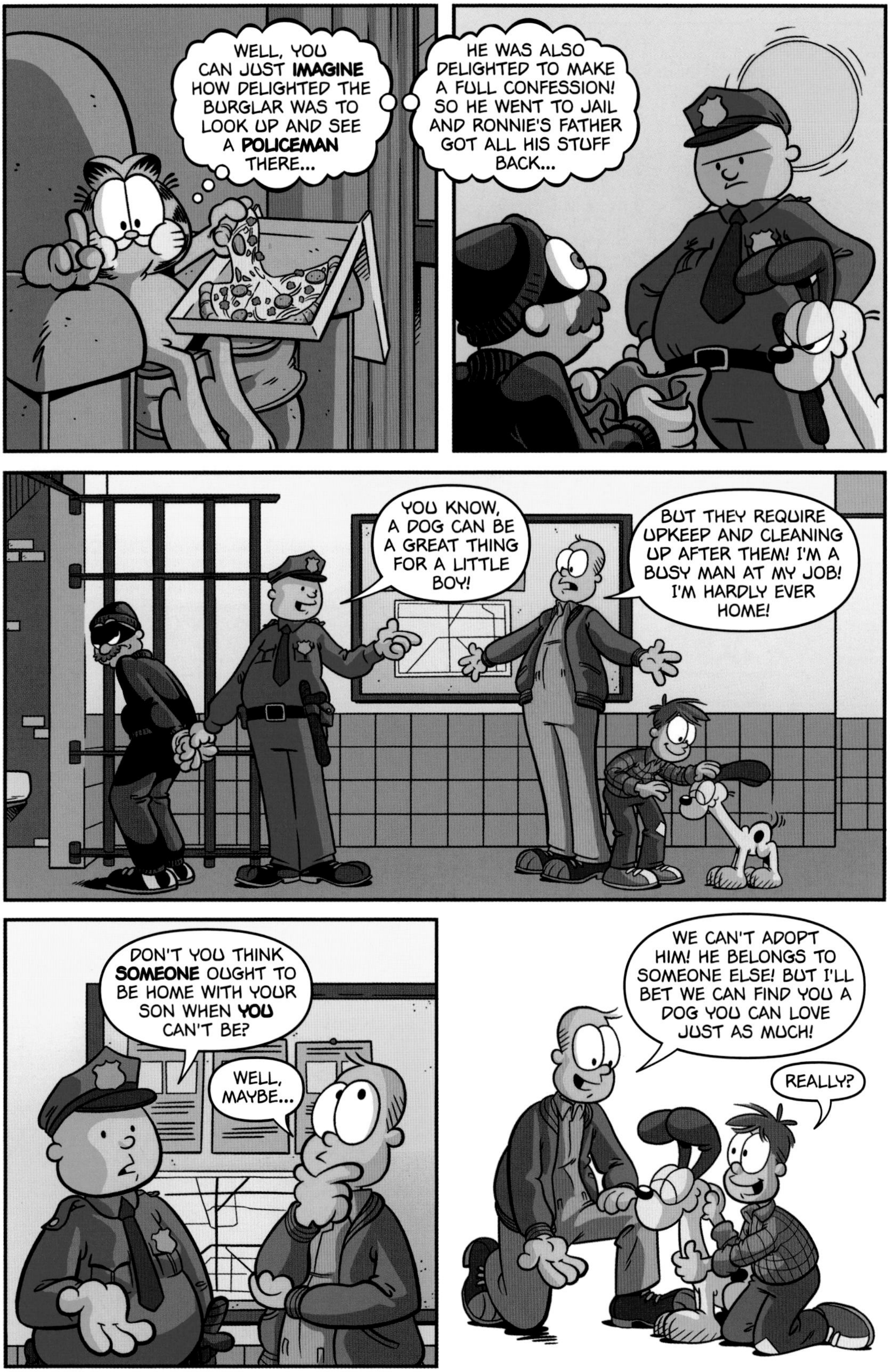
WELL, YOU CAN JUST IMAGINE HOW DELIGHTED THE BURGLAR WAS TO LOOK UP AND SEE A POLICEMAN THERE...
HE WAS ALSO DELIGHTED TO MAKE A FULL CONFESSION! SO HE WENT TO JAIL AND RONNIE'S FATHER GOT ALL HIS STUFF BACK...
YOU KNOW, A DOG CAN BE A GREAT THING FOR A LITTLE BOY!
BUT THEY REQUIRE UPKEEP AND CLEANING UP AFTER THEM! I'M A BUSY MAN AT MY JOB! I'M HARDLY EVER HOME!
DON'T YOU THINK SOMEONE OUGHT TO BE HOME WITH YOUR SON WHEN YOU CAN'T BE?
WELL, MAYBE...
WE CAN'T ADOPT HIM! HE BELONGS TO SOMEONE ELSE! BUT I'LL BET WE CAN FIND YOU A DOG YOU CAN LOVE JUST AS MUCH!
REALLY?

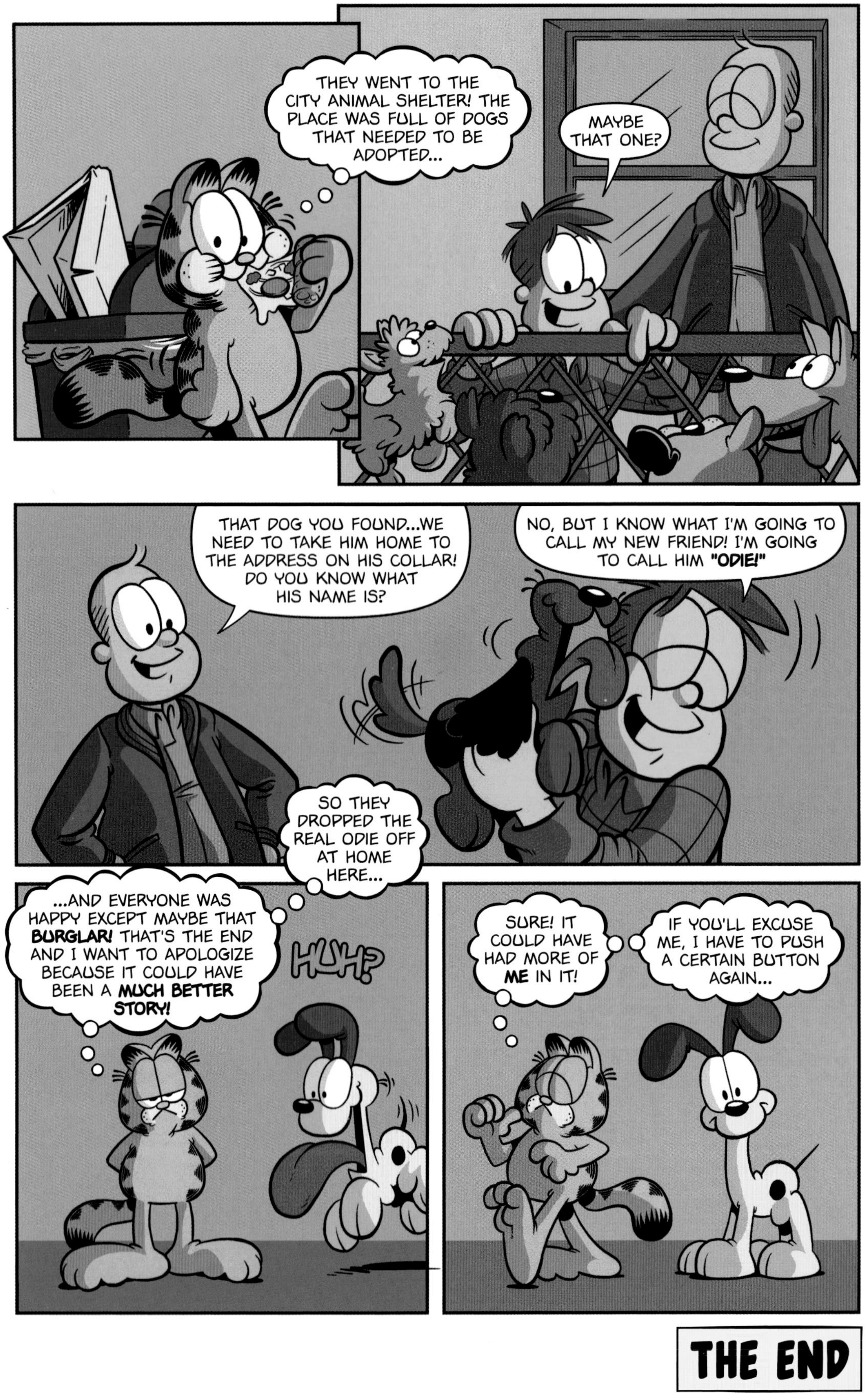
THEY WENT TO THE CITY ANIMAL SHELTER! THE PLACE WAS FULL OF DOGS THAT NEEDED TO BE ADOPTED...
MAYBE THAT ONE?
THAT DOG YOU FOUND...WE NEED TO TAKE HIM HOME TO THE ADDRESS ON HIS COLLAR! DO YOU KNOW WHAT HIS NAME IS?
NO, BUT I KNOW WHAT I'M GOING TO CALL MY NEW FRIEND! I'M GOING TO CALL HIM "ODIE!"
SO THEY DROPPED THE REAL ODIE OFF AT HOME HERE...
...AND EVERYONE WAS HAPPY EXCEPT MAYBE THAT BURGLAR! THAT'S THE END AND I WANT TO APOLOGIZE BECAUSE IT COULD HAVE BEEN A MUCH BETTER STORY!
HUH?
SURE! IT COULD HAVE HAD MORE OF ME IN IT!
IF YOU'LL EXCUSE ME, I HAVE TO PUSH A CERTAIN BUTTON AGAIN...
THE END

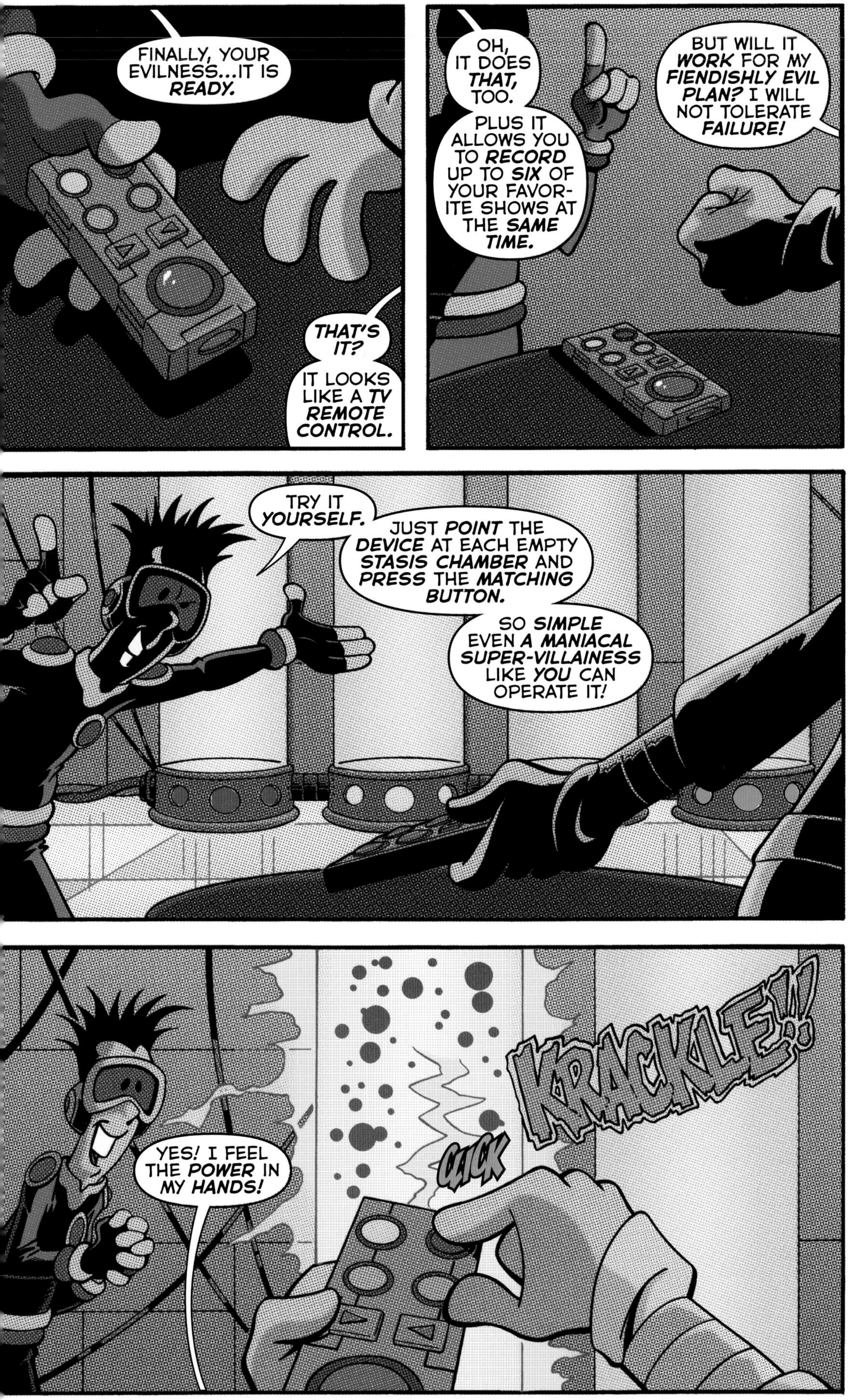
FINALLY, YOUR EVILNESS...IT IS *READY.*
THAT'S IT?
IT LOOKS LIKE A *TV REMOTE CONTROL.*
OH, IT DOES *THAT,* TOO.
PLUS IT ALLOWS YOU TO *RECORD* UP TO *SIX* OF YOUR FAVOR-ITE SHOWS AT THE *SAME TIME.*
BUT WILL IT *WORK* FOR MY *FIENDISHLY EVIL PLAN?* I WILL NOT TOLERATE *FAILURE!*
TRY IT *YOURSELF.*
JUST *POINT* THE *DEVICE* AT EACH EMPTY *STASIS CHAMBER* AND *PRESS* THE *MATCHING BUTTON.*
SO *SIMPLE* EVEN *A MANIACAL SUPER-VILLAINESS* LIKE *YOU* CAN OPERATE IT!
YES! I FEEL THE *POWER* IN MY *HANDS!*
CLICK
KRACKLE!!

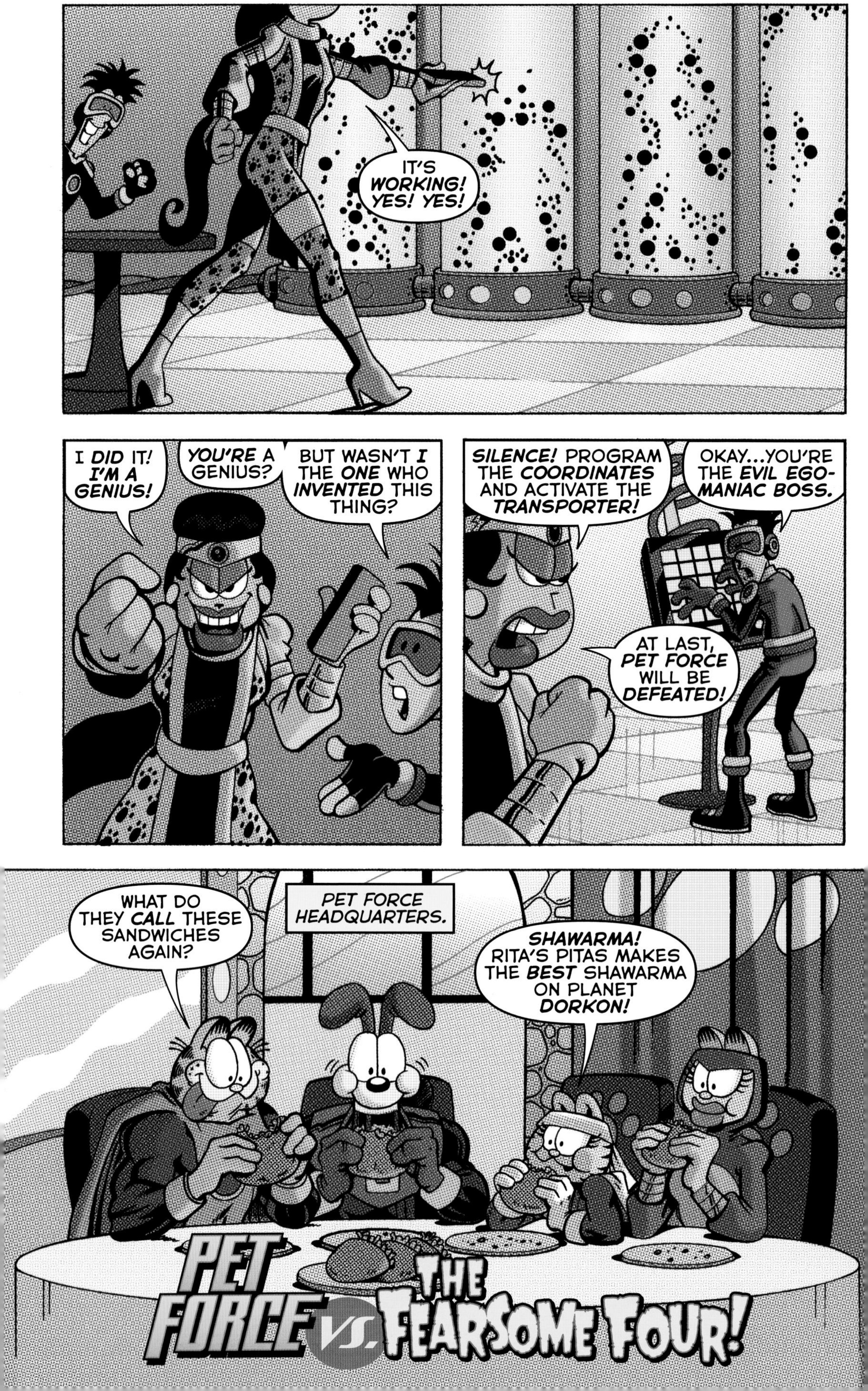
IT'S WORKING! YES! YES!
I DID IT! I'M A GENIUS!
YOU'RE A GENIUS?
BUT WASN'T I THE ONE WHO INVENTED THIS THING?
SILENCE! PROGRAM THE COORDINATES AND ACTIVATE THE TRANSPORTER!
OKAY...YOU'RE THE EVIL EGO-MANIAC BOSS.
AT LAST, PET FORCE WILL BE DEFEATED!
PET FORCE HEADQUARTERS.
WHAT DO THEY CALL THESE SANDWICHES AGAIN?
SHAWARMA! RITA'S PITAS MAKES THE BEST SHAWARMA ON PLANET DORKON!
PET FORCE VS. THE FEARSOME FOUR!

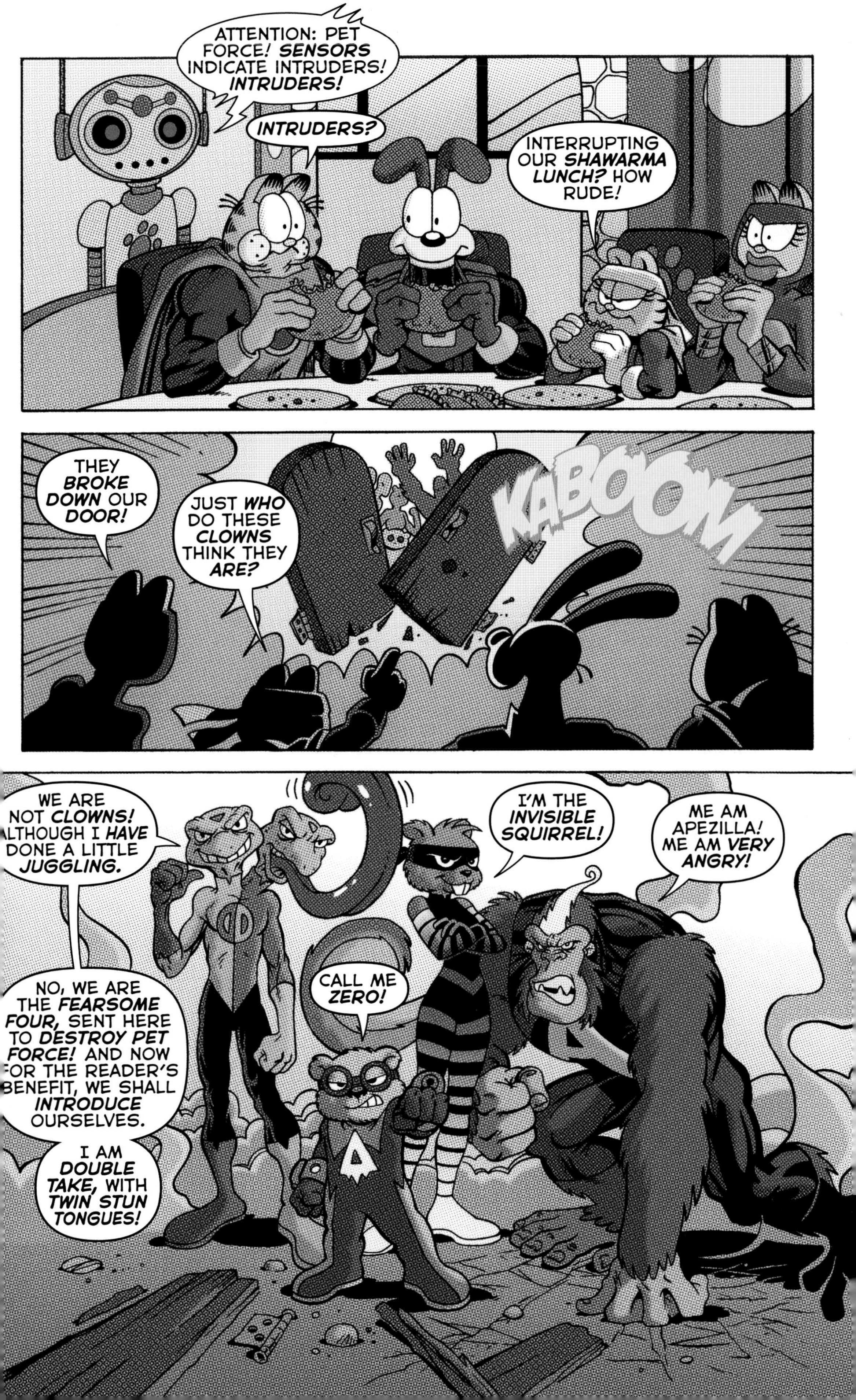

ATTENTION: PET FORCE! SENSORS INDICATE INTRUDERS! INTRUDERS!
INTRUDERS?
INTERRUPTING OUR SHAWARMA LUNCH? HOW RUDE!
THEY BROKE DOWN OUR DOOR!
JUST WHO DO THESE CLOWNS THINK THEY ARE?
KABOOM
WE ARE NOT CLOWNS! ALTHOUGH I HAVE DONE A LITTLE JUGGLING.
NO, WE ARE THE FEARSOME FOUR, SENT HERE TO DESTROY PET FORCE! AND NOW FOR THE READER'S BENEFIT, WE SHALL INTRODUCE OURSELVES.
I AM DOUBLE TAKE, WITH TWIN STUN TONGUES!
CALL ME ZERO!
I'M THE INVISIBLE SQUIRREL!
ME AM APEZILLA! ME AM VERY ANGRY!

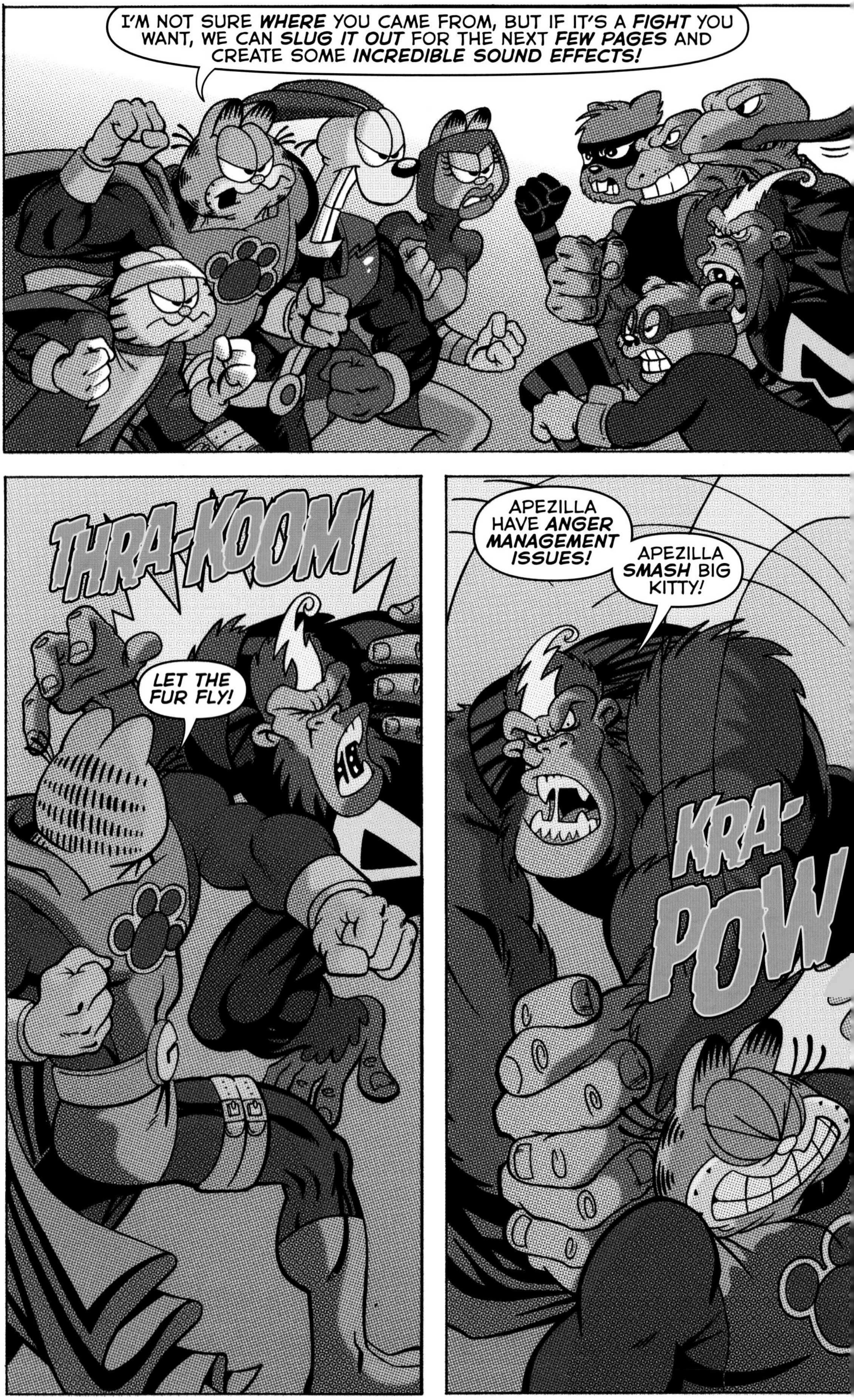
I'M NOT SURE *WHERE* YOU CAME FROM, BUT IF IT'S A *FIGHT* YOU WANT, WE CAN *SLUG IT OUT* FOR THE NEXT *FEW PAGES* AND CREATE SOME *INCREDIBLE SOUND EFFECTS!*
THRA-KOOM
LET THE FUR FLY!
APEZILLA HAVE *ANGER MANAGEMENT ISSUES!*
APEZILLA *SMASH* BIG KITTY!
KRA-POW

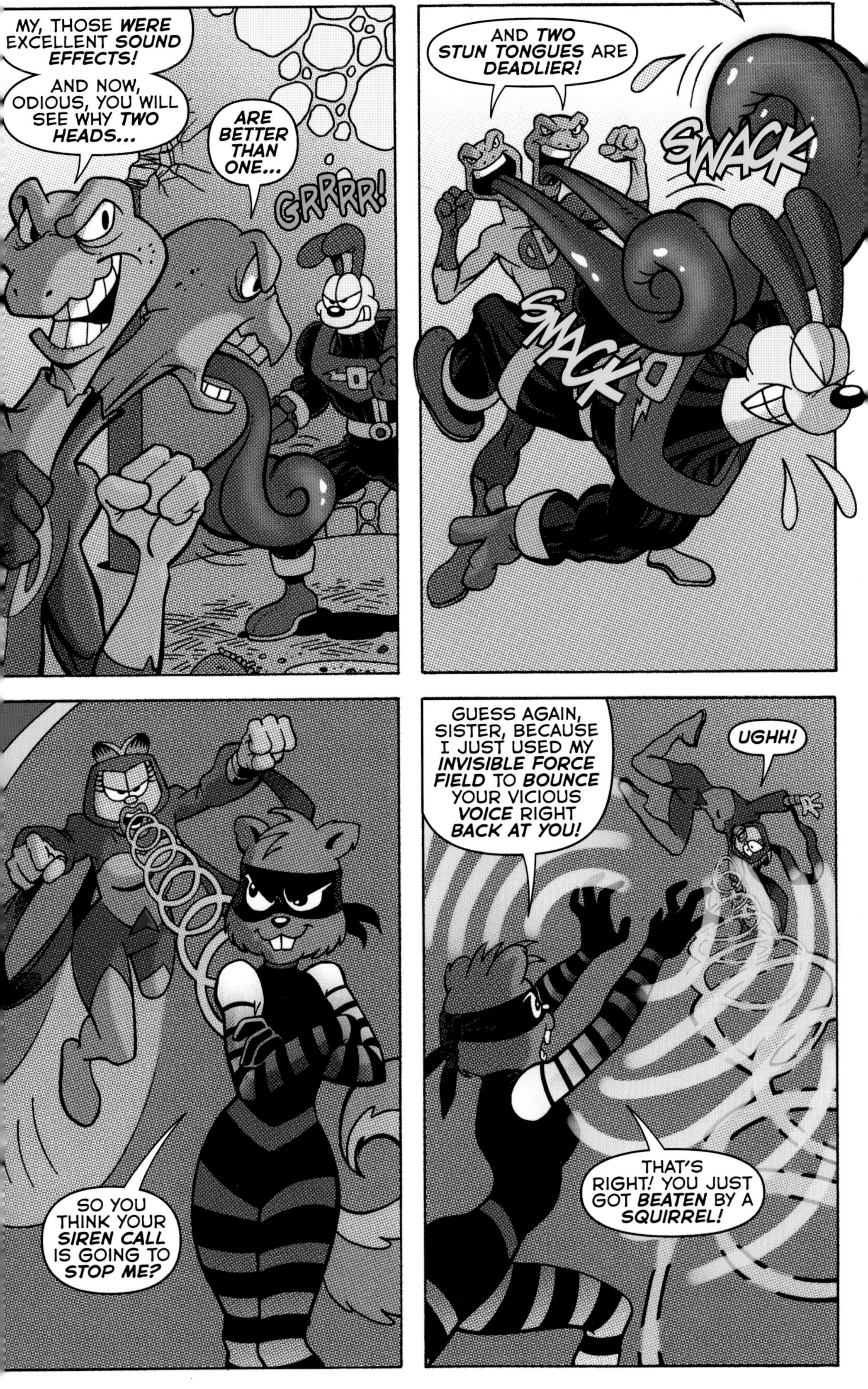
MY, THOSE WERE EXCELLENT SOUND EFFECTS!
AND NOW, ODIOUS, YOU WILL SEE WHY TWO HEADS...
ARE BETTER THAN ONE...
GRRRR!
AND TWO STUN TONGUES ARE DEADLIER!
SWACK
SMACK
SO YOU THINK YOUR SIREN CALL IS GOING TO STOP ME?
GUESS AGAIN, SISTER, BECAUSE I JUST USED MY INVISIBLE FORCE FIELD TO BOUNCE YOUR VICIOUS VOICE RIGHT BACK AT YOU!
UGHH!
THAT'S RIGHT! YOU JUST GOT BEATEN BY A SQUIRREL!

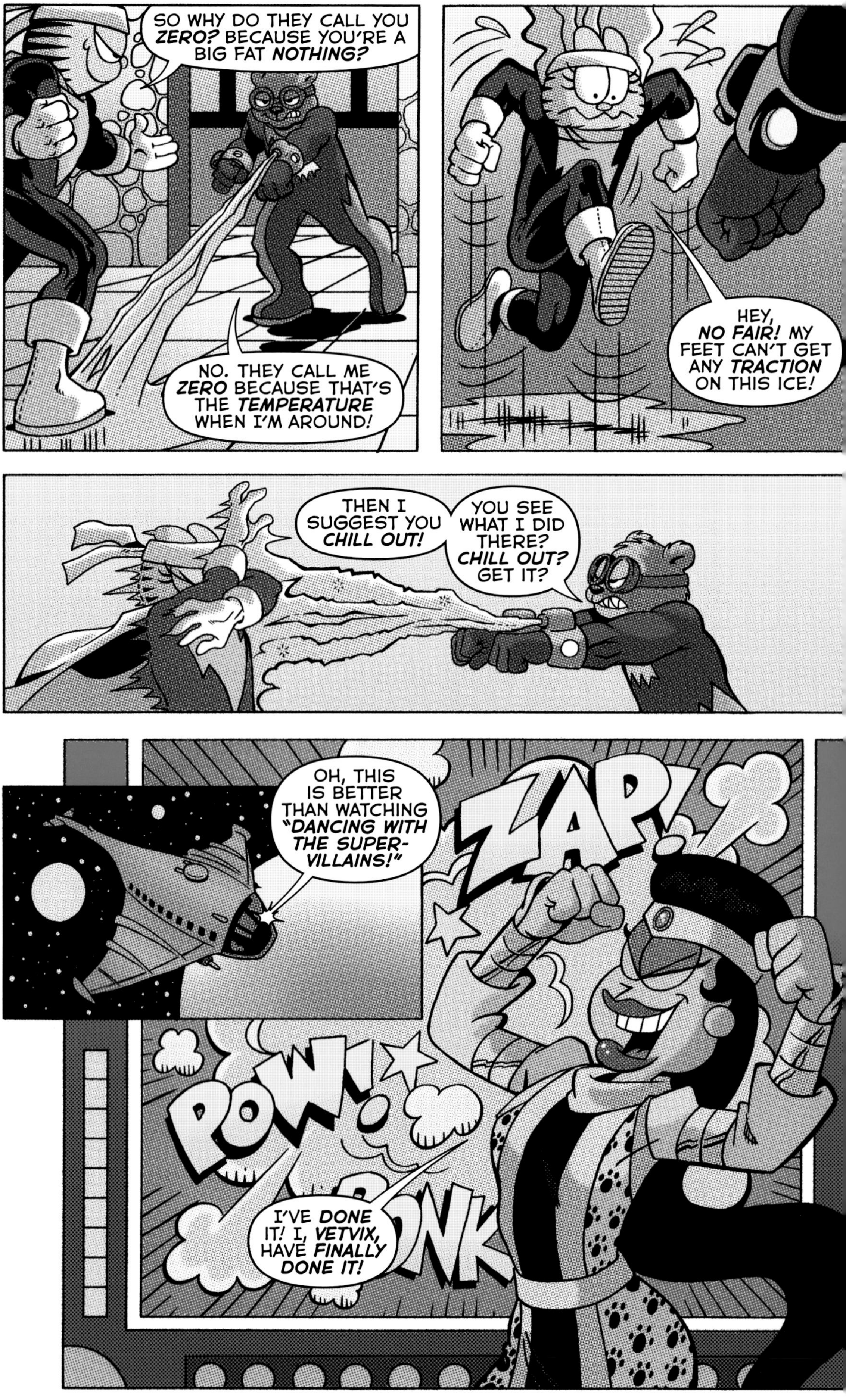
SO WHY DO THEY CALL YOU ZERO? BECAUSE YOU'RE A BIG FAT NOTHING?
NO. THEY CALL ME ZERO BECAUSE THAT'S THE TEMPERATURE WHEN I'M AROUND!
HEY, NO FAIR! MY FEET CAN'T GET ANY TRACTION ON THIS ICE!
THEN I SUGGEST YOU CHILL OUT!
YOU SEE WHAT I DID THERE? CHILL OUT? GET IT?
OH, THIS IS BETTER THAN WATCHING "DANCING WITH THE SUPER-VILLAINS!"
ZAP!
POW!
I'VE DONE IT! I, VETVIX, HAVE FINALLY DONE IT!

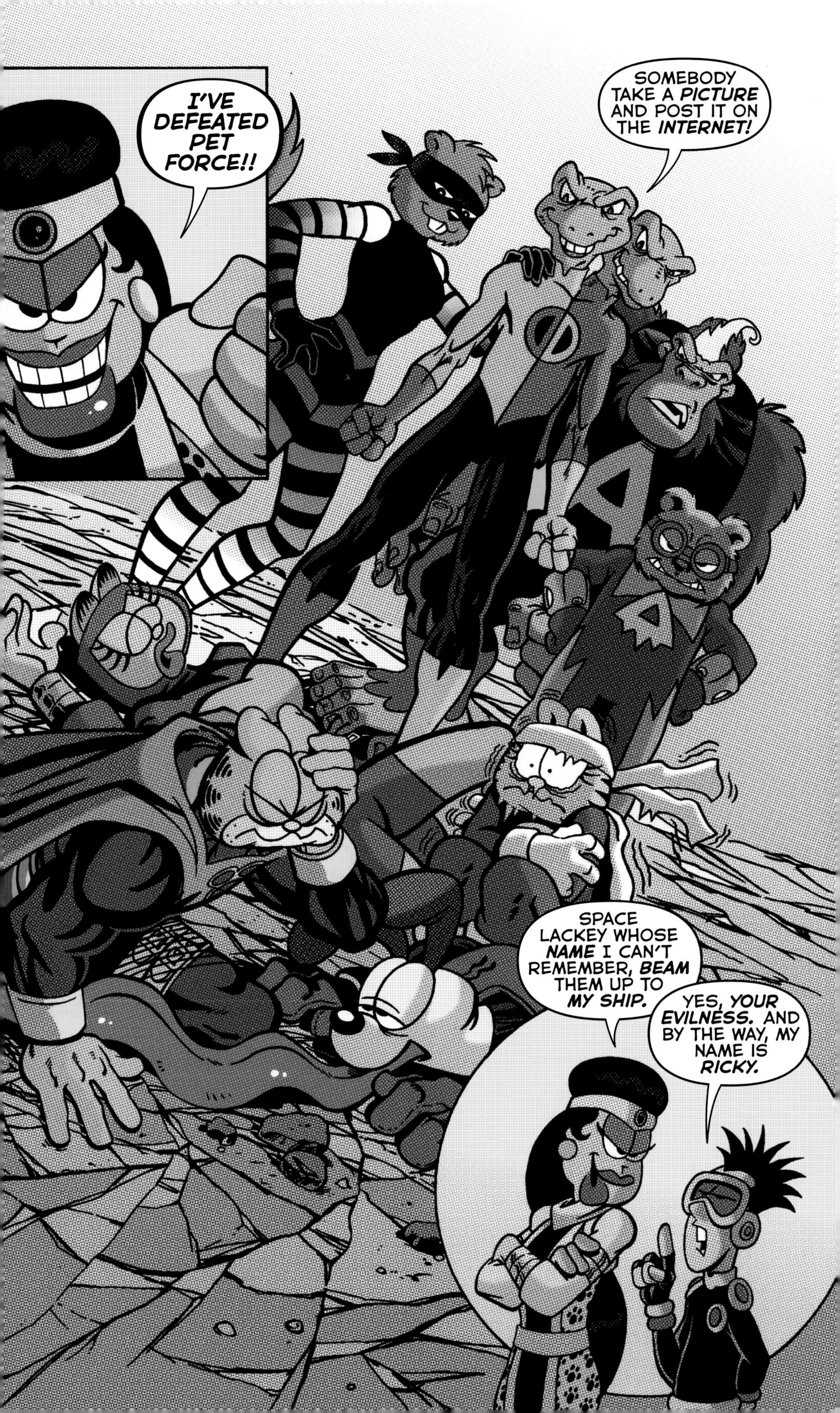
I'VE DEFEATED PET FORCE!!
SOMEBODY TAKE A PICTURE AND POST IT ON THE INTERNET!
SPACE LACKEY WHOSE NAME I CAN'T REMEMBER, BEAM THEM UP TO MY SHIP.
YES, YOUR EVILNESS. AND BY THE WAY, MY NAME IS RICKY.

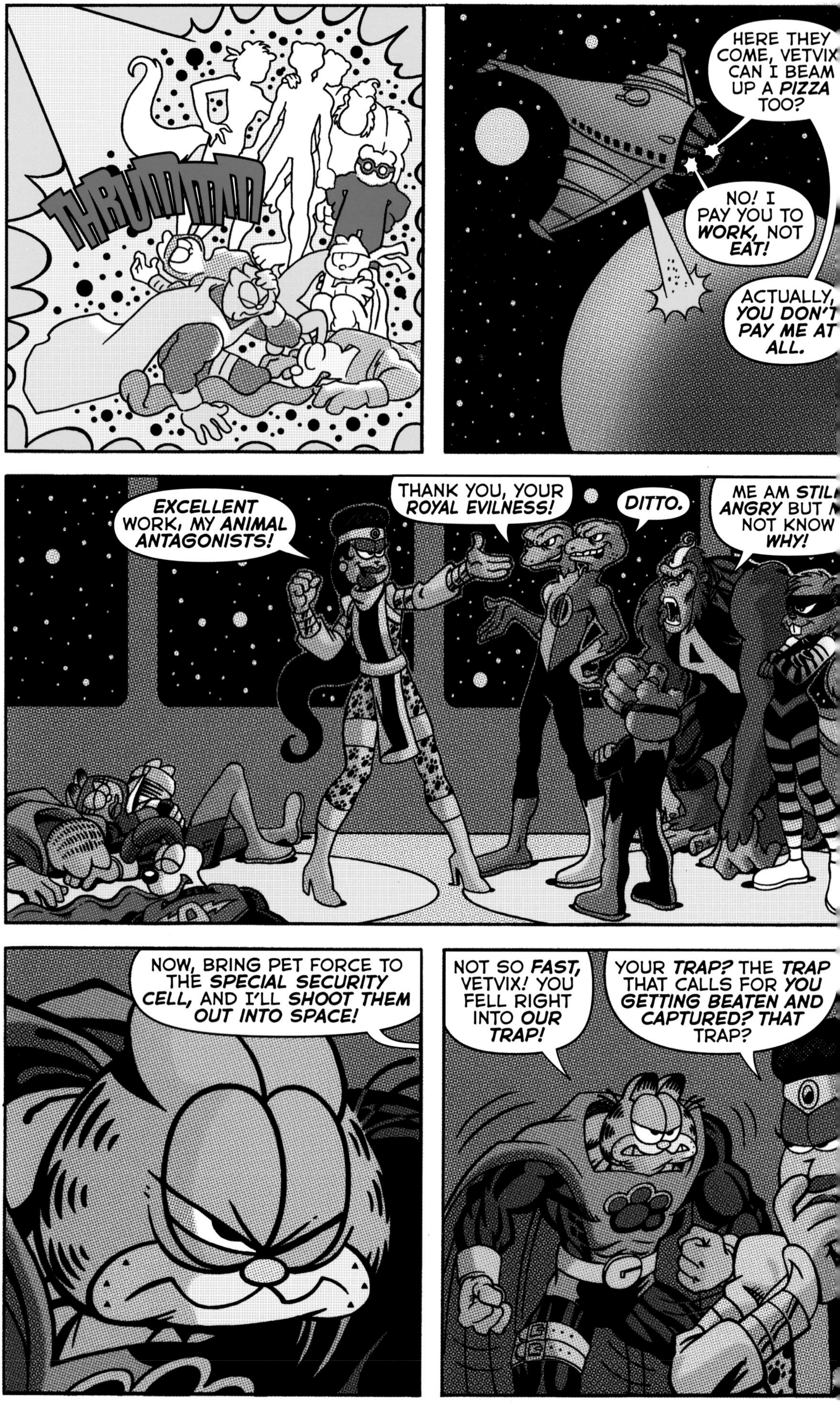
THRUMMMM
HERE THEY COME, VETVIX CAN I BEAM UP A PIZZA TOO?
NO! I PAY YOU TO WORK, NOT EAT!
ACTUALLY, YOU DON'T PAY ME AT ALL.
EXCELLENT WORK, MY ANIMAL ANTAGONISTS!
THANK YOU, YOUR ROYAL EVILNESS!
DITTO.
ME AM STILL ANGRY BUT ME NOT KNOW WHY!
NOW, BRING PET FORCE TO THE SPECIAL SECURITY CELL, AND I'LL SHOOT THEM OUT INTO SPACE!
NOT SO FAST, VETVIX! YOU FELL RIGHT INTO OUR TRAP!
YOUR TRAP? THE TRAP THAT CALLS FOR YOU GETTING BEATEN AND CAPTURED? THAT TRAP?

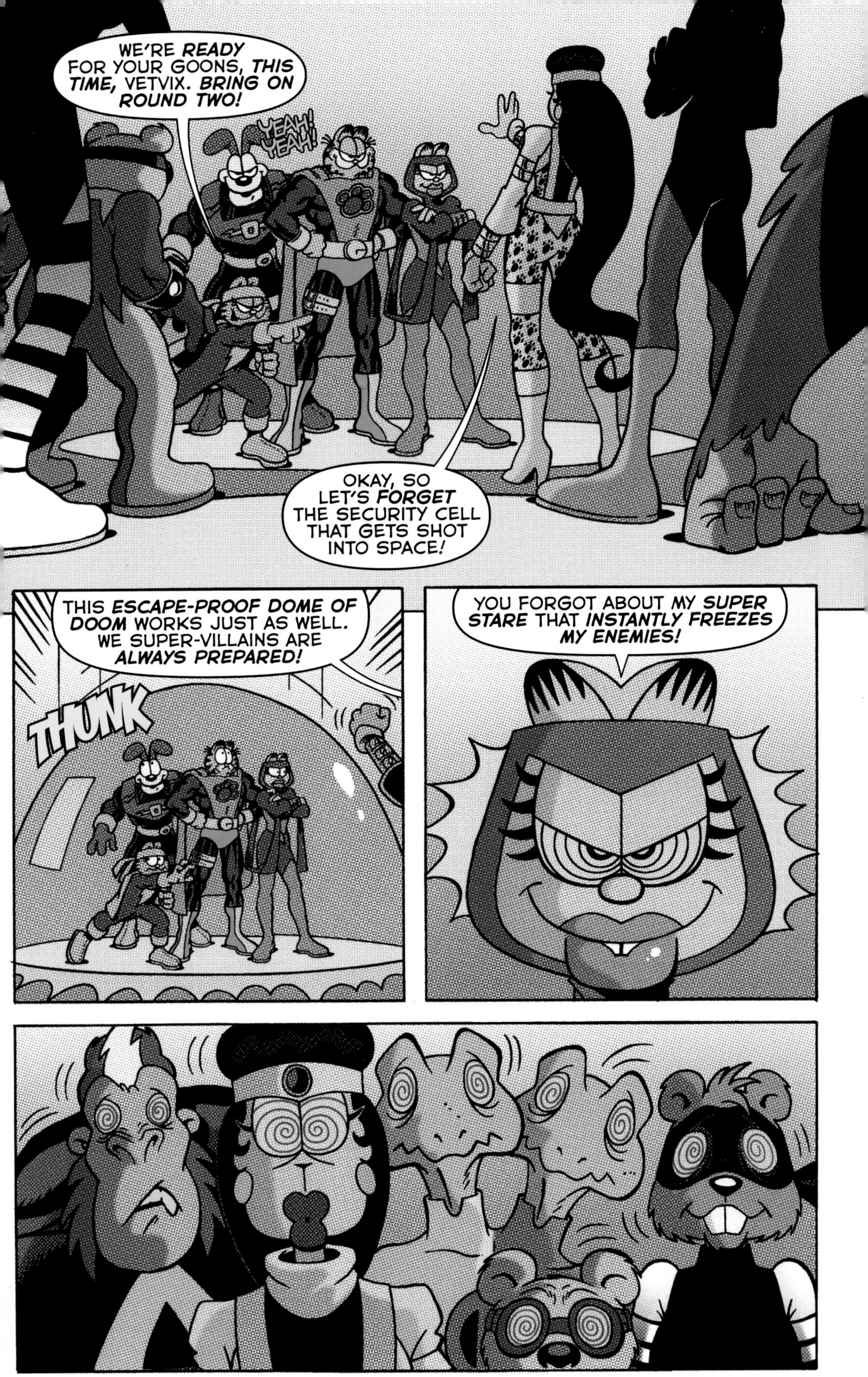
WE'RE READY FOR YOUR GOONS, THIS TIME, VETVIX. BRING ON ROUND TWO!
YEAH! YEAH!
OKAY, SO LET'S FORGET THE SECURITY CELL THAT GETS SHOT INTO SPACE!
THIS ESCAPE-PROOF DOME OF DOOM WORKS JUST AS WELL. WE SUPER-VILLAINS ARE ALWAYS PREPARED!
THUNK
YOU FORGOT ABOUT MY SUPER STARE THAT INSTANTLY FREEZES MY ENEMIES!

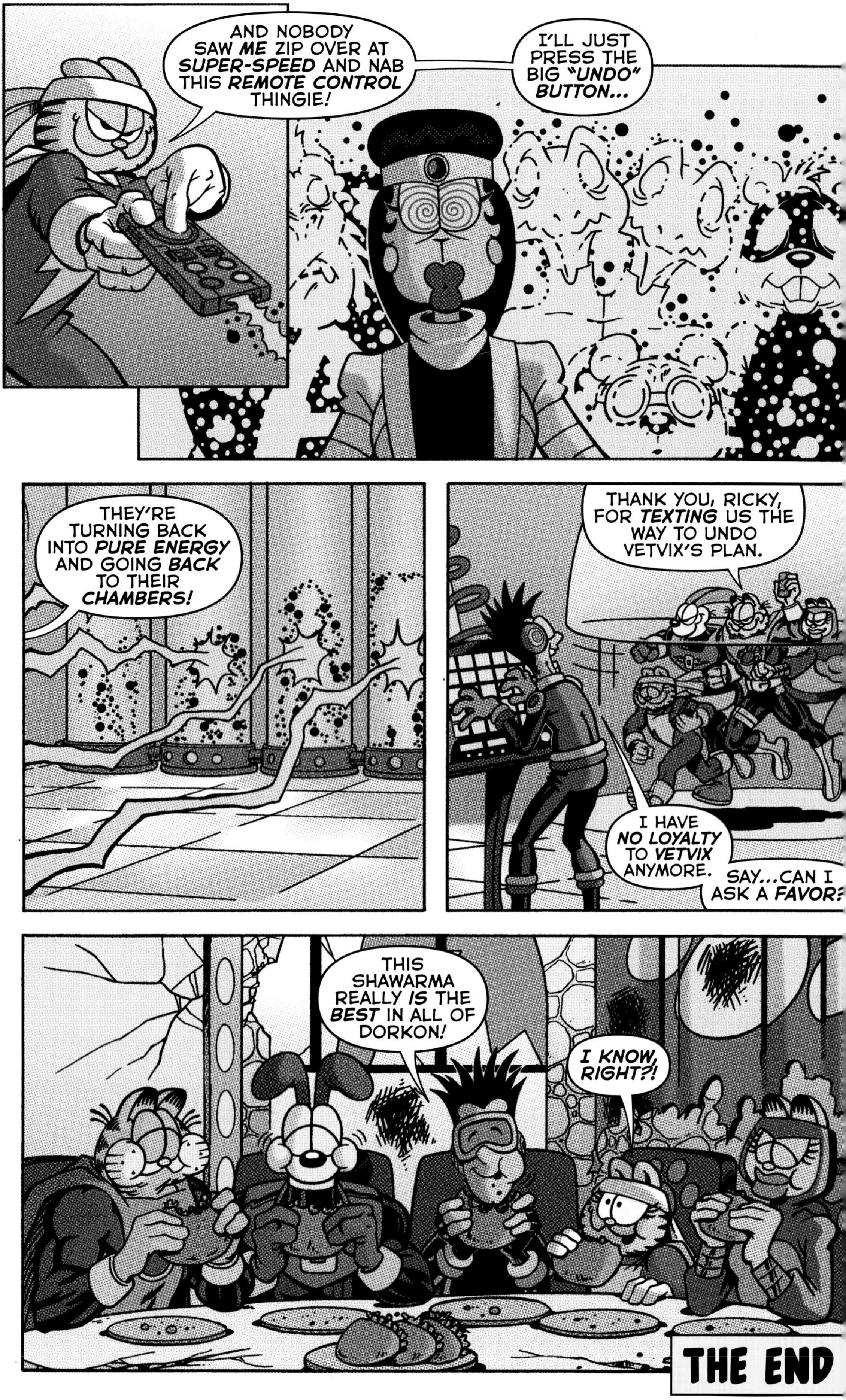
AND NOBODY SAW ME ZIP OVER AT SUPER-SPEED AND NAB THIS REMOTE CONTROL THINGIE!
I'LL JUST PRESS THE BIG "UNDO" BUTTON...
THEY'RE TURNING BACK INTO PURE ENERGY AND GOING BACK TO THEIR CHAMBERS!
THANK YOU, RICKY, FOR TEXTING US THE WAY TO UNDO VETVIX'S PLAN.
I HAVE NO LOYALTY TO VETVIX ANYMORE.
SAY...CAN I ASK A FAVOR?
THIS SHAWARMA REALLY IS THE BEST IN ALL OF DORKON!
I KNOW, RIGHT?!
THE END

CHAPTER 2

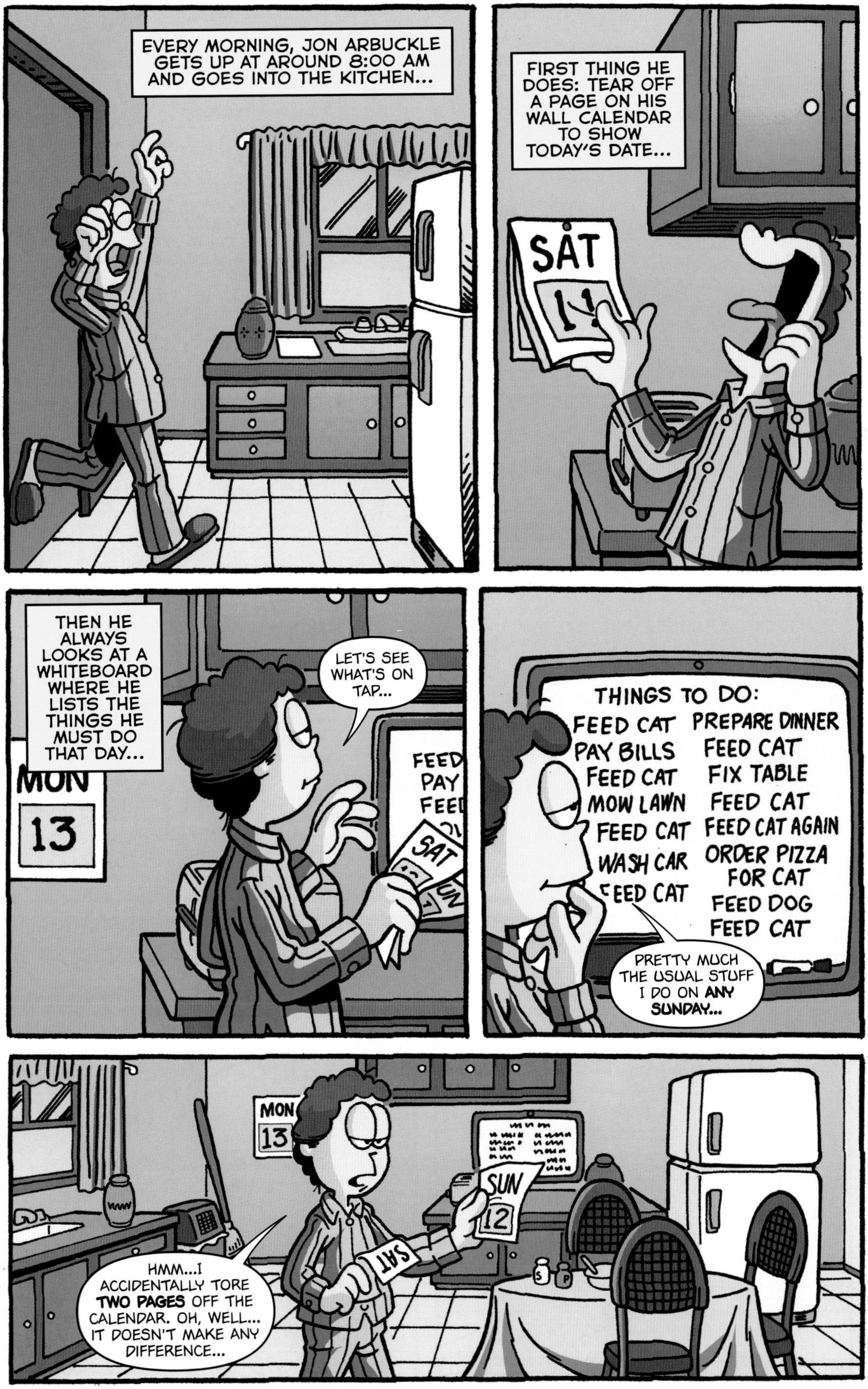

EVERY MORNING, JON ARBUCKLE GETS UP AT AROUND 8:00 AM AND GOES INTO THE KITCHEN...
FIRST THING HE DOES: TEAR OFF A PAGE ON HIS WALL CALENDAR TO SHOW TODAY'S DATE...
SAT
THEN HE ALWAYS LOOKS AT A WHITEBOARD WHERE HE LISTS THE THINGS HE MUST DO THAT DAY...
LET'S SEE WHAT'S ON TAP...
MON
13
THINGS TO DO:
FEED CAT
PAY BILLS
FEED CAT
MOW LAWN
FEED CAT
WASH CAR
FEED CAT
PREPARE DINNER
FEED CAT
FIX TABLE
FEED CAT
FEED CAT AGAIN
ORDER PIZZA FOR CAT
FEED DOG
FEED CAT
PRETTY MUCH THE USUAL STUFF I DO ON **ANY SUNDAY...**
MON
13
SUN
12
SAT
HMM...I ACCIDENTALLY TORE **TWO PAGES** OFF THE CALENDAR. OH, WELL... IT DOESN'T MAKE ANY DIFFERENCE...

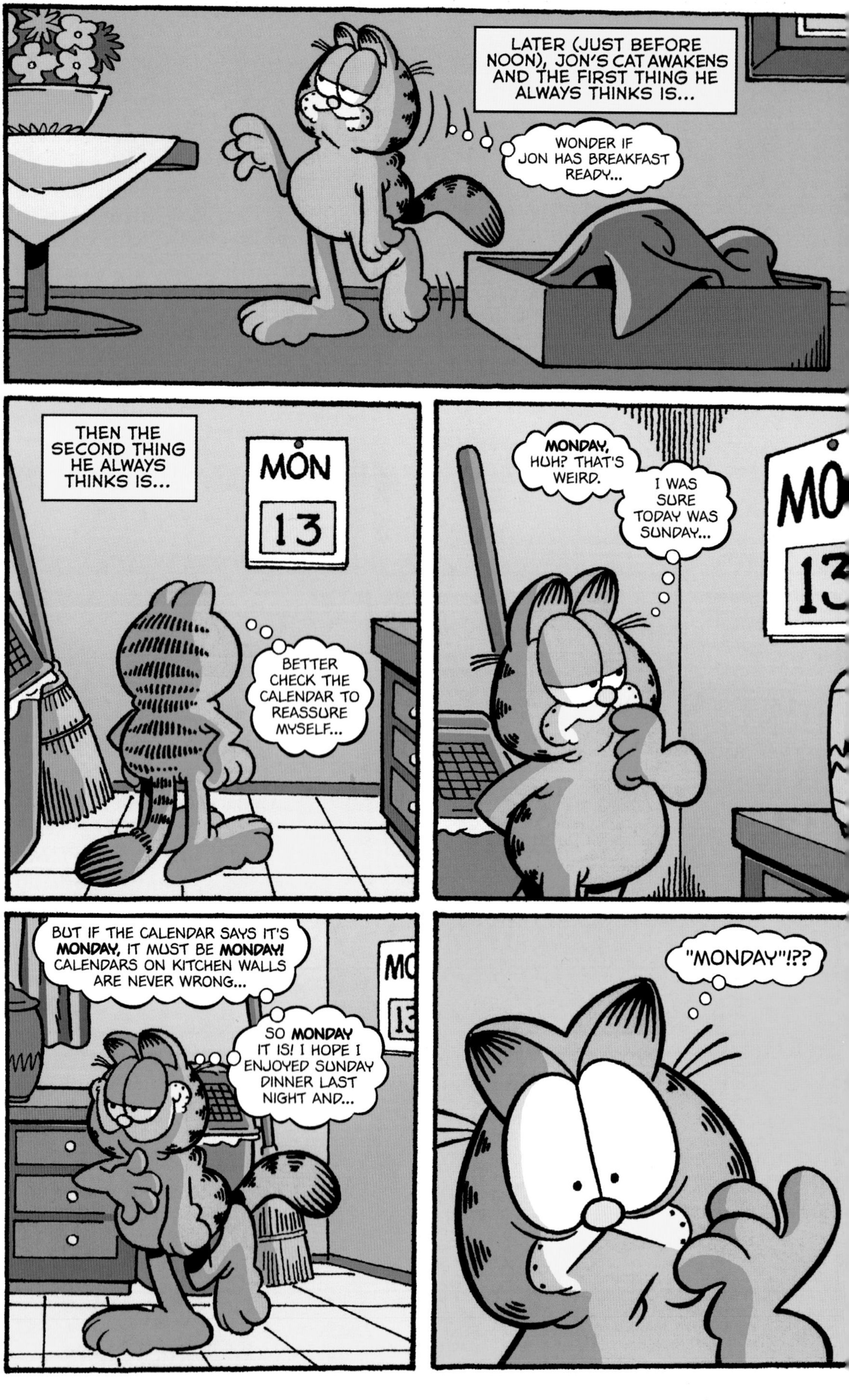
LATER (JUST BEFORE NOON), JON'S CAT AWAKENS AND THE FIRST THING HE ALWAYS THINKS IS...
WONDER IF JON HAS BREAKFAST READY...
THEN THE SECOND THING HE ALWAYS THINKS IS...
MON
13
BETTER CHECK THE CALENDAR TO REASSURE MYSELF...
MONDAY, HUH? THAT'S WEIRD.
I WAS SURE TODAY WAS SUNDAY...
BUT IF THE CALENDAR SAYS IT'S MONDAY, IT MUST BE MONDAY! CALENDARS ON KITCHEN WALLS ARE NEVER WRONG...
SO MONDAY IT IS! I HOPE I ENJOYED SUNDAY DINNER LAST NIGHT AND...
"MONDAY"!??

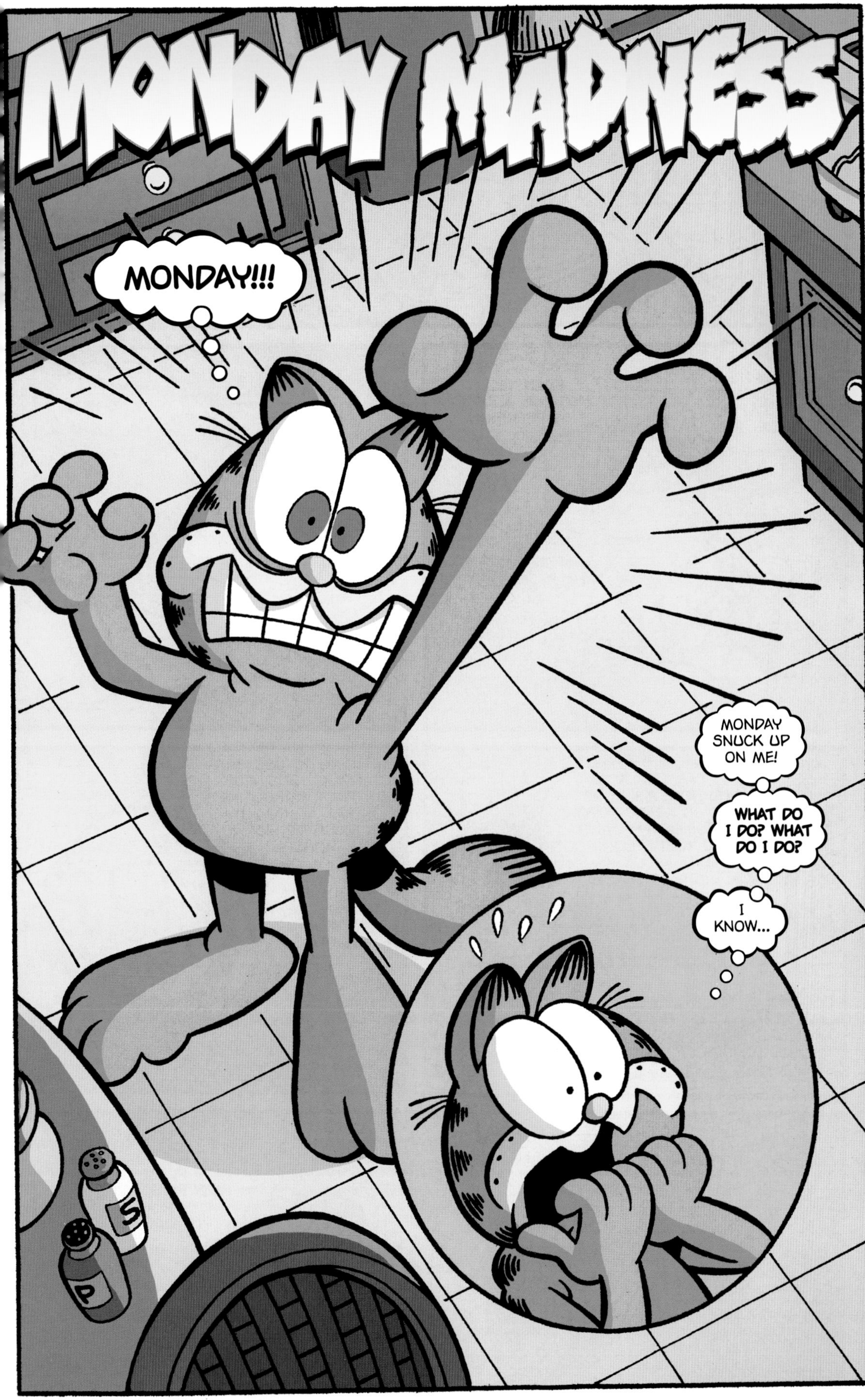
MONDAY MADNESS
MONDAY!!!
MONDAY SNUCK UP ON ME!
WHAT DO I DO? WHAT DO I DO?
I KNOW...

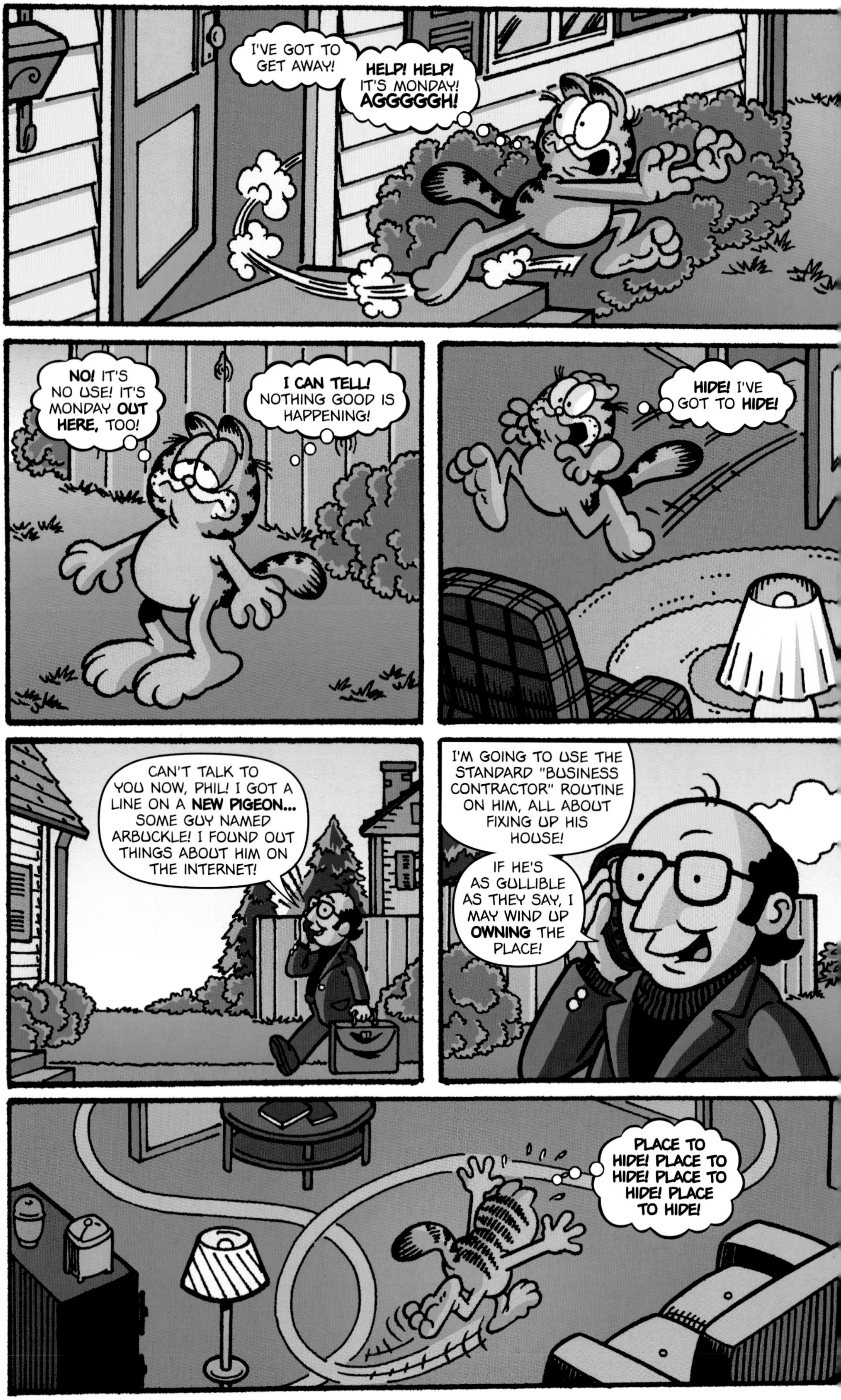
I'VE GOT TO GET AWAY!
HELP! HELP! IT'S MONDAY! AGGGGGH!
NO! IT'S NO USE! IT'S MONDAY OUT HERE, TOO!
I CAN TELL! NOTHING GOOD IS HAPPENING!
HIDE! I'VE GOT TO HIDE!
CAN'T TALK TO YOU NOW, PHIL! I GOT A LINE ON A NEW PIGEON... SOME GUY NAMED ARBUCKLE! I FOUND OUT THINGS ABOUT HIM ON THE INTERNET!
I'M GOING TO USE THE STANDARD "BUSINESS CONTRACTOR" ROUTINE ON HIM, ALL ABOUT FIXING UP HIS HOUSE!
IF HE'S AS GULLIBLE AS THEY SAY, I MAY WIND UP OWNING THE PLACE!
PLACE TO HIDE! PLACE TO HIDE! PLACE TO HIDE! PLACE TO HIDE!

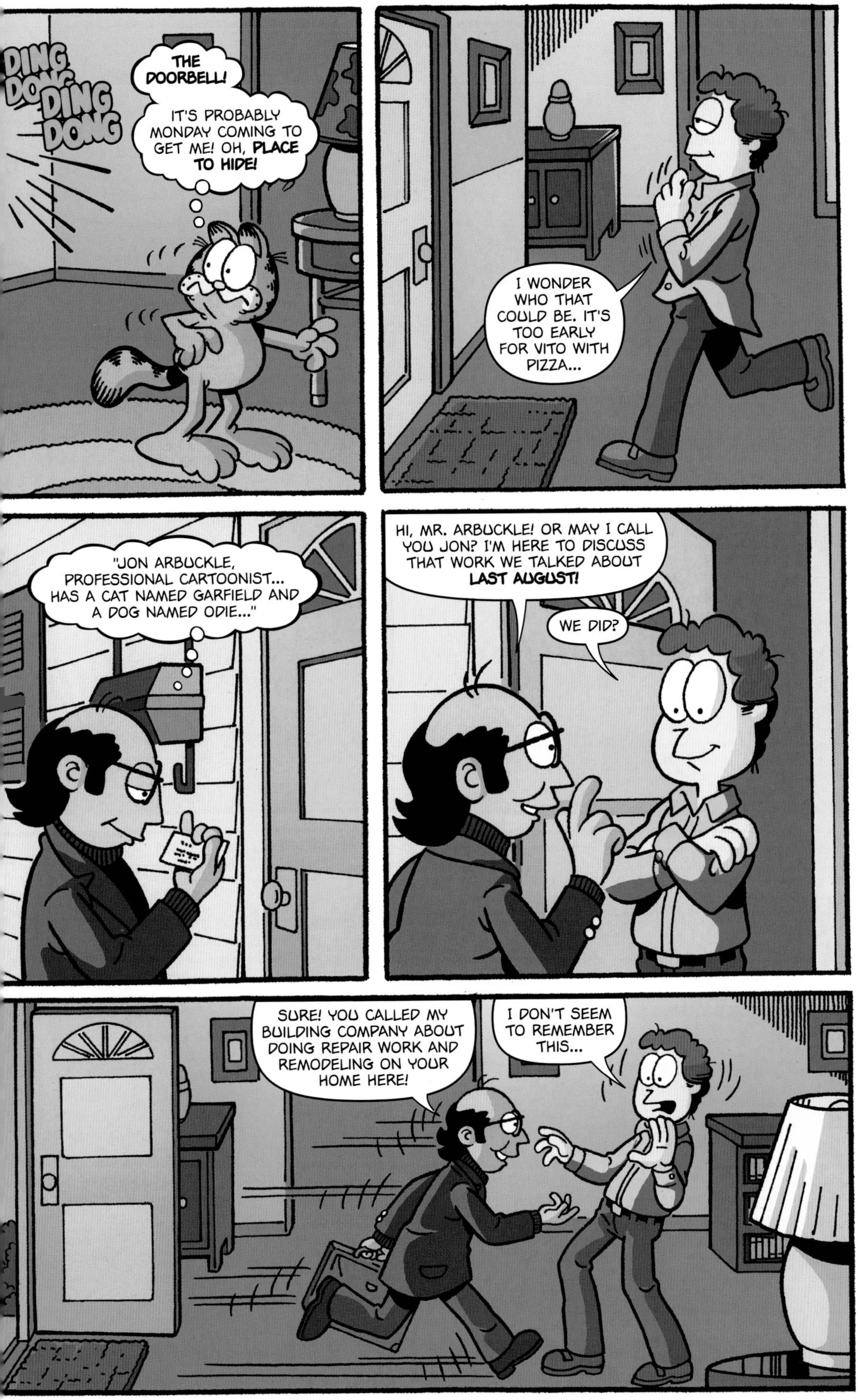
DING DONG DING DONG
THE DOORBELL!
IT'S PROBABLY MONDAY COMING TO GET ME! OH, PLACE TO HIDE!
I WONDER WHO THAT COULD BE. IT'S TOO EARLY FOR VITO WITH PIZZA...
"JON ARBUCKLE, PROFESSIONAL CARTOONIST... HAS A CAT NAMED GARFIELD AND A DOG NAMED ODIE..."
HI, MR. ARBUCKLE! OR MAY I CALL YOU JON? I'M HERE TO DISCUSS THAT WORK WE TALKED ABOUT LAST AUGUST!
WE DID?
SURE! YOU CALLED MY BUILDING COMPANY ABOUT DOING REPAIR WORK AND REMODELING ON YOUR HOME HERE!
I DON'T SEEM TO REMEMBER THIS...

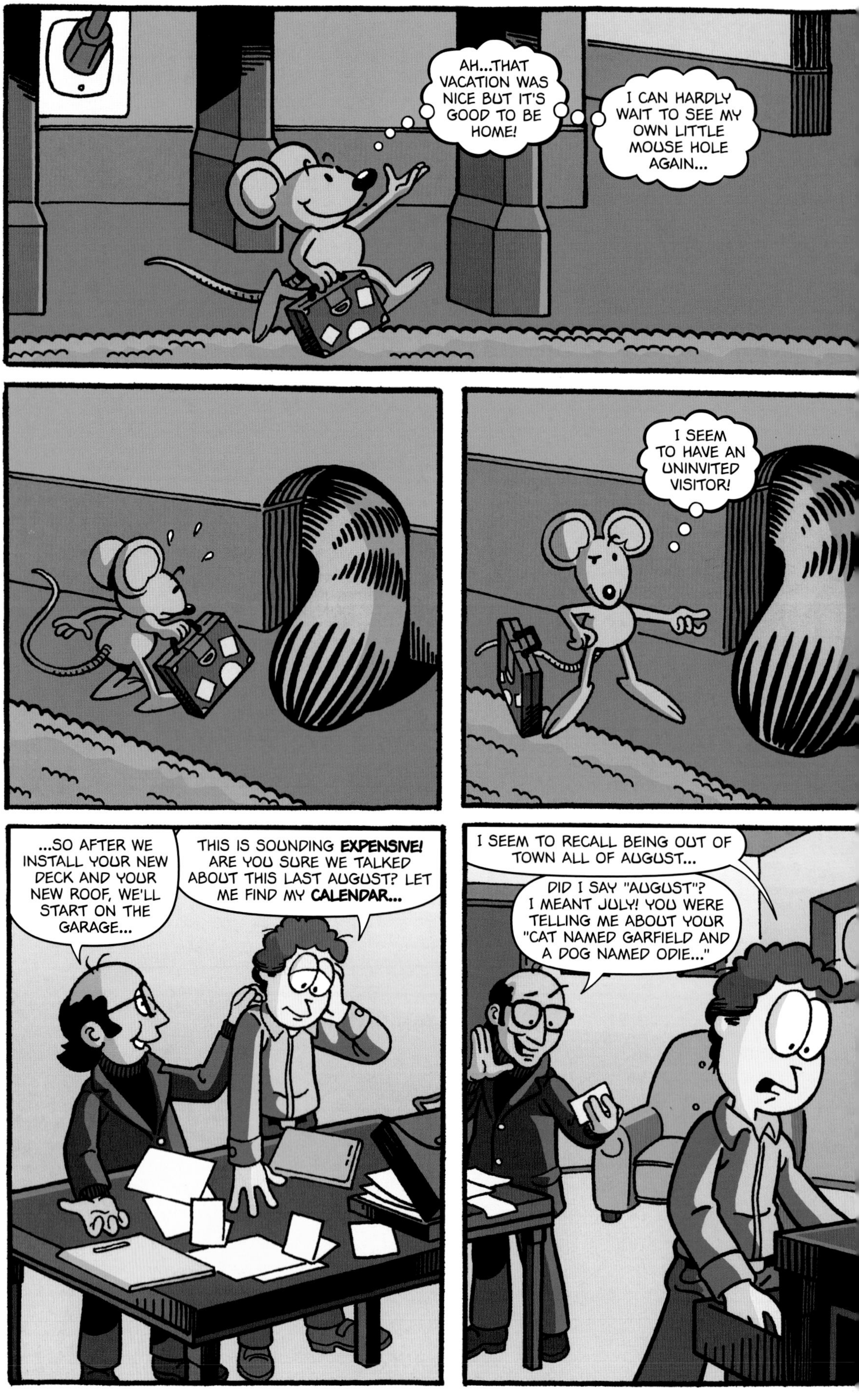

AH...THAT VACATION WAS NICE BUT IT'S GOOD TO BE HOME!
I CAN HARDLY WAIT TO SEE MY OWN LITTLE MOUSE HOLE AGAIN...
I SEEM TO HAVE AN UNINVITED VISITOR!
...SO AFTER WE INSTALL YOUR NEW DECK AND YOUR NEW ROOF, WE'LL START ON THE GARAGE...
THIS IS SOUNDING **EXPENSIVE!** ARE YOU SURE WE TALKED ABOUT THIS LAST AUGUST? LET ME FIND MY **CALENDAR...**
I SEEM TO RECALL BEING OUT OF TOWN ALL OF AUGUST...
DID I SAY "AUGUST"? I MEANT JULY! YOU WERE TELLING ME ABOUT YOUR "CAT NAMED GARFIELD AND A DOG NAMED ODIE..."

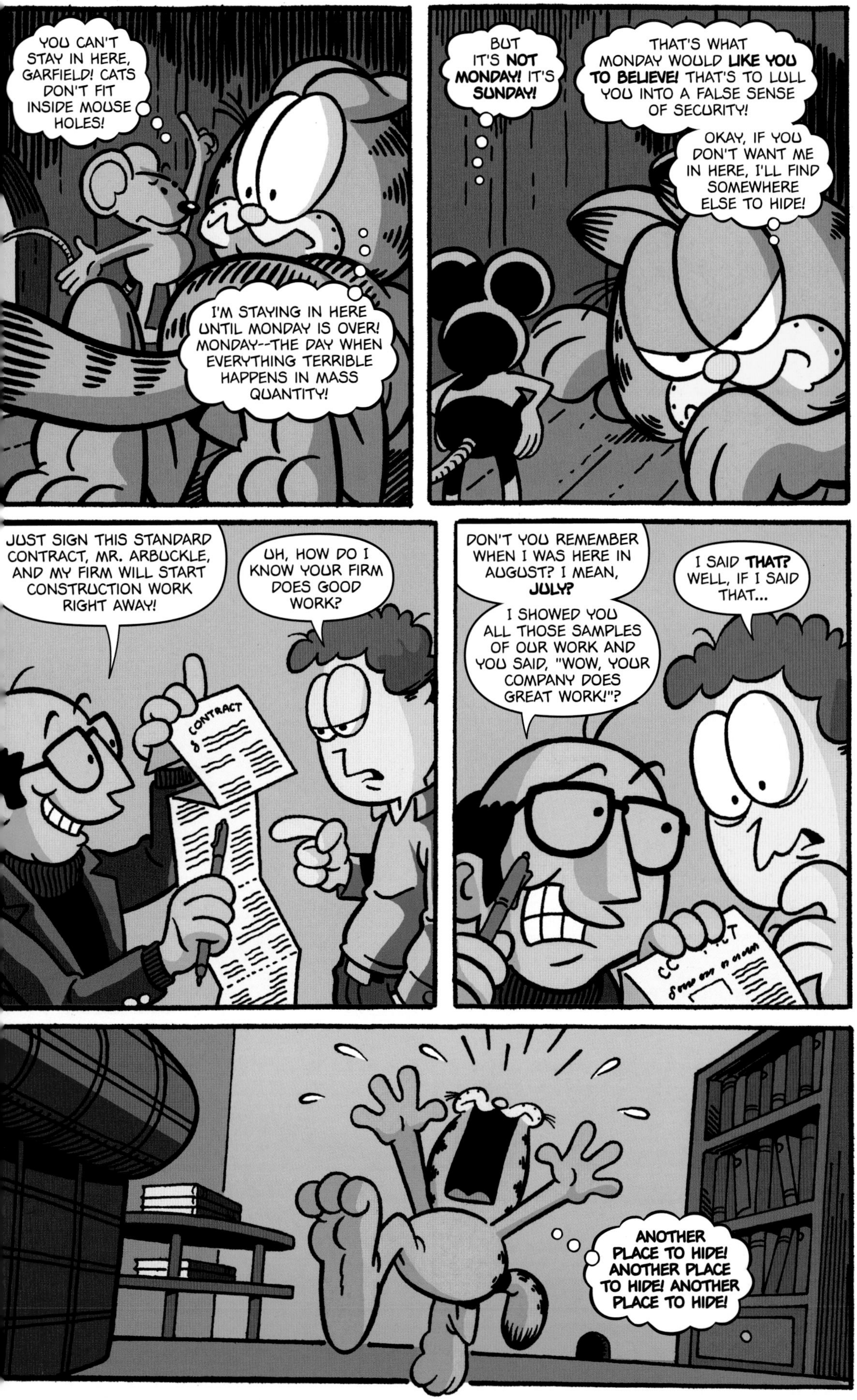

YOU CAN'T STAY IN HERE, GARFIELD! CATS DON'T FIT INSIDE MOUSE HOLES!
I'M STAYING IN HERE UNTIL MONDAY IS OVER! MONDAY--THE DAY WHEN EVERYTHING TERRIBLE HAPPENS IN MASS QUANTITY!
BUT IT'S NOT MONDAY! IT'S SUNDAY!
THAT'S WHAT MONDAY WOULD LIKE YOU TO BELIEVE! THAT'S TO LULL YOU INTO A FALSE SENSE OF SECURITY!
OKAY, IF YOU DON'T WANT ME IN HERE, I'LL FIND SOMEWHERE ELSE TO HIDE!
JUST SIGN THIS STANDARD CONTRACT, MR. ARBUCKLE, AND MY FIRM WILL START CONSTRUCTION WORK RIGHT AWAY!
CONTRACT
UH, HOW DO I KNOW YOUR FIRM DOES GOOD WORK?
DON'T YOU REMEMBER WHEN I WAS HERE IN AUGUST? I MEAN, JULY?
I SHOWED YOU ALL THOSE SAMPLES OF OUR WORK AND YOU SAID, "WOW, YOUR COMPANY DOES GREAT WORK!"?
I SAID THAT? WELL, IF I SAID THAT...
ANOTHER PLACE TO HIDE! ANOTHER PLACE TO HIDE! ANOTHER PLACE TO HIDE!

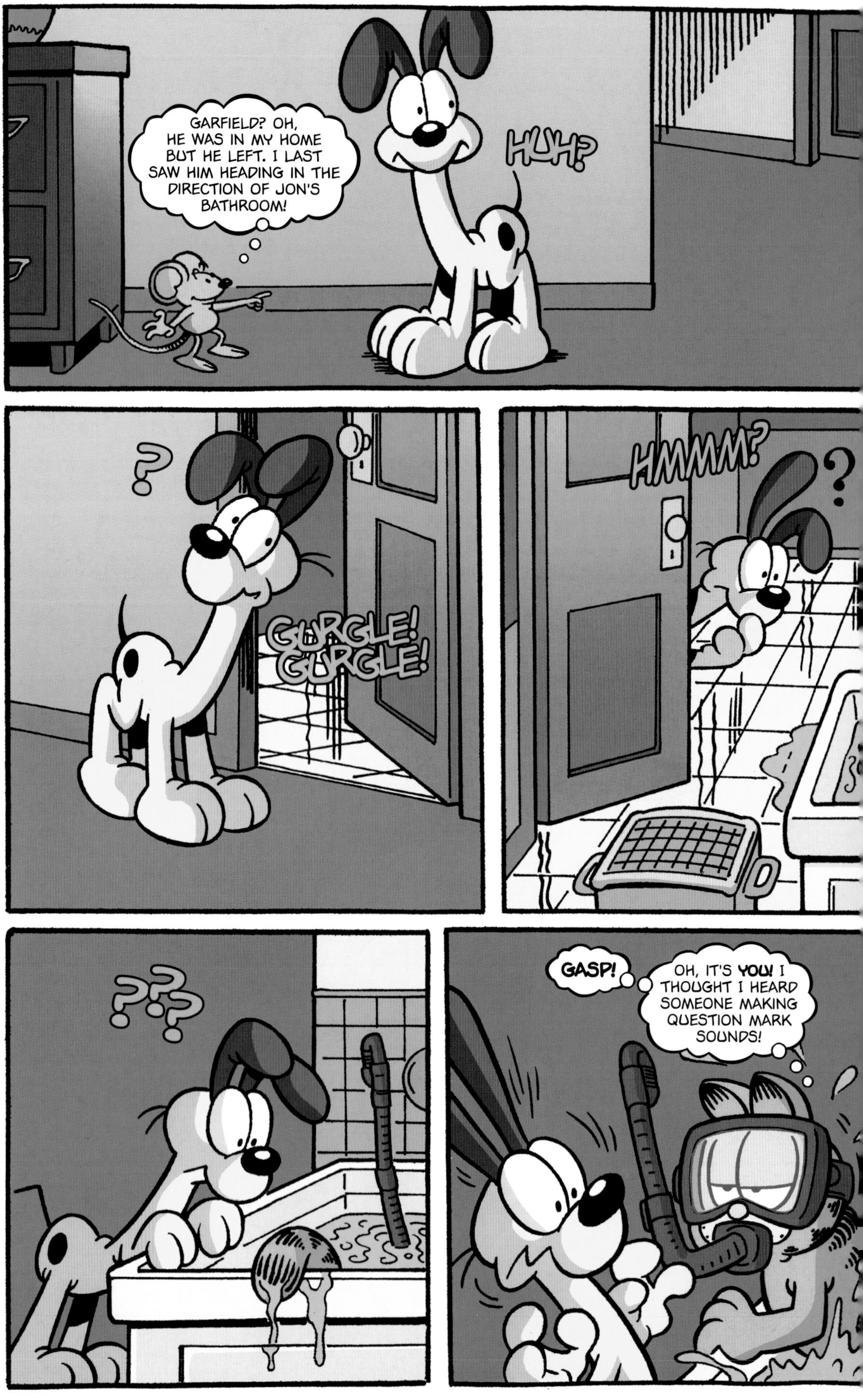
GARFIELD? OH, HE WAS IN MY HOME BUT HE LEFT. I LAST SAW HIM HEADING IN THE DIRECTION OF JON'S BATHROOM!
HUH?
?
GURGLE! GURGLE!
HMMM?
?
???
GASP!
OH, IT'S **YOU!** I THOUGHT I HEARD SOMEONE MAKING QUESTION MARK SOUNDS!

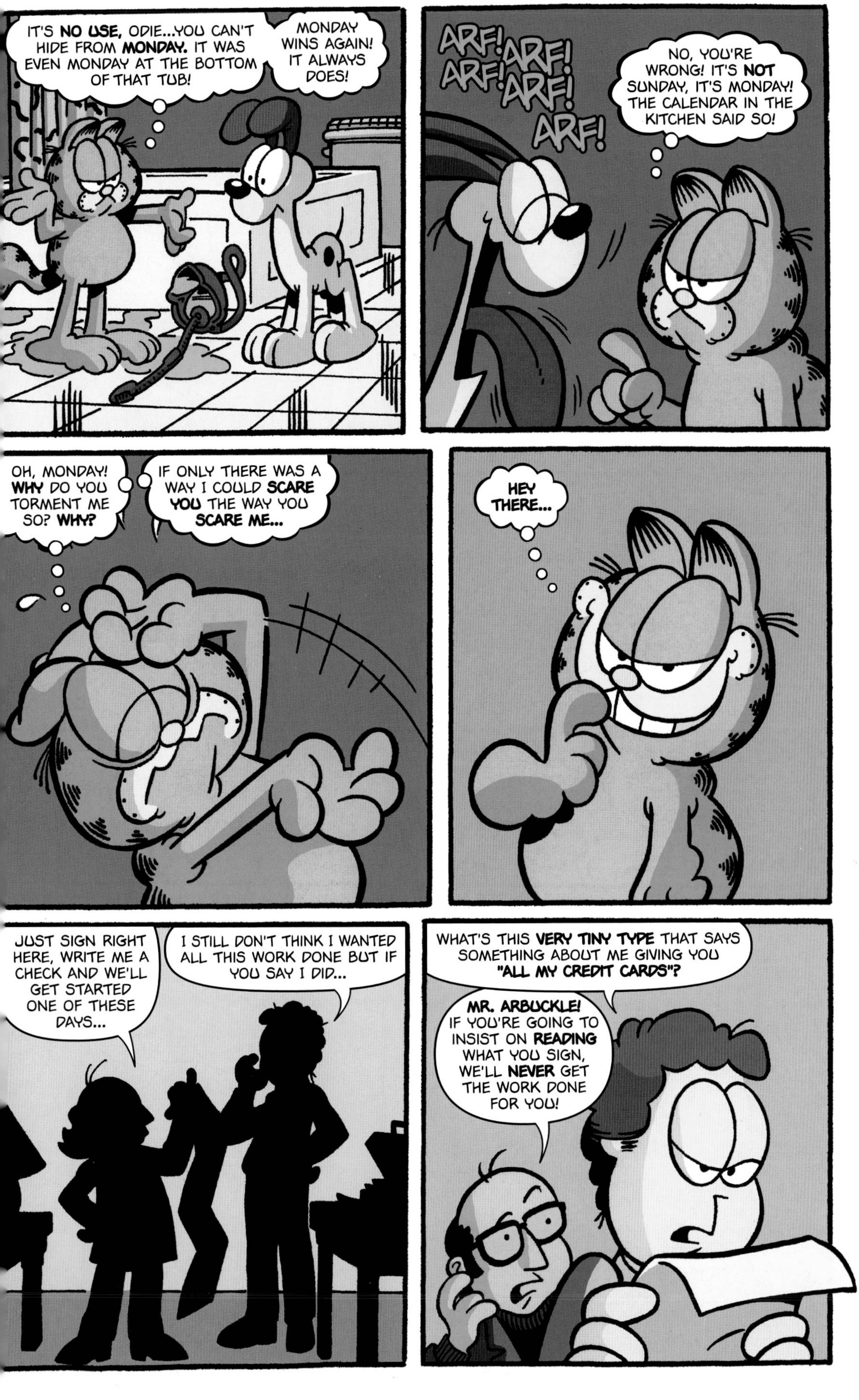
IT'S NO USE, ODIE...YOU CAN'T HIDE FROM MONDAY. IT WAS EVEN MONDAY AT THE BOTTOM OF THAT TUB!
MONDAY WINS AGAIN! IT ALWAYS DOES!
ARF! ARF! ARF! ARF! ARF!
NO, YOU'RE WRONG! IT'S NOT SUNDAY, IT'S MONDAY! THE CALENDAR IN THE KITCHEN SAID SO!
OH, MONDAY! WHY DO YOU TORMENT ME SO? WHY?
IF ONLY THERE WAS A WAY I COULD SCARE YOU THE WAY YOU SCARE ME...
HEY THERE...
JUST SIGN RIGHT HERE, WRITE ME A CHECK AND WE'LL GET STARTED ONE OF THESE DAYS...
I STILL DON'T THINK I WANTED ALL THIS WORK DONE BUT IF YOU SAY I DID...
WHAT'S THIS VERY TINY TYPE THAT SAYS SOMETHING ABOUT ME GIVING YOU "ALL MY CREDIT CARDS"?
MR. ARBUCKLE! IF YOU'RE GOING TO INSIST ON READING WHAT YOU SIGN, WE'LL NEVER GET THE WORK DONE FOR YOU!

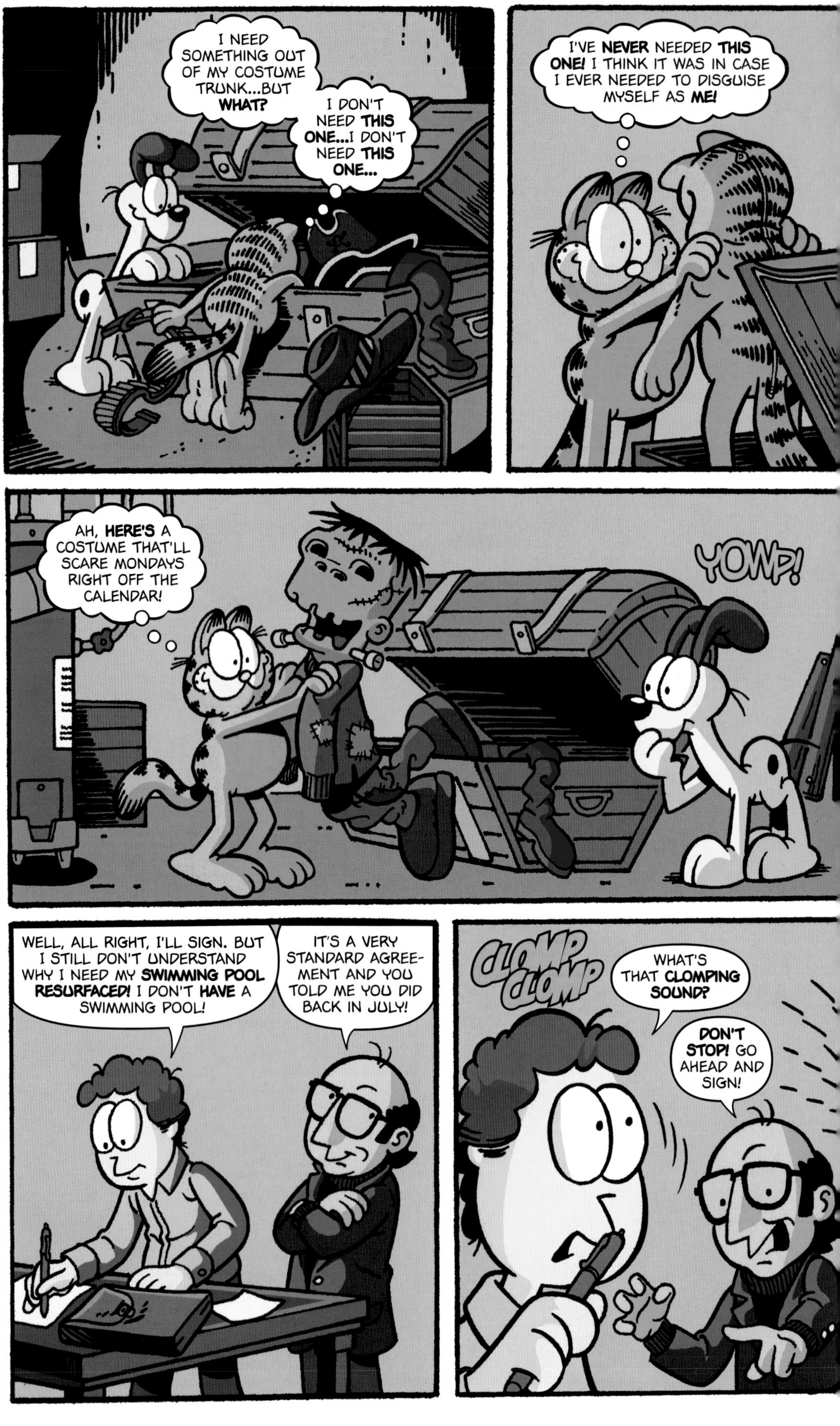

I NEED SOMETHING OUT OF MY COSTUME TRUNK...BUT **WHAT?**
I DON'T NEED **THIS ONE...**I DON'T NEED **THIS ONE...**
I'VE **NEVER** NEEDED **THIS ONE!** I THINK IT WAS IN CASE I EVER NEEDED TO DISGUISE MYSELF AS **ME!**
AH, **HERE'S** A COSTUME THAT'LL SCARE MONDAYS RIGHT OFF THE CALENDAR!
YOWP!
WELL, ALL RIGHT, I'LL SIGN. BUT I STILL DON'T UNDERSTAND WHY I NEED MY **SWIMMING POOL RESURFACED!** I DON'T **HAVE** A SWIMMING POOL!
IT'S A VERY STANDARD AGREE-MENT AND YOU TOLD ME YOU DID BACK IN JULY!
CLOMP CLOMP
WHAT'S THAT **CLOMPING SOUND?**
DON'T STOP! GO AHEAD AND SIGN!

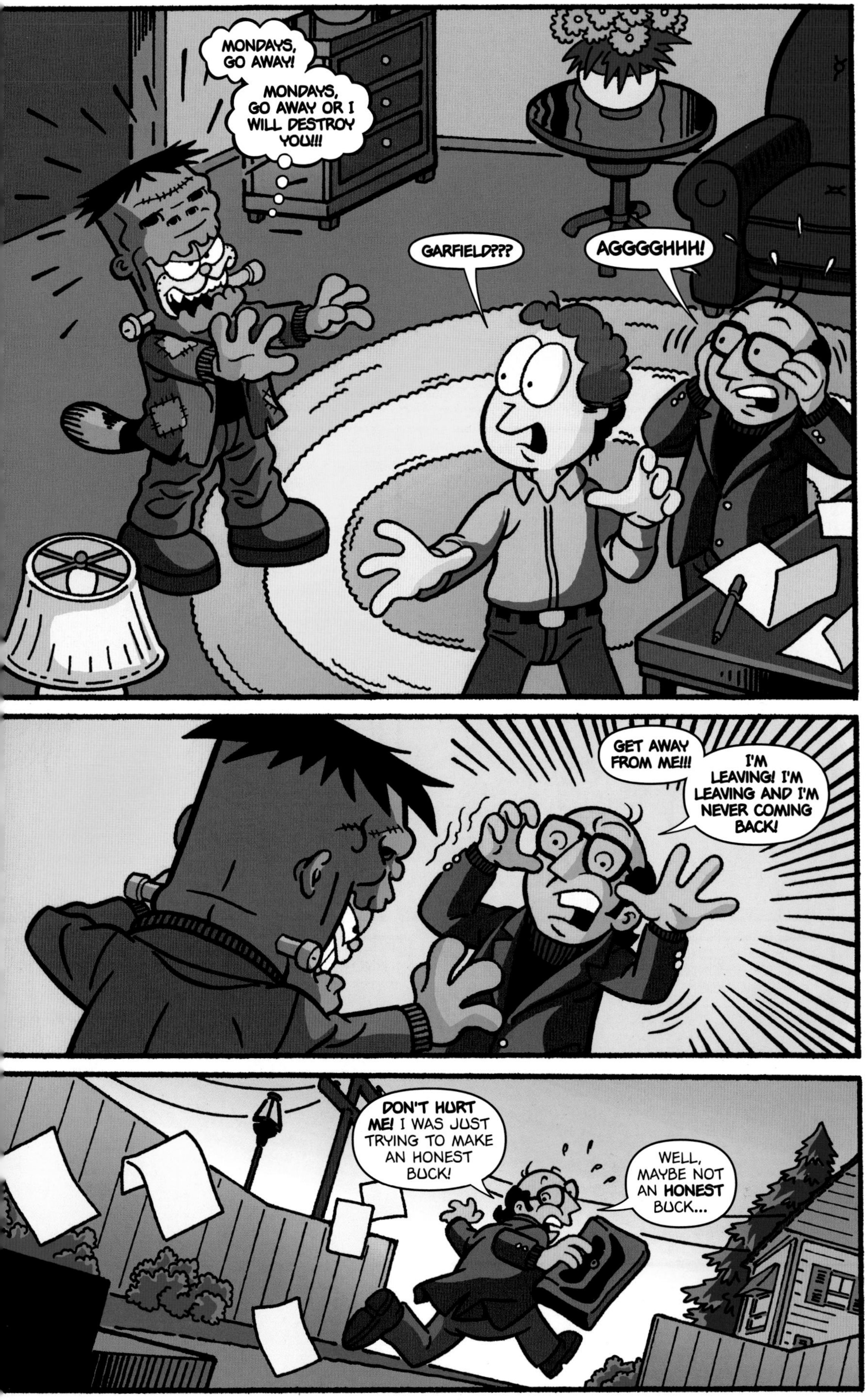
MONDAYS, GO AWAY!
MONDAYS, GO AWAY OR I WILL DESTROY YOU!!!
GARFIELD???
AGGGGHHH!
GET AWAY FROM ME!!!
I'M LEAVING! I'M LEAVING AND I'M NEVER COMING BACK!
DON'T HURT ME! I WAS JUST TRYING TO MAKE AN HONEST BUCK!
WELL, MAYBE NOT AN HONEST BUCK...

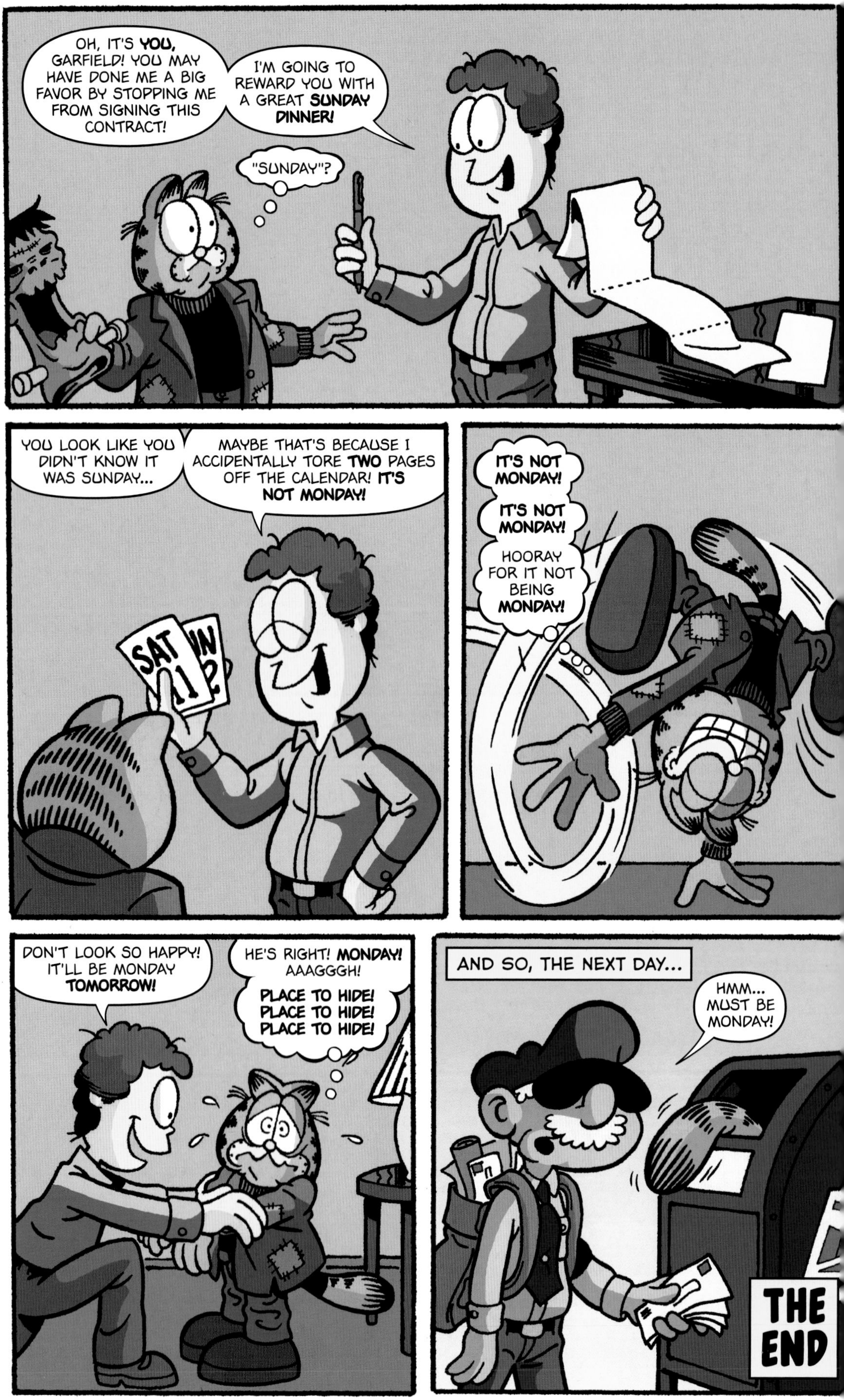
OH, IT'S **YOU,** GARFIELD! YOU MAY HAVE DONE ME A BIG FAVOR BY STOPPING ME FROM SIGNING THIS CONTRACT!
I'M GOING TO REWARD YOU WITH A GREAT **SUNDAY DINNER!**
"SUNDAY"?
YOU LOOK LIKE YOU DIDN'T KNOW IT WAS SUNDAY...
MAYBE THAT'S BECAUSE I ACCIDENTALLY TORE **TWO** PAGES OFF THE CALENDAR! **IT'S NOT MONDAY!**
SAT 11
IT'S NOT MONDAY!
IT'S NOT MONDAY!
HOORAY FOR IT NOT BEING **MONDAY!**
DON'T LOOK SO HAPPY! IT'LL BE MONDAY **TOMORROW!**
HE'S RIGHT! **MONDAY!** AAAGGGH!
PLACE TO HIDE! PLACE TO HIDE! PLACE TO HIDE!
AND SO, THE NEXT DAY...
HMM... MUST BE MONDAY!
THE END

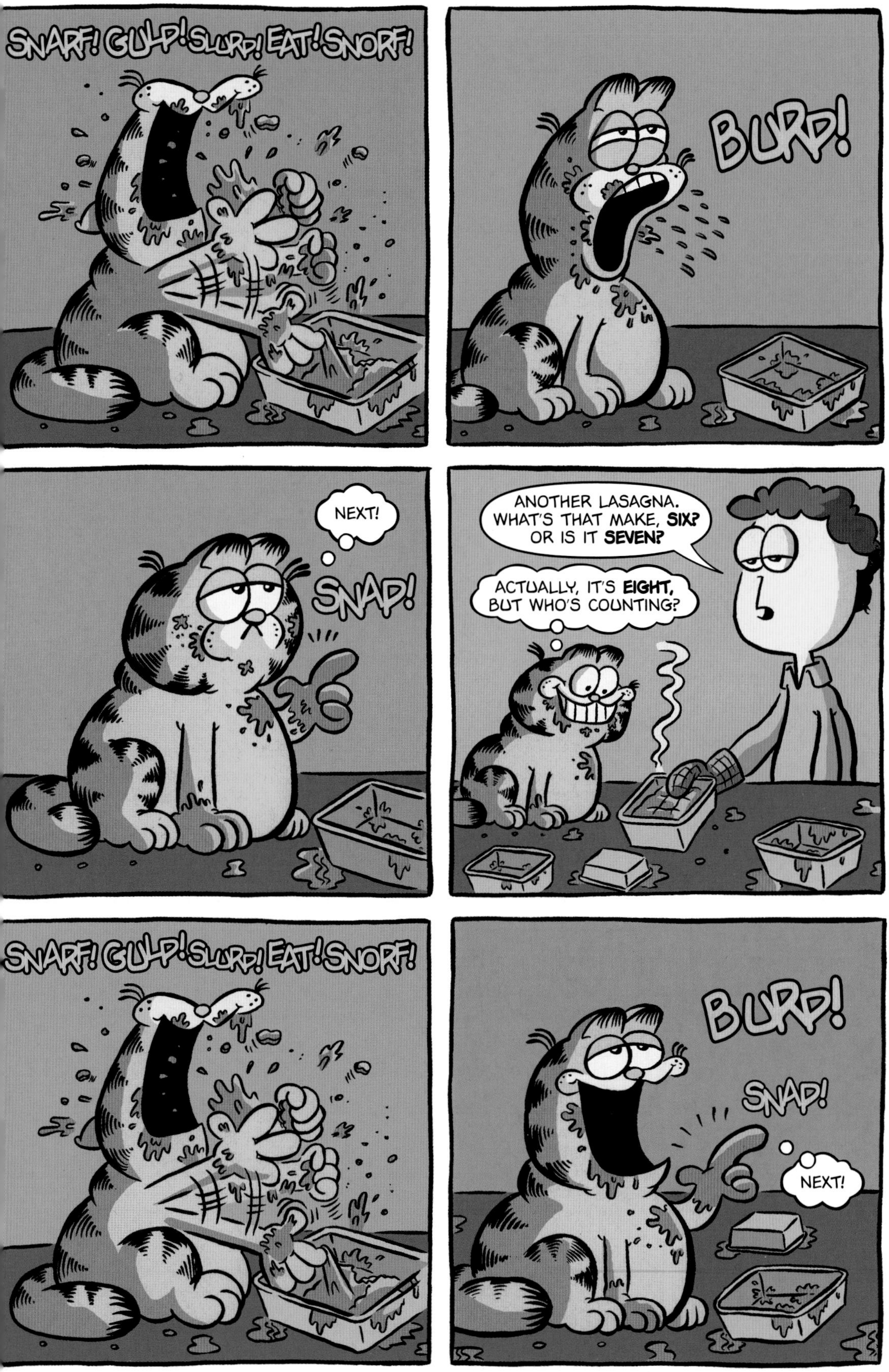
SNARF! GULP! SLURP! EAT! SNORF!
BURP!
NEXT!
SNAP!
ANOTHER LASAGNA. WHAT'S THAT MAKE, **SIX?** OR IS IT **SEVEN?**
ACTUALLY, IT'S **EIGHT**, BUT WHO'S COUNTING?
SNARF! GULP! SLURP! EAT! SNORF!
BURP!
SNAP!
NEXT!

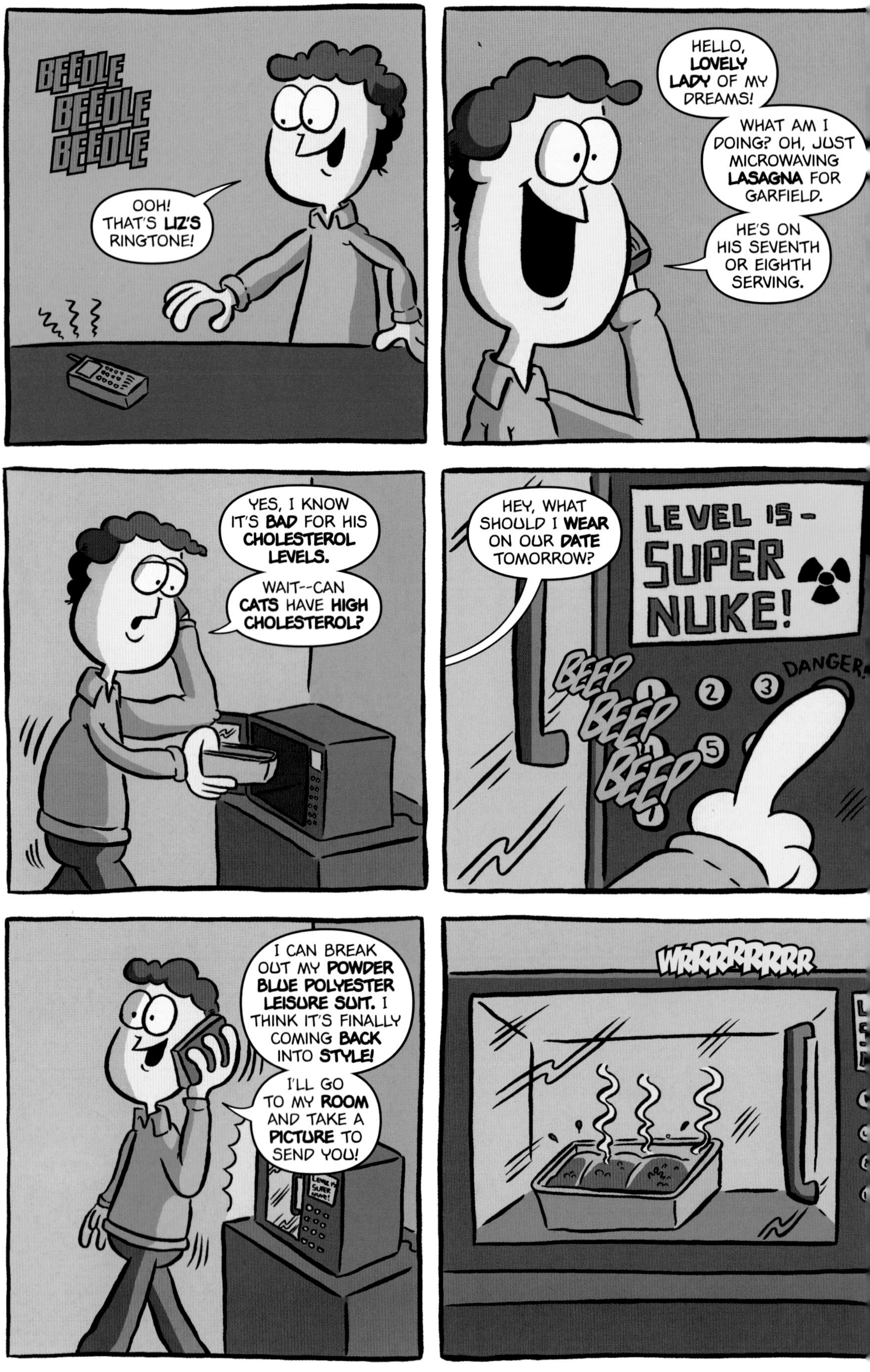

BEEDLE BEEDLE BEEDLE
OOH! THAT'S LIZ'S RINGTONE!
HELLO, LOVELY LADY OF MY DREAMS!
WHAT AM I DOING? OH, JUST MICROWAVING LASAGNA FOR GARFIELD.
HE'S ON HIS SEVENTH OR EIGHTH SERVING.
YES, I KNOW IT'S BAD FOR HIS CHOLESTEROL LEVELS.
WAIT--CAN CATS HAVE HIGH CHOLESTEROL?
HEY, WHAT SHOULD I WEAR ON OUR DATE TOMORROW?
LEVEL IS - SUPER NUKE!
DANGER!
BEEP BEEP BEEP
I CAN BREAK OUT MY POWDER BLUE POLYESTER LEISURE SUIT. I THINK IT'S FINALLY COMING BACK INTO STYLE!
I'LL GO TO MY ROOM AND TAKE A PICTURE TO SEND YOU!
WRRRRRRRR

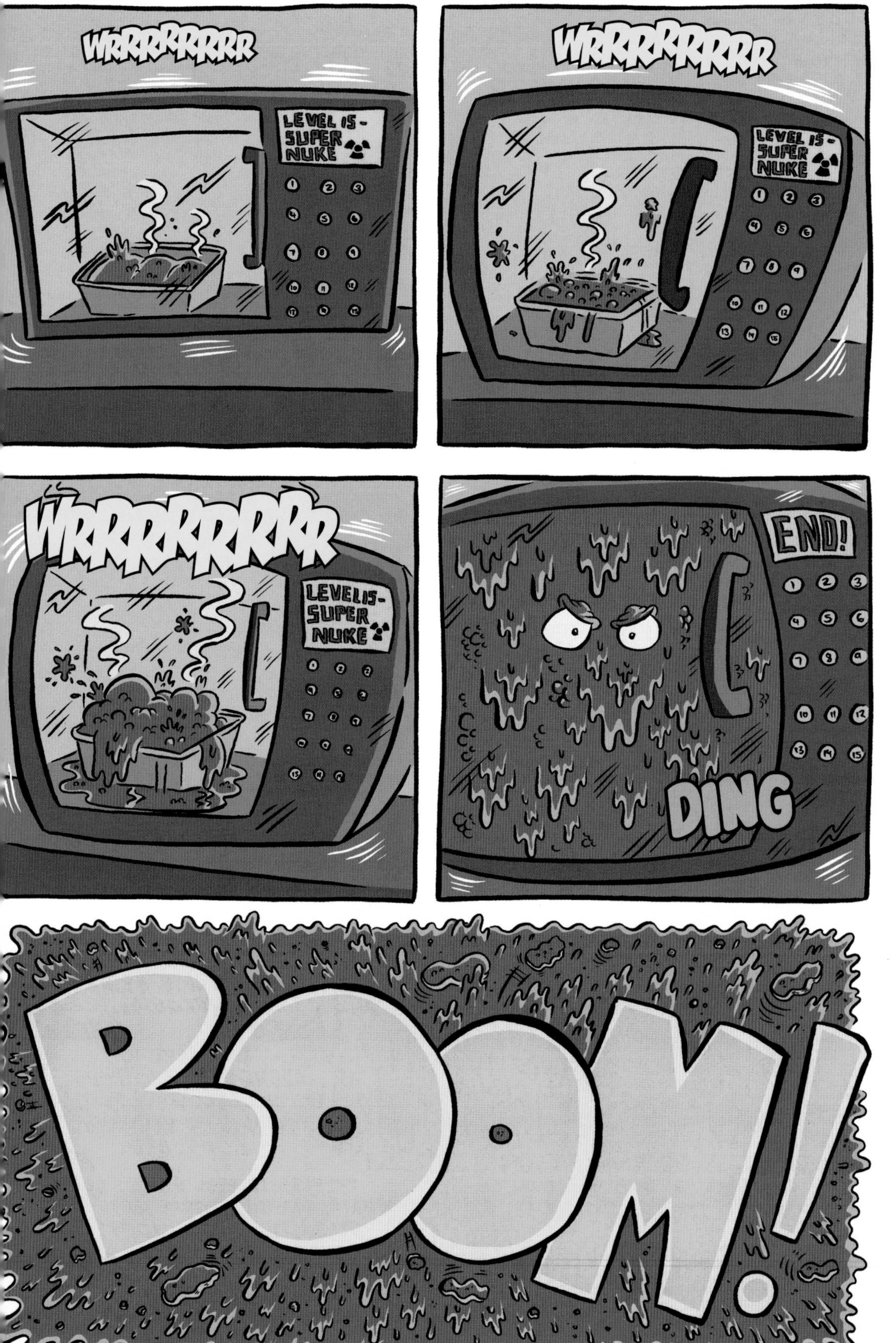
WRRRRRRRR
LEVEL IS - SUPER NUKE
WRRRRRRRRR
LEVEL IS - SUPER NUKE
WRRRRRRRRR
LEVEL IS - SUPER NUKE
END!
DING
BOOM!!

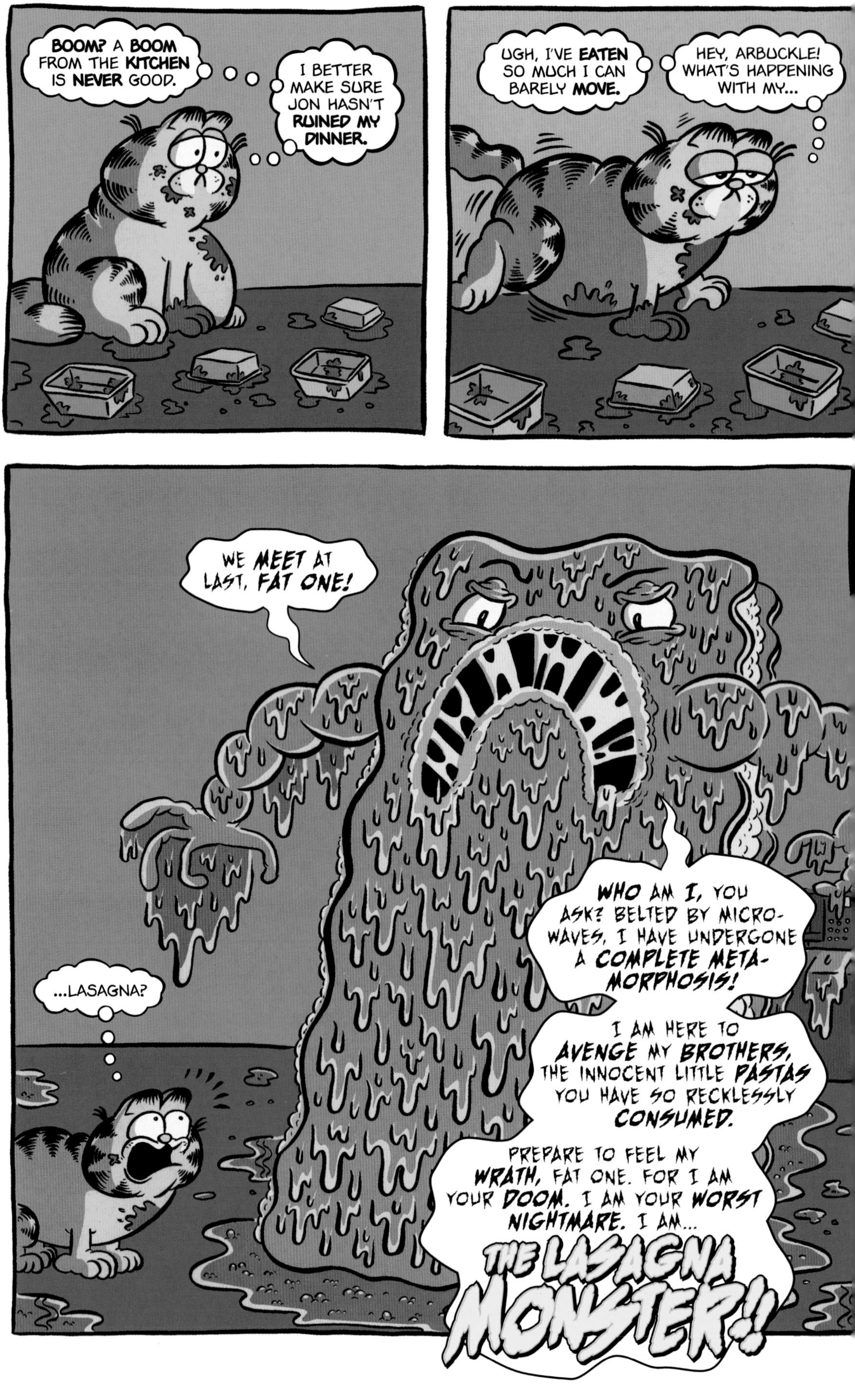

BOOM? A BOOM FROM THE KITCHEN IS NEVER GOOD.
I BETTER MAKE SURE JON HASN'T RUINED MY DINNER.
UGH, I'VE EATEN SO MUCH I CAN BARELY MOVE.
HEY, ARBUCKLE! WHAT'S HAPPENING WITH MY...
WE MEET AT LAST, FAT ONE!
...LASAGNA?
WHO AM I, YOU ASK? BELTED BY MICRO-WAVES, I HAVE UNDERGONE A COMPLETE META-MORPHOSIS!
I AM HERE TO AVENGE MY BROTHERS, THE INNOCENT LITTLE PASTAS YOU HAVE SO RECKLESSLY CONSUMED.
PREPARE TO FEEL MY WRATH, FAT ONE. FOR I AM YOUR DOOM. I AM YOUR WORST NIGHTMARE. I AM...
THE LASAGNA MONSTER!!

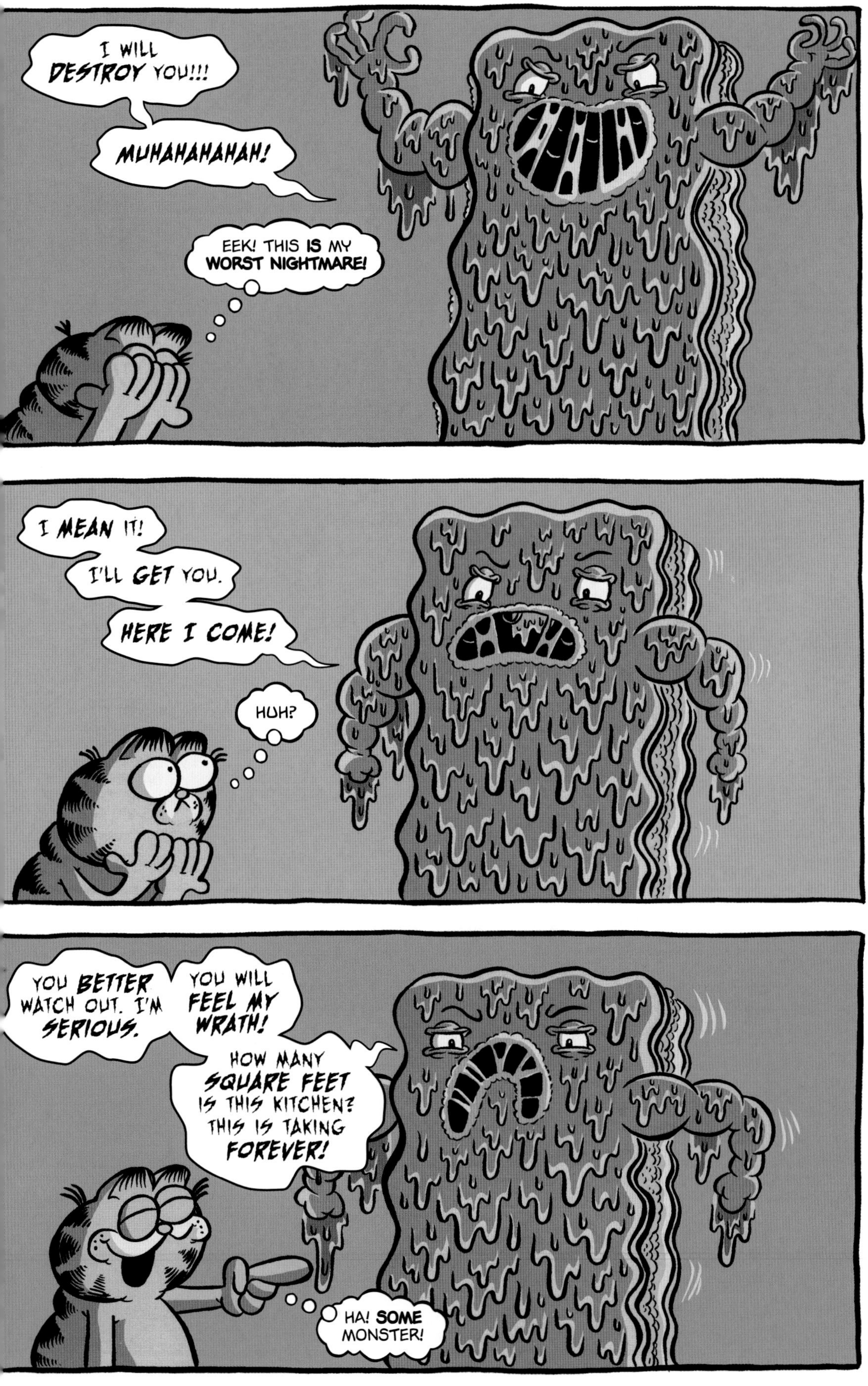
I WILL DESTROY YOU!!!
MUHAHAHAHAH!
EEK! THIS IS MY WORST NIGHTMARE!
I MEAN IT!
I'LL GET YOU.
HERE I COME!
HUH?
YOU BETTER WATCH OUT. I'M SERIOUS.
YOU WILL FEEL MY WRATH!
HOW MANY SQUARE FEET IS THIS KITCHEN? THIS IS TAKING FOREVER!
HA! SOME MONSTER!

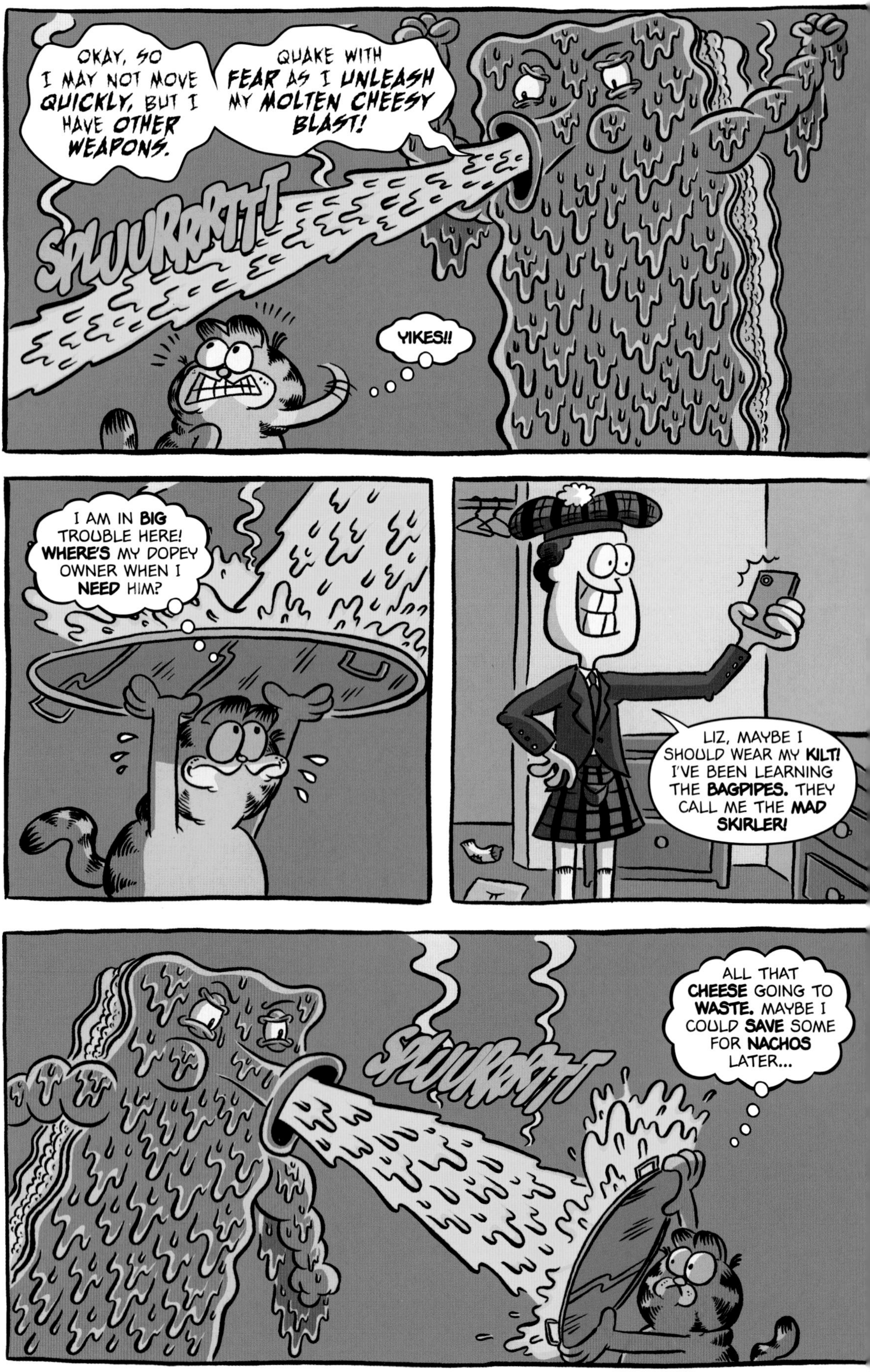

OKAY, SO I MAY NOT MOVE QUICKLY, BUT I HAVE OTHER WEAPONS.
QUAKE WITH FEAR AS I UNLEASH MY MOLTEN CHEESY BLAST!
SPLUURRRTTT
YIKES!!
I AM IN BIG TROUBLE HERE! WHERE'S MY DOPEY OWNER WHEN I NEED HIM?
LIZ, MAYBE I SHOULD WEAR MY KILT! I'VE BEEN LEARNING THE BAGPIPES. THEY CALL ME THE MAD SKIRLER!
SPLUURRRTTT
ALL THAT CHEESE GOING TO WASTE. MAYBE I COULD SAVE SOME FOR NACHOS LATER...

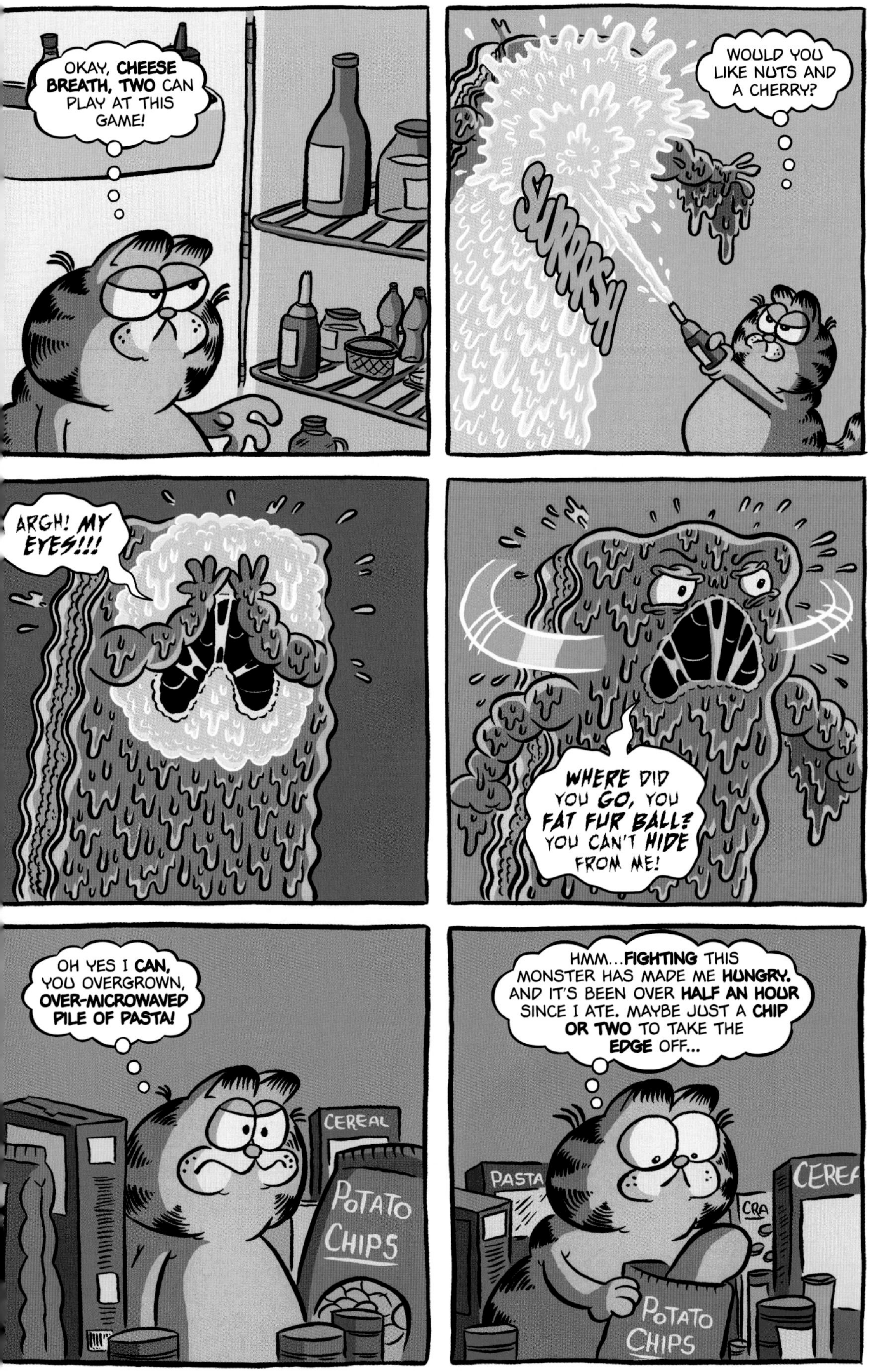

OKAY, CHEESE BREATH, TWO CAN PLAY AT THIS GAME!
SPLURRSH
WOULD YOU LIKE NUTS AND A CHERRY?
ARGH! MY EYES!!!
WHERE DID YOU GO, YOU FAT FUR BALL? YOU CAN'T HIDE FROM ME!
OH YES I CAN, YOU OVERGROWN, OVER-MICROWAVED PILE OF PASTA!
CEREAL
POTATO CHIPS
HMM...FIGHTING THIS MONSTER HAS MADE ME HUNGRY. AND IT'S BEEN OVER HALF AN HOUR SINCE I ATE. MAYBE JUST A CHIP OR TWO TO TAKE THE EDGE OFF...
PASTA
CRA
CEREA
POTATO CHIPS

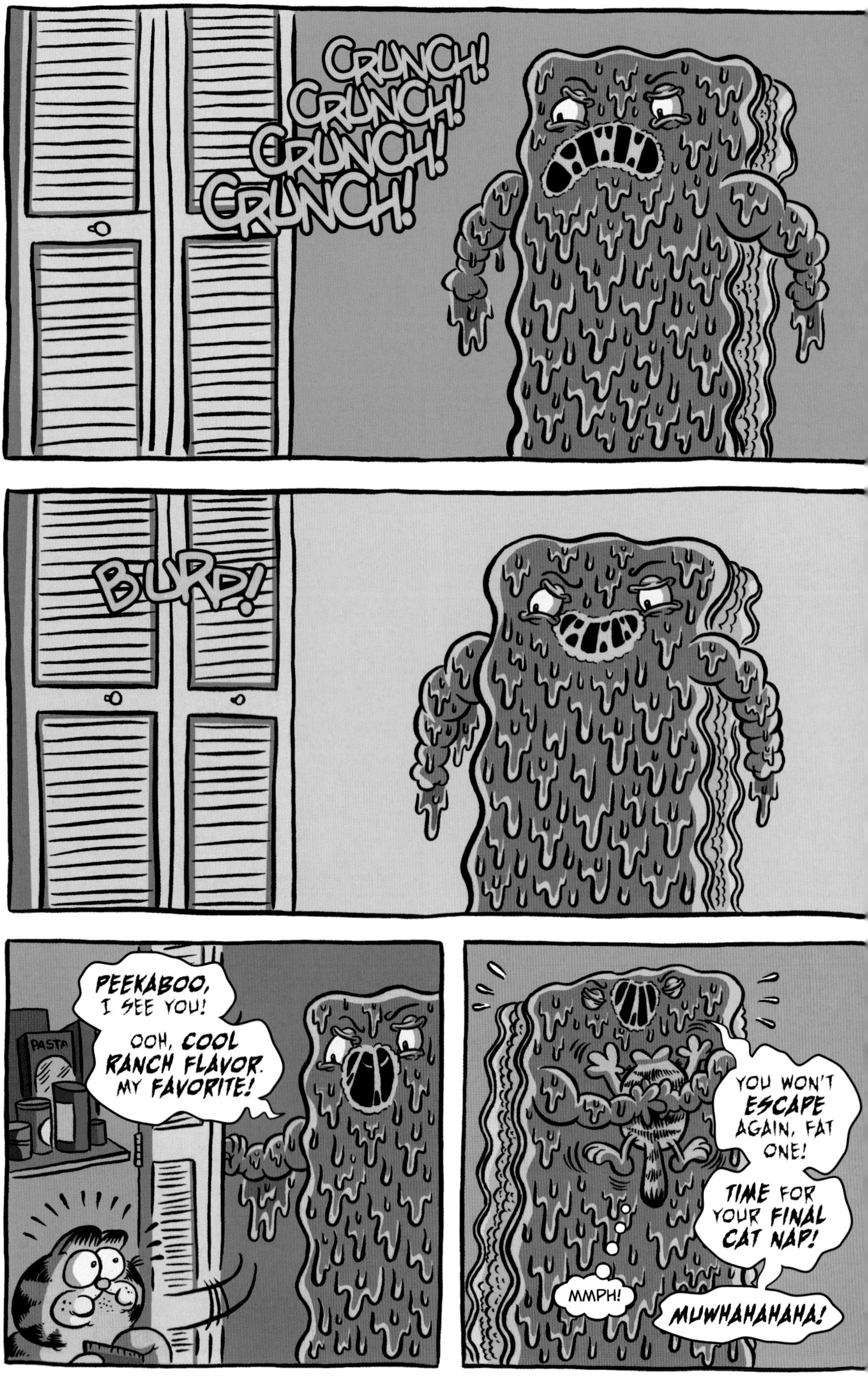
CRUNCH!
CRUNCH!
CRUNCH!
CRUNCH!
BURP!
PEEKABOO, I SEE YOU!
OOH, COOL RANCH FLAVOR. MY FAVORITE!
PASTA
YOU WON'T ESCAPE AGAIN, FAT ONE!
TIME FOR YOUR FINAL CAT NAP!
MMPH!
MUWHAHAHAHA!

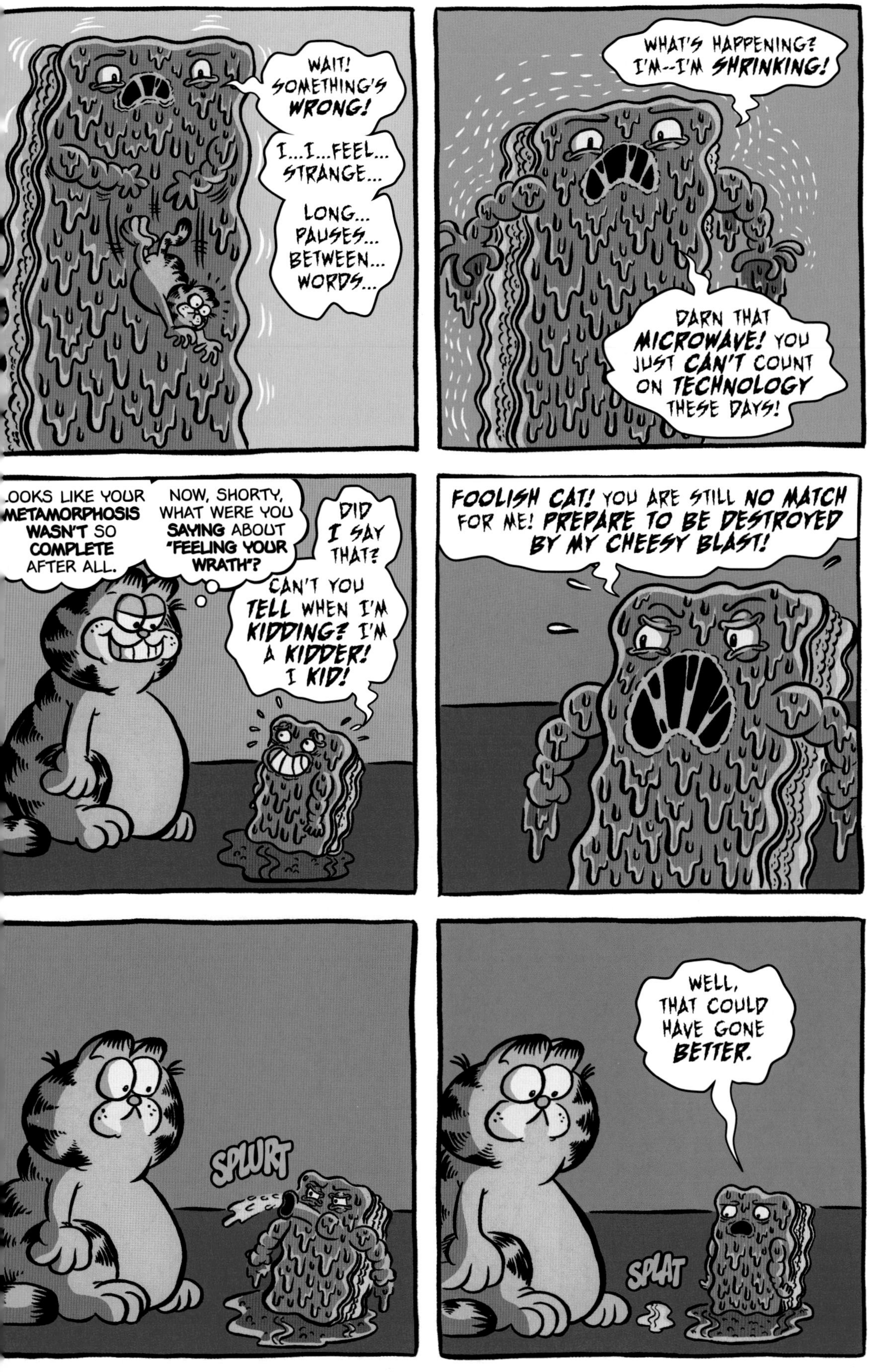
WAIT! SOMETHING'S WRONG!
I...I...FEEL... STRANGE...
LONG... PAUSES... BETWEEN... WORDS...
WHAT'S HAPPENING? I'M--I'M SHRINKING!
DARN THAT MICROWAVE! YOU JUST CAN'T COUNT ON TECHNOLOGY THESE DAYS!
LOOKS LIKE YOUR METAMORPHOSIS WASN'T SO COMPLETE AFTER ALL.
NOW, SHORTY, WHAT WERE YOU SAYING ABOUT "FEELING YOUR WRATH"?
DID I SAY THAT?
CAN'T YOU TELL WHEN I'M KIDDING? I'M A KIDDER! I KID!
FOOLISH CAT! YOU ARE STILL NO MATCH FOR ME! PREPARE TO BE DESTROYED BY MY CHEESY BLAST!
SPLURT
WELL, THAT COULD HAVE GONE BETTER.
SPLAT

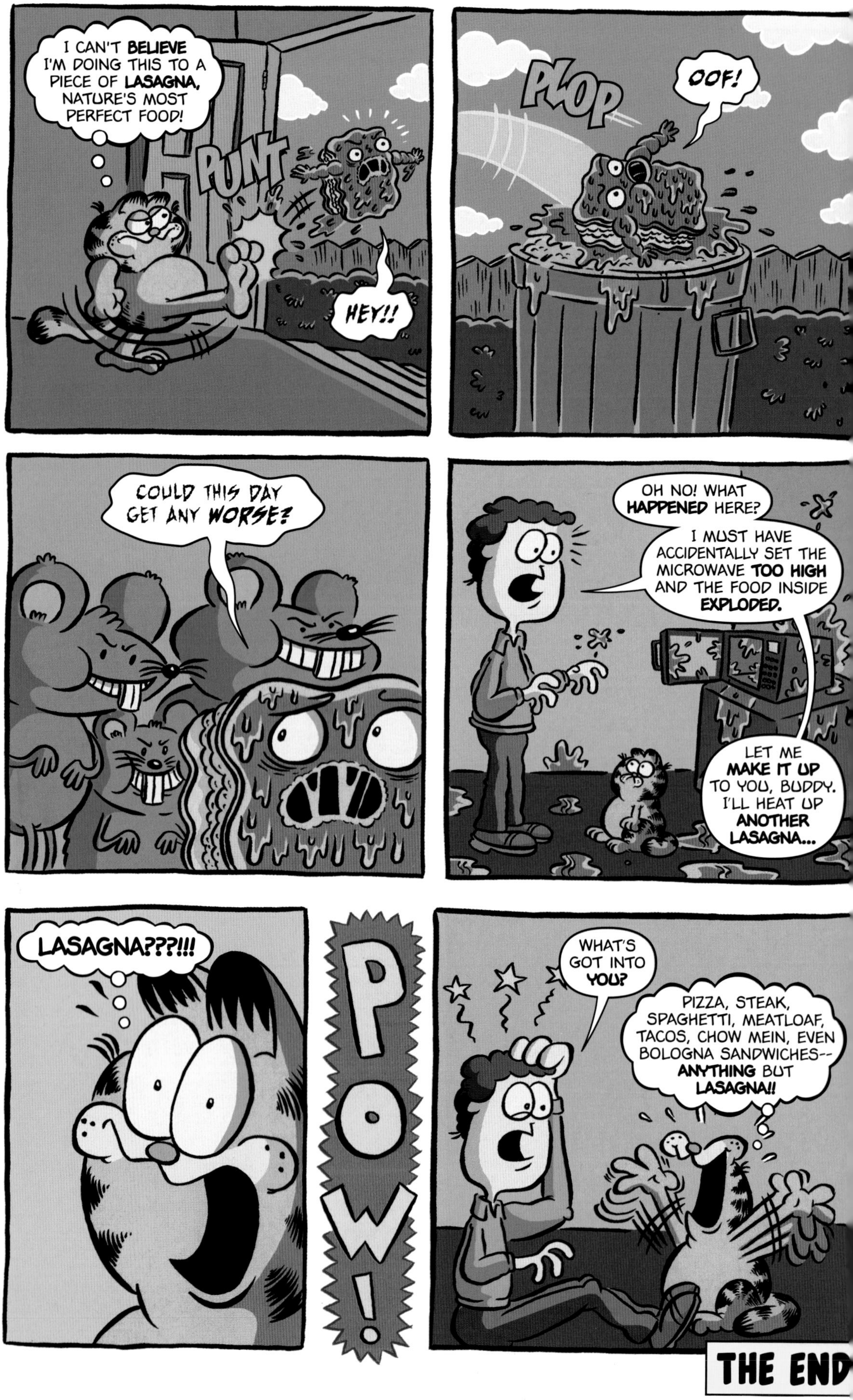
I CAN'T BELIEVE I'M DOING THIS TO A PIECE OF LASAGNA, NATURE'S MOST PERFECT FOOD!
PUNT
HEY!!
PLOP
OOF!
COULD THIS DAY GET ANY WORSE?
OH NO! WHAT HAPPENED HERE?
I MUST HAVE ACCIDENTALLY SET THE MICROWAVE TOO HIGH AND THE FOOD INSIDE EXPLODED.
LET ME MAKE IT UP TO YOU, BUDDY. I'LL HEAT UP ANOTHER LASAGNA...
LASAGNA???!!!
POW!
WHAT'S GOT INTO YOU?
PIZZA, STEAK, SPAGHETTI, MEATLOAF, TACOS, CHOW MEIN, EVEN BOLOGNA SANDWICHES--ANYTHING BUT LASAGNA!!
THE END

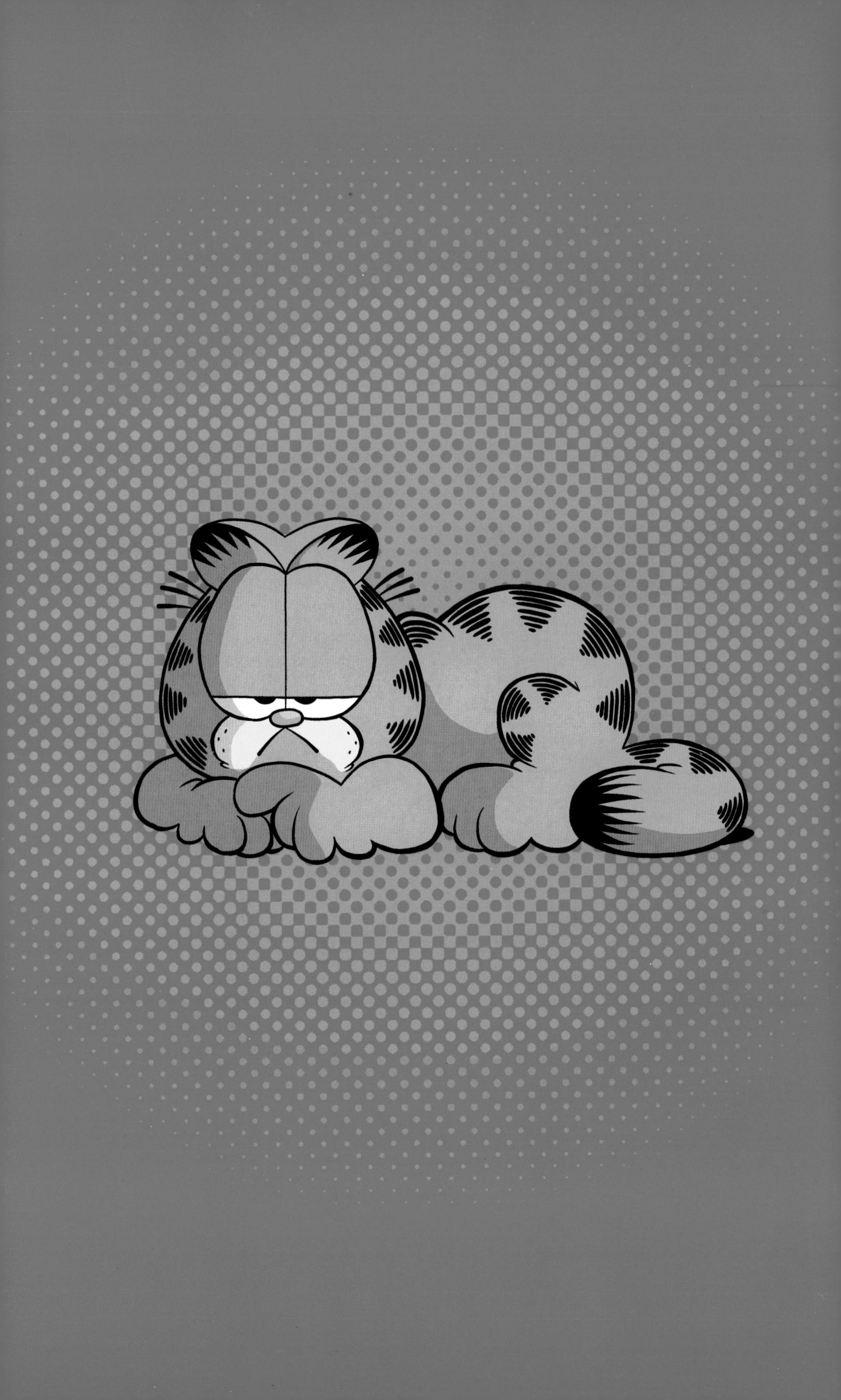

CHAPTER 3

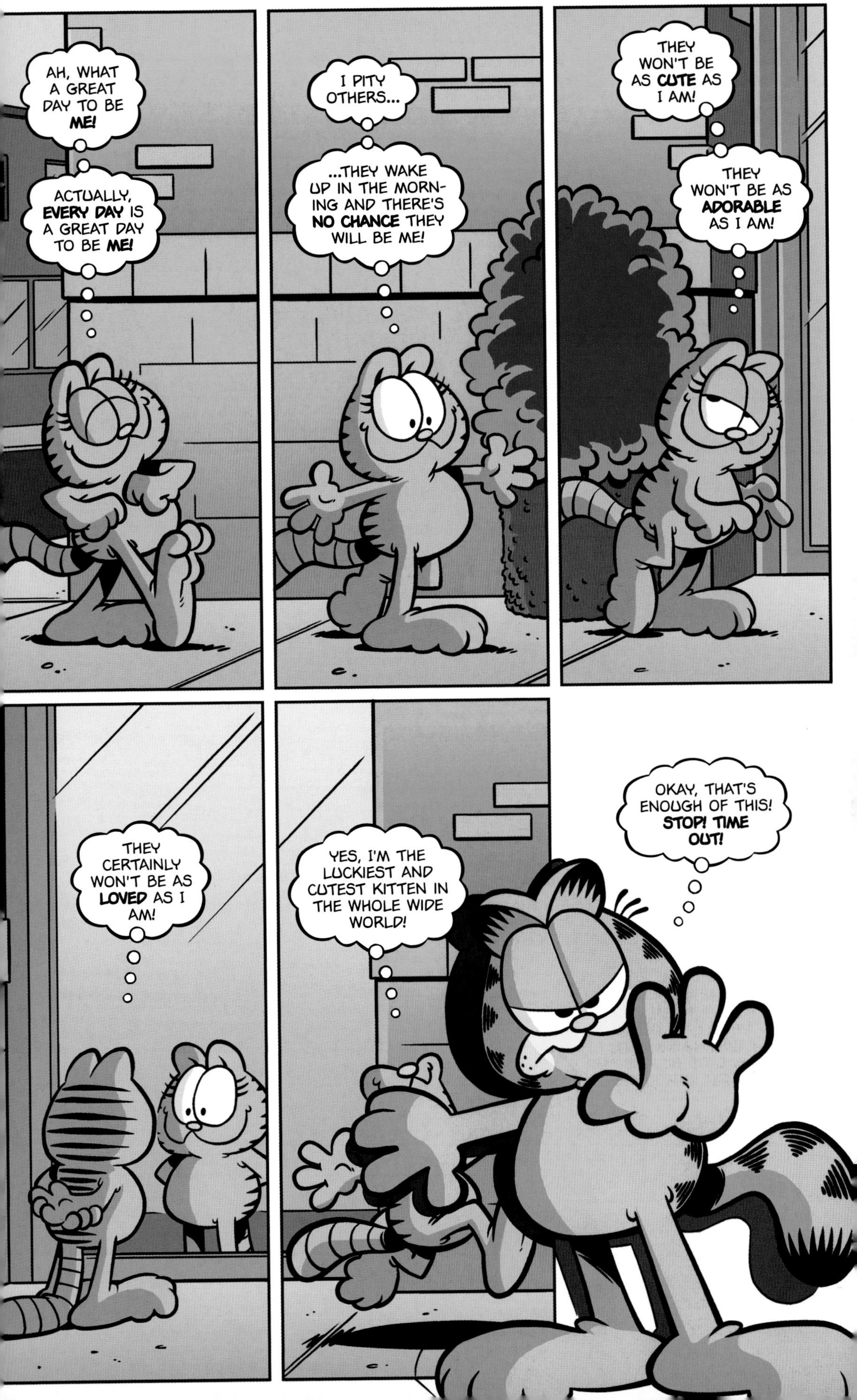
AH, WHAT A GREAT DAY TO BE **ME!**
ACTUALLY, **EVERY DAY** IS A GREAT DAY TO BE **ME!**
I PITY OTHERS...
...THEY WAKE UP IN THE MORNING AND THERE'S **NO CHANCE** THEY WILL BE ME!
THEY WON'T BE AS **CUTE** AS I AM!
THEY WON'T BE AS **ADORABLE** AS I AM!
THEY CERTAINLY WON'T BE AS **LOVED** AS I AM!
YES, I'M THE LUCKIEST AND CUTEST KITTEN IN THE WHOLE WIDE WORLD!
OKAY, THAT'S ENOUGH OF THIS! **STOP! TIME OUT!**

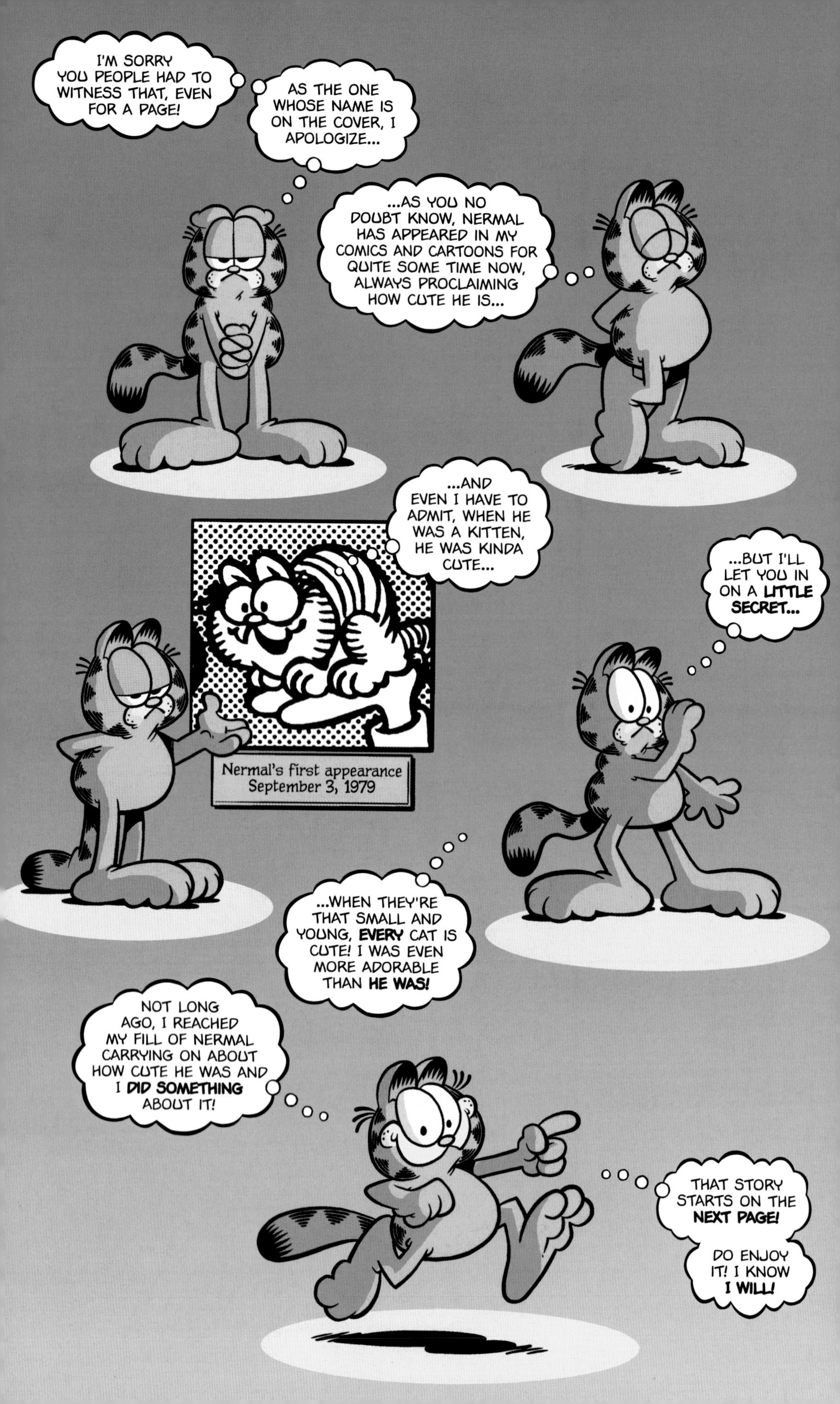

I'M SORRY YOU PEOPLE HAD TO WITNESS THAT, EVEN FOR A PAGE!
AS THE ONE WHOSE NAME IS ON THE COVER, I APOLOGIZE...
...AS YOU NO DOUBT KNOW, NERMAL HAS APPEARED IN MY COMICS AND CARTOONS FOR QUITE SOME TIME NOW, ALWAYS PROCLAIMING HOW CUTE HE IS...
...AND EVEN I HAVE TO ADMIT, WHEN HE WAS A KITTEN, HE WAS KINDA CUTE...
Nermal's first appearance September 3, 1979
...BUT I'LL LET YOU IN ON A **LITTLE SECRET...**
...WHEN THEY'RE THAT SMALL AND YOUNG, **EVERY** CAT IS CUTE! I WAS EVEN MORE ADORABLE THAN **HE WAS!**
NOT LONG AGO, I REACHED MY FILL OF NERMAL CARRYING ON ABOUT HOW CUTE HE WAS AND I **DID SOMETHING** ABOUT IT!
THAT STORY STARTS ON THE **NEXT PAGE!**
DO ENJOY IT! I KNOW **I WILL!**

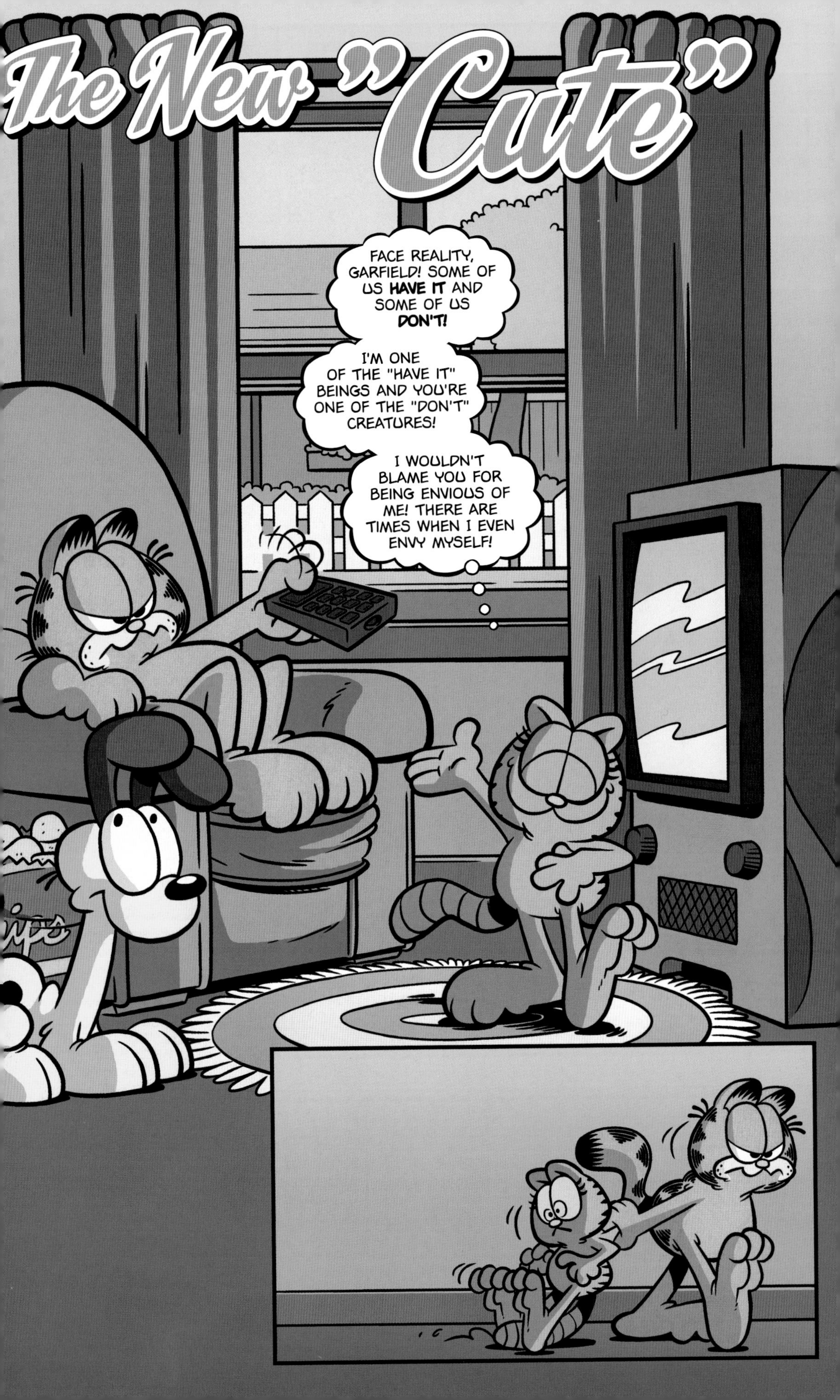
The New "Cute"
FACE REALITY, GARFIELD! SOME OF US **HAVE IT** AND SOME OF US **DON'T!**
I'M ONE OF THE "HAVE IT" BEINGS AND YOU'RE ONE OF THE "DON'T" CREATURES!
I WOULDN'T BLAME YOU FOR BEING ENVIOUS OF ME! THERE ARE TIMES WHEN I EVEN ENVY MYSELF!

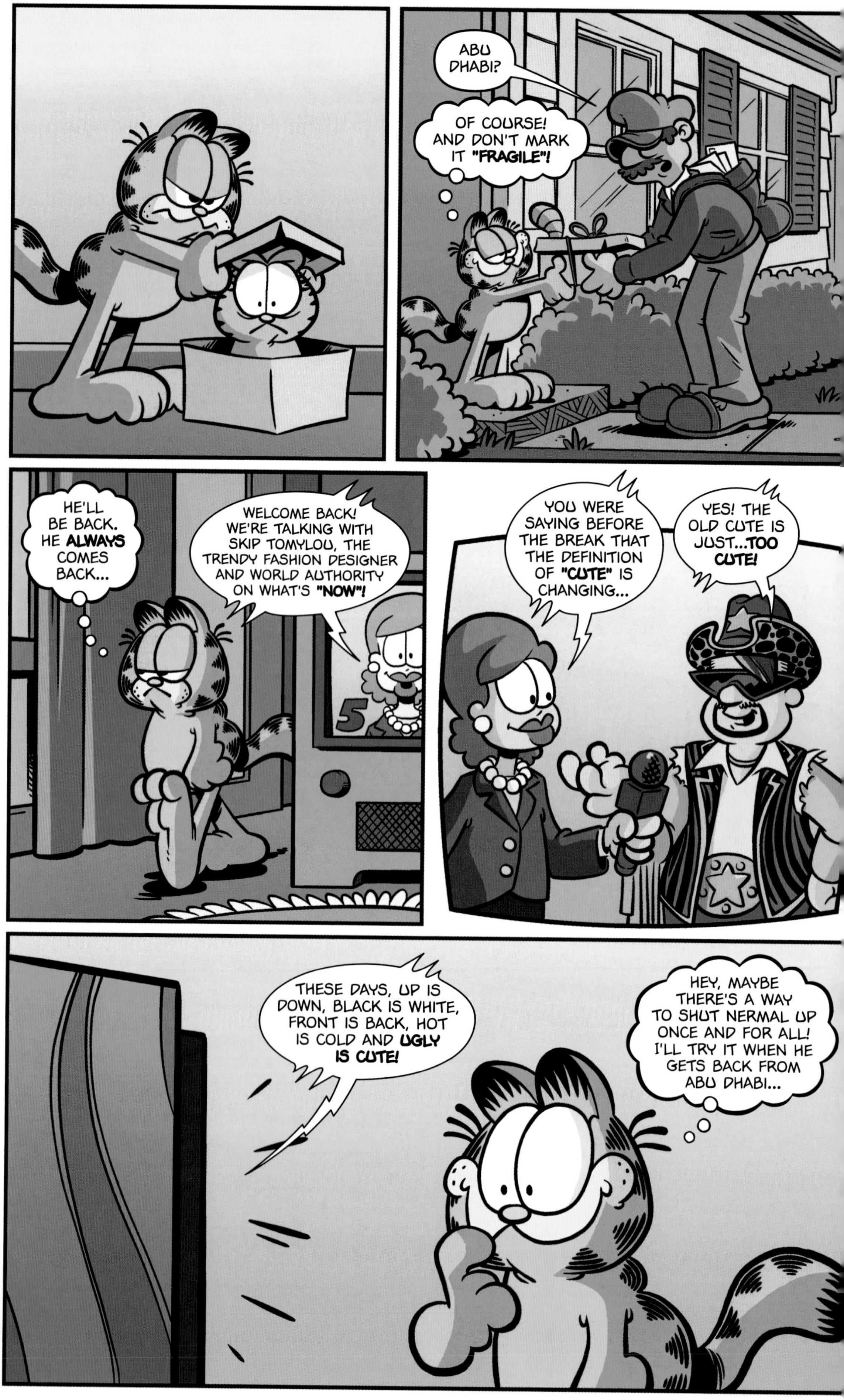

ABU DHABI?
OF COURSE! AND DON'T MARK IT "FRAGILE"!
HE'LL BE BACK. HE ALWAYS COMES BACK...
WELCOME BACK! WE'RE TALKING WITH SKIP TOMYLOU, THE TRENDY FASHION DESIGNER AND WORLD AUTHORITY ON WHAT'S "NOW"!
5
YOU WERE SAYING BEFORE THE BREAK THAT THE DEFINITION OF "CUTE" IS CHANGING...
YES! THE OLD CUTE IS JUST...TOO CUTE!
THESE DAYS, UP IS DOWN, BLACK IS WHITE, FRONT IS BACK, HOT IS COLD AND UGLY IS CUTE!
HEY, MAYBE THERE'S A WAY TO SHUT NERMAL UP ONCE AND FOR ALL! I'LL TRY IT WHEN HE GETS BACK FROM ABU DHABI...

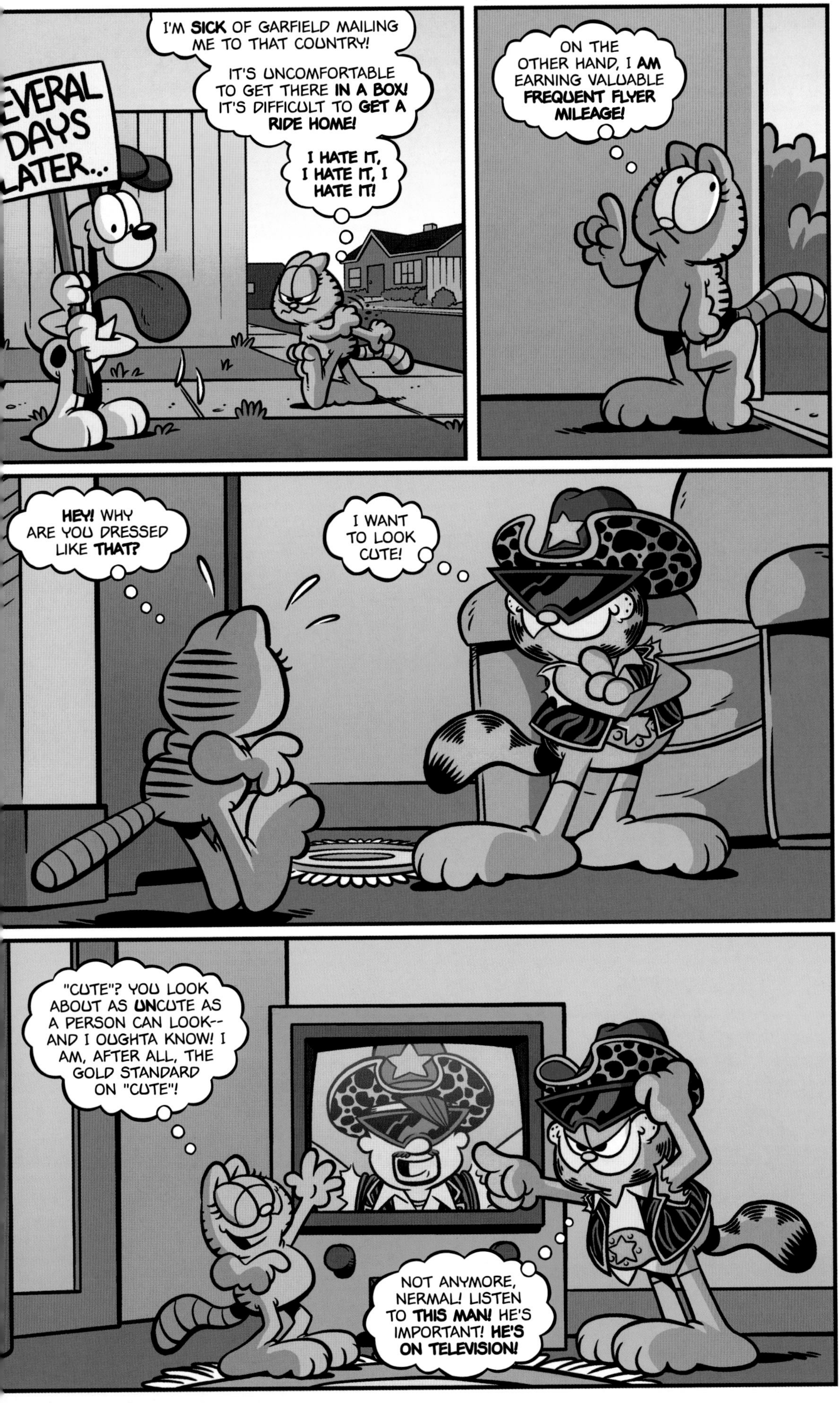

SEVERAL DAYS LATER...
I'M SICK OF GARFIELD MAILING ME TO THAT COUNTRY!
IT'S UNCOMFORTABLE TO GET THERE IN A BOX! IT'S DIFFICULT TO GET A RIDE HOME!
I HATE IT, I HATE IT, I HATE IT!
ON THE OTHER HAND, I AM EARNING VALUABLE FREQUENT FLYER MILEAGE!
HEY! WHY ARE YOU DRESSED LIKE THAT?
I WANT TO LOOK CUTE!
"CUTE"? YOU LOOK ABOUT AS UNCUTE AS A PERSON CAN LOOK-- AND I OUGHTA KNOW! I AM, AFTER ALL, THE GOLD STANDARD ON "CUTE"!
NOT ANYMORE, NERMAL! LISTEN TO THIS MAN! HE'S IMPORTANT! HE'S ON TELEVISION!

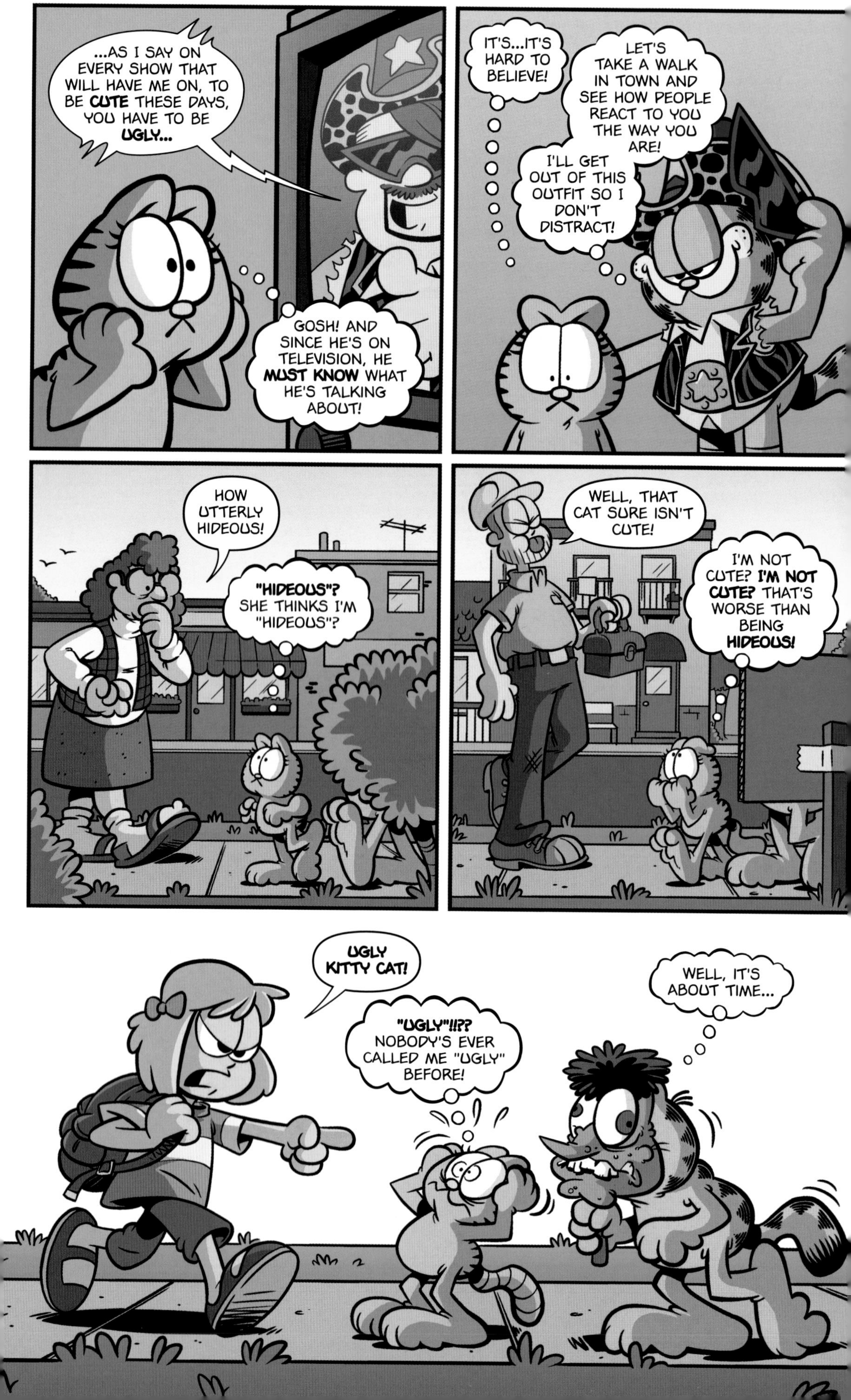
...AS I SAY ON EVERY SHOW THAT WILL HAVE ME ON, TO BE CUTE THESE DAYS, YOU HAVE TO BE UGLY...
GOSH! AND SINCE HE'S ON TELEVISION, HE MUST KNOW WHAT HE'S TALKING ABOUT!
IT'S...IT'S HARD TO BELIEVE!
LET'S TAKE A WALK IN TOWN AND SEE HOW PEOPLE REACT TO YOU THE WAY YOU ARE!
I'LL GET OUT OF THIS OUTFIT SO I DON'T DISTRACT!
HOW UTTERLY HIDEOUS!
"HIDEOUS"? SHE THINKS I'M "HIDEOUS"?
WELL, THAT CAT SURE ISN'T CUTE!
I'M NOT CUTE? I'M NOT CUTE? THAT'S WORSE THAN BEING HIDEOUS!
UGLY KITTY CAT!
"UGLY"!!?? NOBODY'S EVER CALLED ME "UGLY" BEFORE!
WELL, IT'S ABOUT TIME...

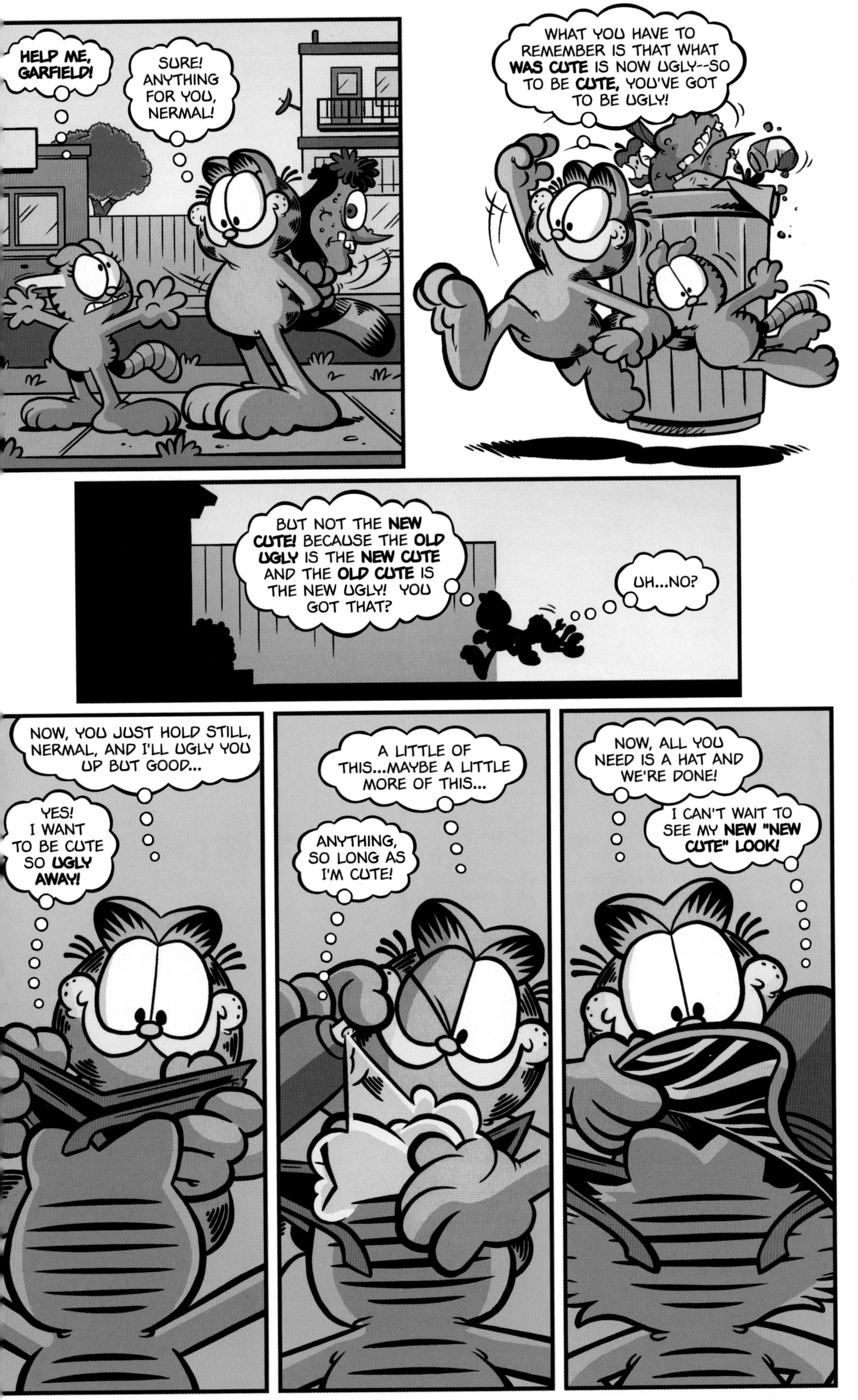

HELP ME, GARFIELD!
SURE! ANYTHING FOR YOU, NERMAL!
WHAT YOU HAVE TO REMEMBER IS THAT WHAT WAS CUTE IS NOW UGLY--SO TO BE CUTE, YOU'VE GOT TO BE UGLY!
BUT NOT THE NEW CUTE! BECAUSE THE OLD UGLY IS THE NEW CUTE AND THE OLD CUTE IS THE NEW UGLY! YOU GOT THAT?
UH...NO?
NOW, YOU JUST HOLD STILL, NERMAL, AND I'LL UGLY YOU UP BUT GOOD...
YES! I WANT TO BE CUTE SO UGLY AWAY!
A LITTLE OF THIS...MAYBE A LITTLE MORE OF THIS...
ANYTHING, SO LONG AS I'M CUTE!
NOW, ALL YOU NEED IS A HAT AND WE'RE DONE!
I CAN'T WAIT TO SEE MY NEW "NEW CUTE" LOOK!

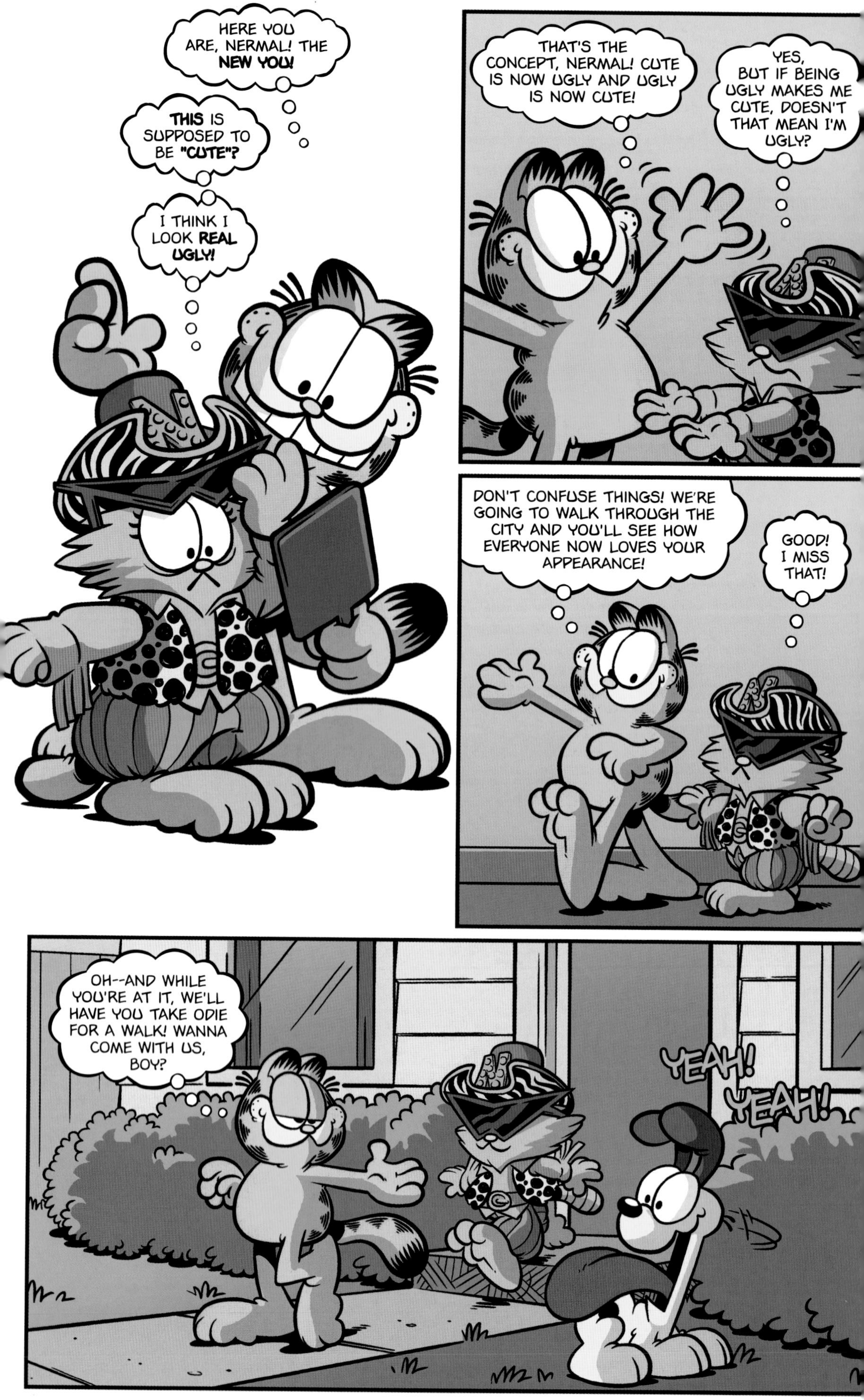
HERE YOU ARE, NERMAL! THE **NEW YOU!**
THIS IS SUPPOSED TO BE **"CUTE"?**
I THINK I LOOK **REAL UGLY!**
THAT'S THE CONCEPT, NERMAL! CUTE IS NOW UGLY AND UGLY IS NOW CUTE!
YES, BUT IF BEING UGLY MAKES ME CUTE, DOESN'T THAT MEAN I'M UGLY?
DON'T CONFUSE THINGS! WE'RE GOING TO WALK THROUGH THE CITY AND YOU'LL SEE HOW EVERYONE NOW LOVES YOUR APPEARANCE!
GOOD! I MISS THAT!
OH--AND WHILE YOU'RE AT IT, WE'LL HAVE YOU TAKE ODIE FOR A WALK! WANNA COME WITH US, BOY?
YEAH! YEAH!

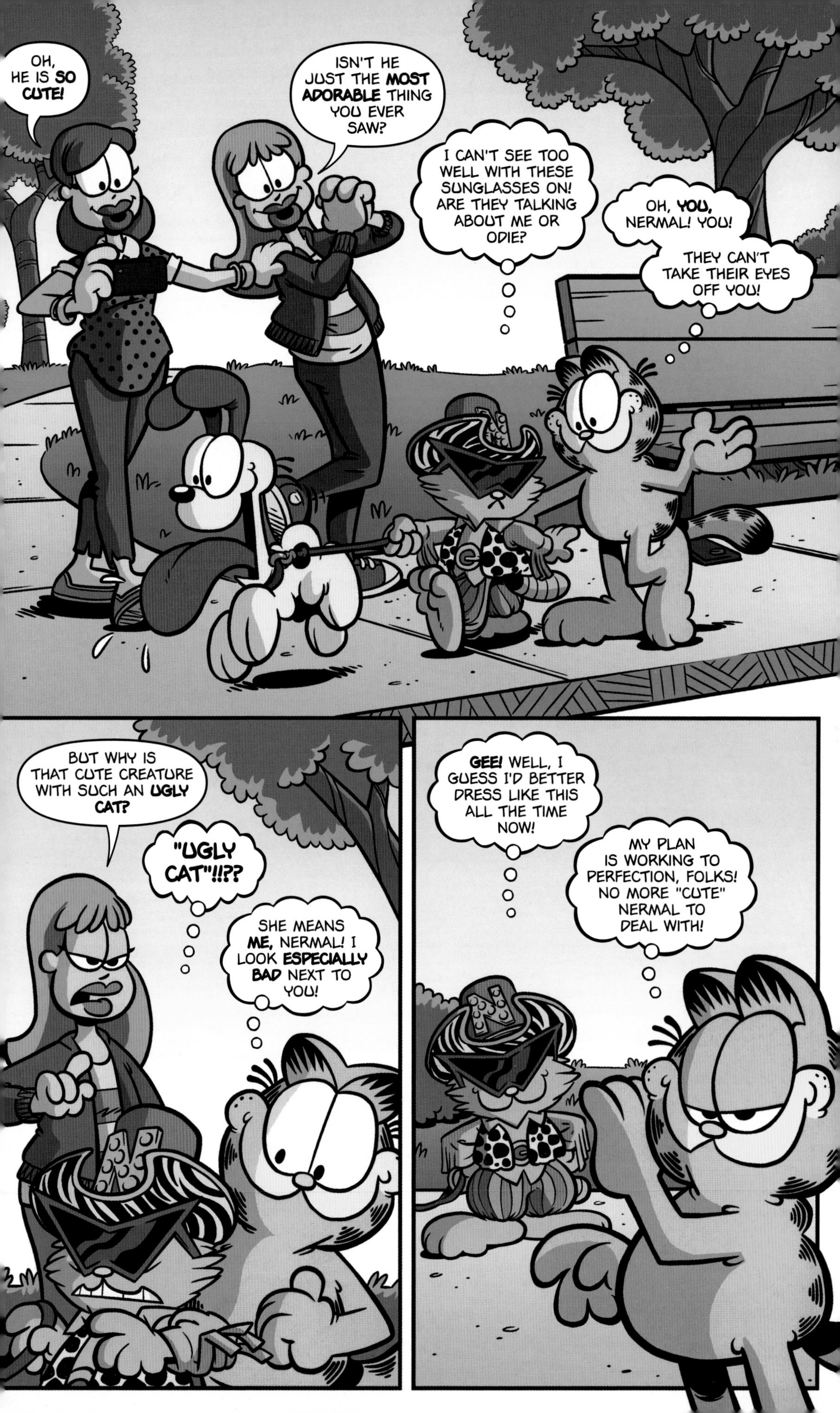
OH, HE IS **SO CUTE!**
ISN'T HE JUST THE **MOST ADORABLE** THING YOU EVER SAW?
I CAN'T SEE TOO WELL WITH THESE SUNGLASSES ON! ARE THEY TALKING ABOUT ME OR ODIE?
OH, **YOU,** NERMAL! YOU!
THEY CAN'T TAKE THEIR EYES OFF YOU!
BUT WHY IS THAT CUTE CREATURE WITH SUCH AN **UGLY CAT?**
"UGLY CAT"!!??
SHE MEANS **ME,** NERMAL! I LOOK **ESPECIALLY BAD** NEXT TO YOU!
GEE! WELL, I GUESS I'D BETTER DRESS LIKE THIS ALL THE TIME NOW!
MY PLAN IS WORKING TO PERFECTION, FOLKS! NO MORE "CUTE" NERMAL TO DEAL WITH!

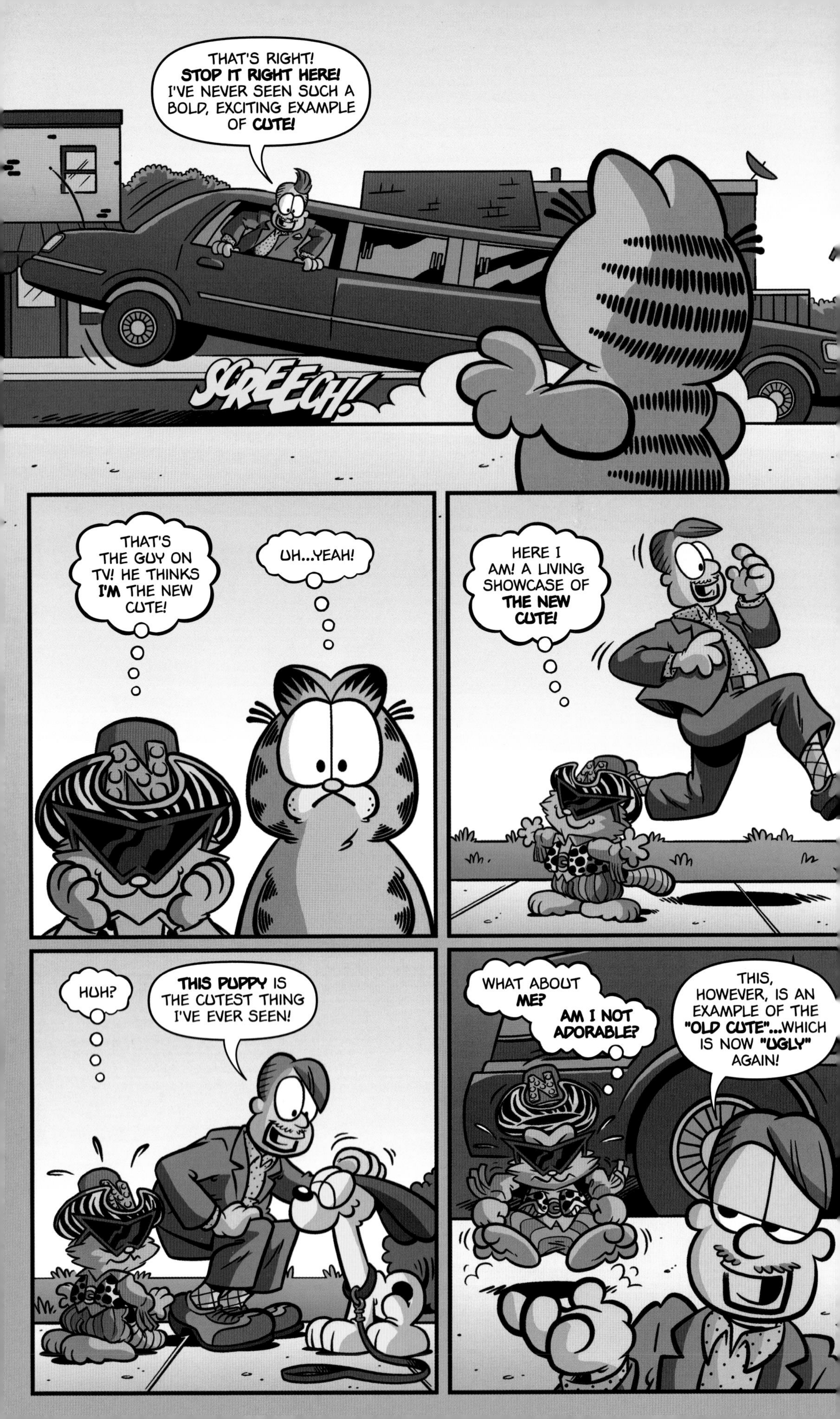
THAT'S RIGHT! STOP IT RIGHT HERE! I'VE NEVER SEEN SUCH A BOLD, EXCITING EXAMPLE OF CUTE!
SCREEECH!
THAT'S THE GUY ON TV! HE THINKS I'M THE NEW CUTE!
UH...YEAH!
HERE I AM! A LIVING SHOWCASE OF THE NEW CUTE!
HUH?
THIS PUPPY IS THE CUTEST THING I'VE EVER SEEN!
WHAT ABOUT ME?
AM I NOT ADORABLE?
THIS, HOWEVER, IS AN EXAMPLE OF THE "OLD CUTE"...WHICH IS NOW "UGLY" AGAIN!

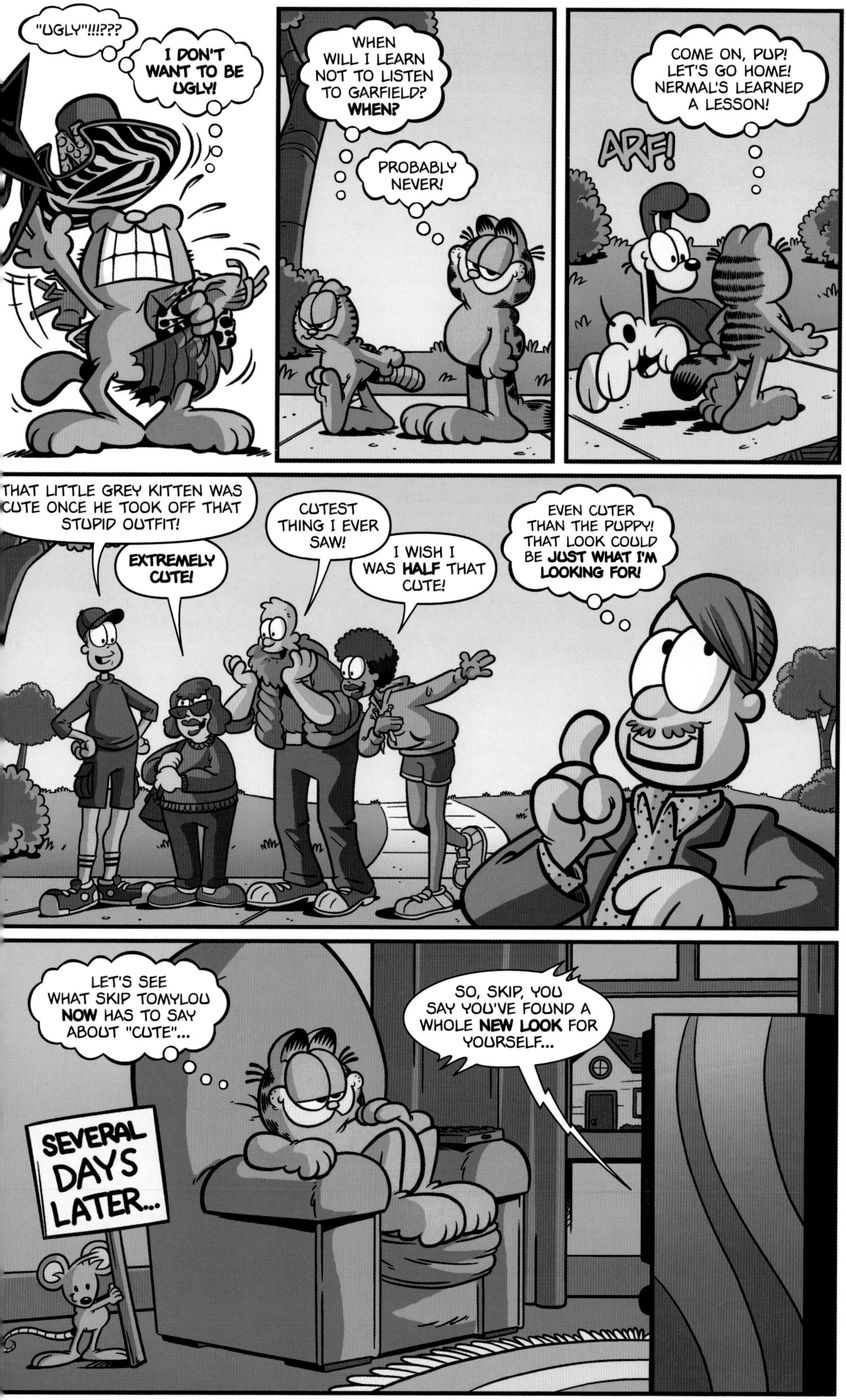
"UGLY"!!!???
I DON'T WANT TO BE UGLY!
WHEN WILL I LEARN NOT TO LISTEN TO GARFIELD? WHEN?
PROBABLY NEVER!
COME ON, PUP! LET'S GO HOME! NERMAL'S LEARNED A LESSON!
ARF!
THAT LITTLE GREY KITTEN WAS CUTE ONCE HE TOOK OFF THAT STUPID OUTFIT!
EXTREMELY CUTE!
CUTEST THING I EVER SAW!
I WISH I WAS HALF THAT CUTE!
EVEN CUTER THAN THE PUPPY! THAT LOOK COULD BE JUST WHAT I'M LOOKING FOR!
LET'S SEE WHAT SKIP TOMYLOU NOW HAS TO SAY ABOUT "CUTE"...
SO, SKIP, YOU SAY YOU'VE FOUND A WHOLE NEW LOOK FOR YOURSELF...
SEVERAL DAYS LATER...

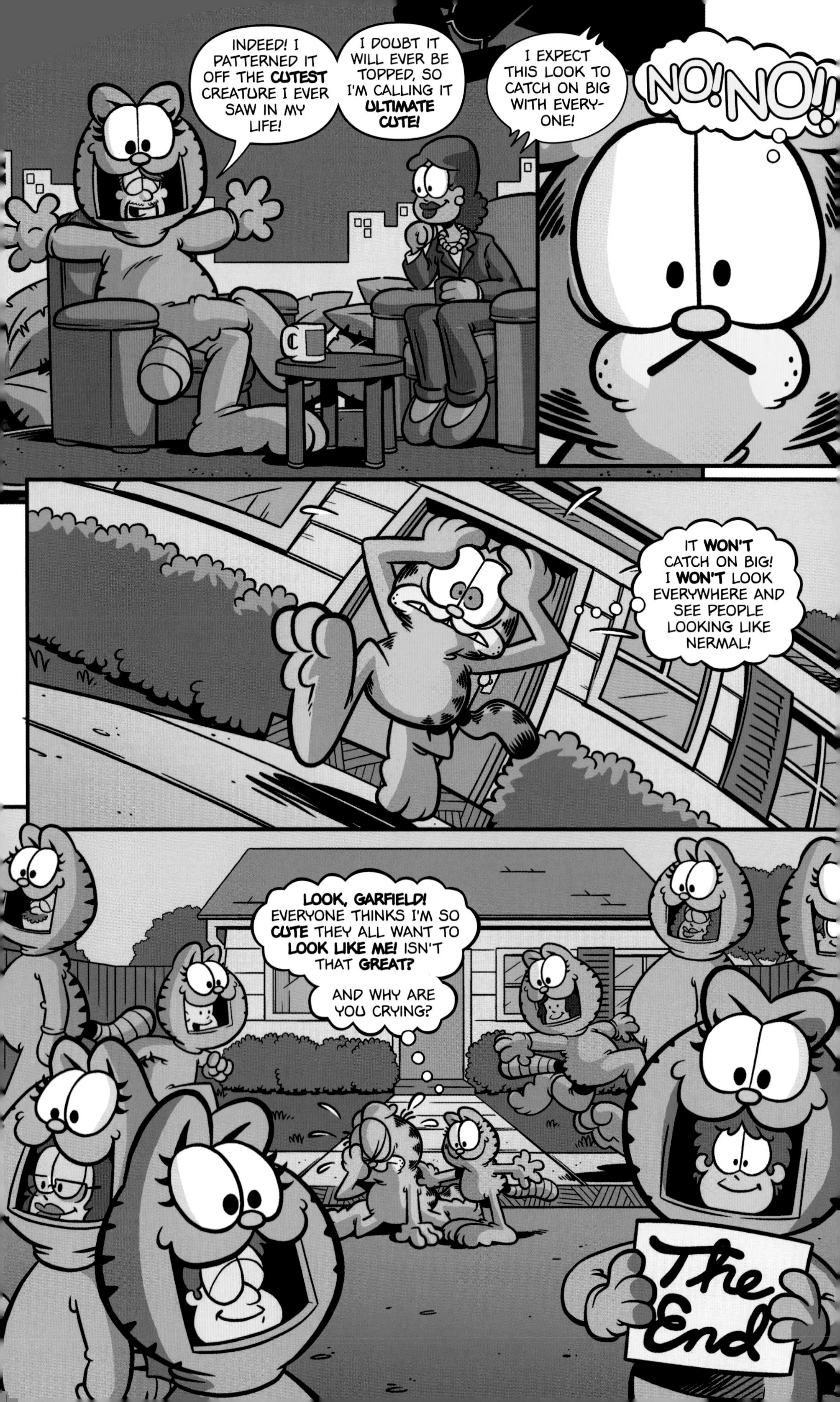

INDEED! I PATTERNED IT OFF THE **CUTEST** CREATURE I EVER SAW IN MY LIFE!
I DOUBT IT WILL EVER BE TOPPED, SO I'M CALLING IT **ULTIMATE CUTE!**
I EXPECT THIS LOOK TO CATCH ON BIG WITH EVERY-ONE!
NO! NO!!
IT **WON'T** CATCH ON BIG! I **WON'T** LOOK EVERYWHERE AND SEE PEOPLE LOOKING LIKE NERMAL!
LOOK, GARFIELD! EVERYONE THINKS I'M SO **CUTE** THEY ALL WANT TO **LOOK LIKE ME!** ISN'T THAT **GREAT?**
AND WHY ARE YOU CRYING?
The End

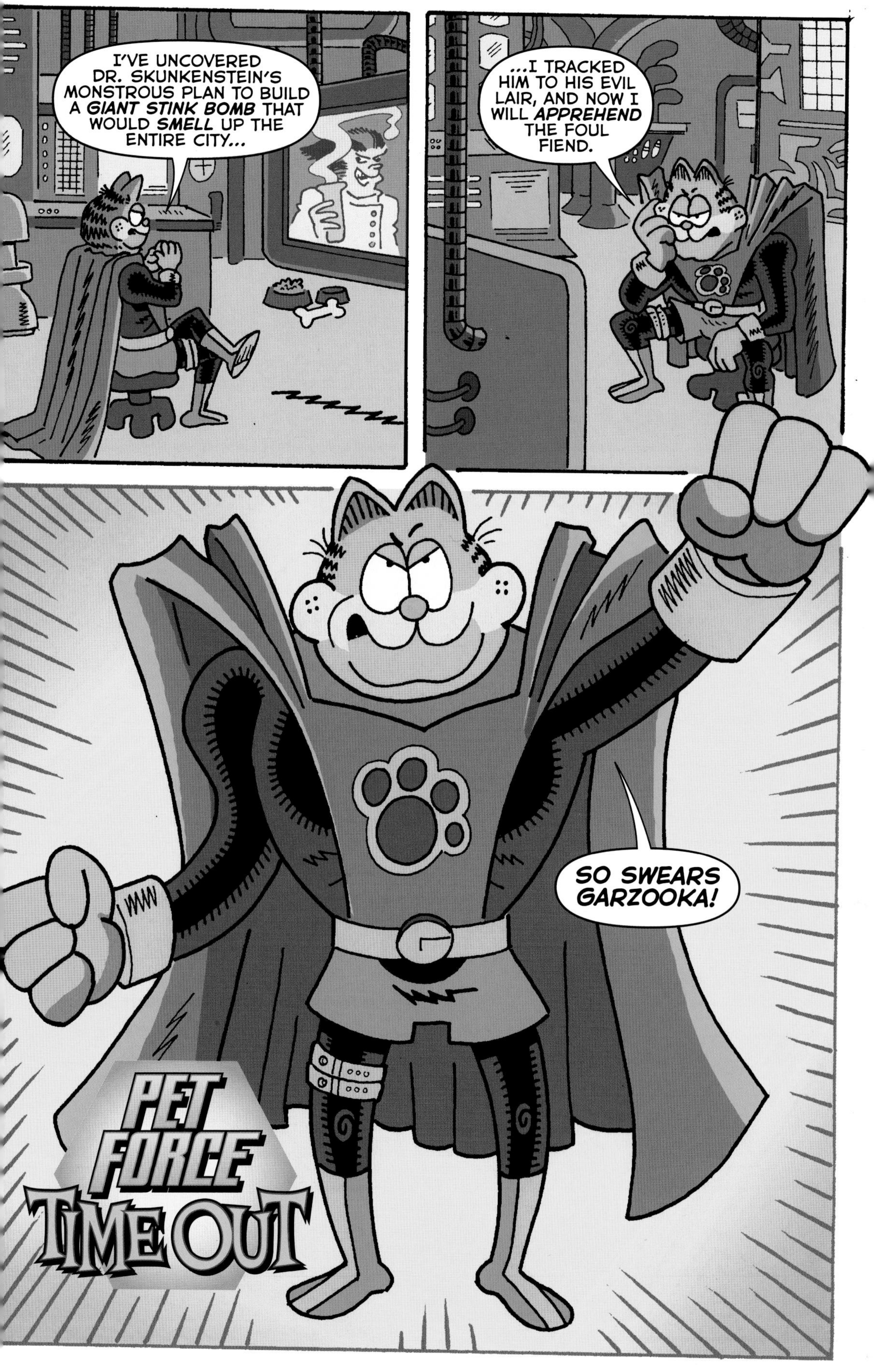
I'VE UNCOVERED DR. SKUNKENSTEIN'S MONSTROUS PLAN TO BUILD A GIANT STINK BOMB THAT WOULD SMELL UP THE ENTIRE CITY...
...I TRACKED HIM TO HIS EVIL LAIR, AND NOW I WILL APPREHEND THE FOUL FIEND.
SO SWEARS GARZOOKA!
PET FORCE
TIME OUT

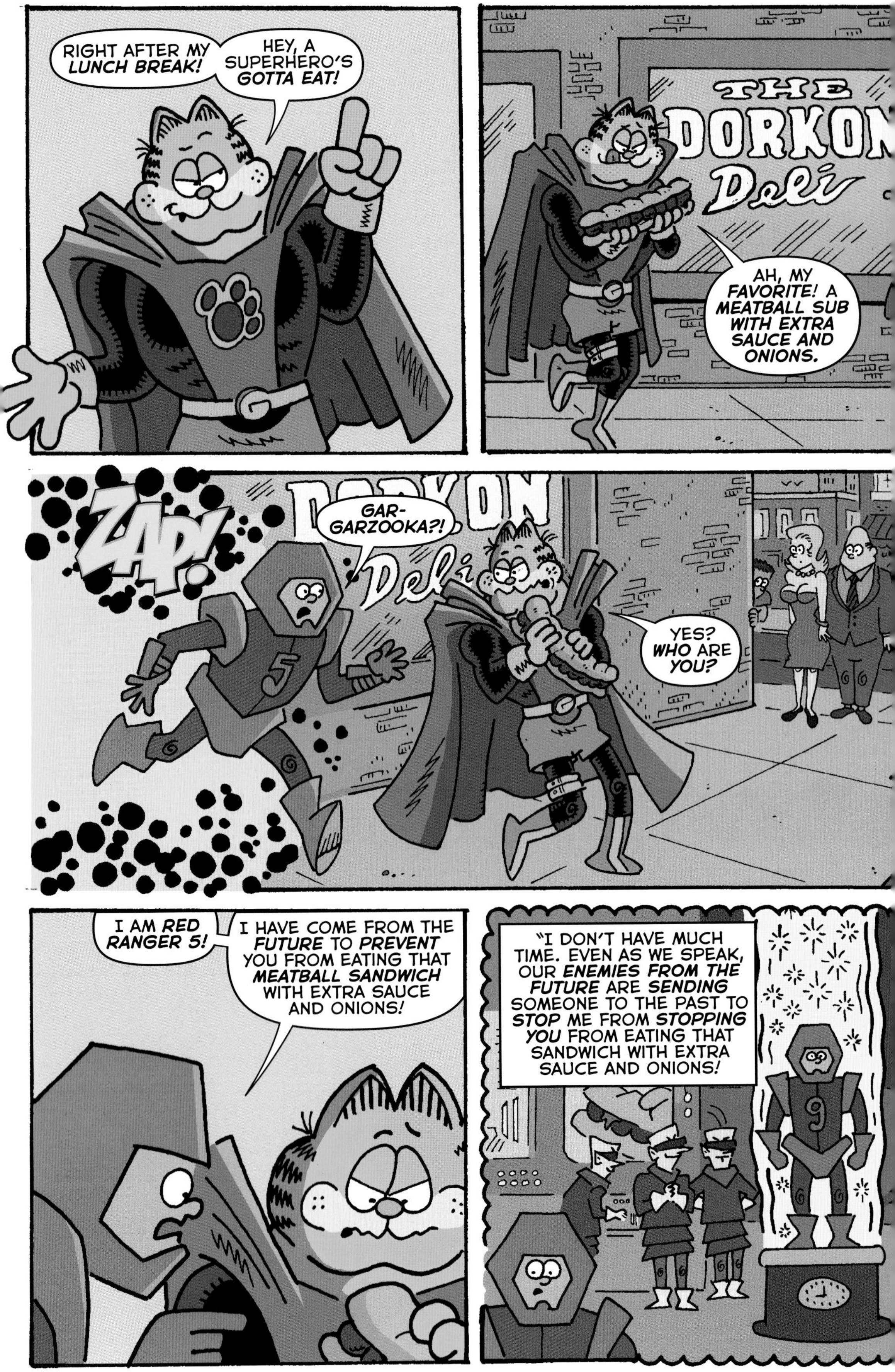

RIGHT AFTER MY *LUNCH BREAK!*
HEY, A SUPERHERO'S *GOTTA EAT!*
THE DORKON Deli
AH, MY *FAVORITE!* A *MEATBALL SUB WITH EXTRA SAUCE AND ONIONS.*
ZAP!
DORKON Deli
GAR-GARZOOKA?!
YES? *WHO* ARE *YOU?*
I AM *RED RANGER 5!*
I HAVE COME FROM THE *FUTURE* TO *PREVENT* YOU FROM EATING THAT *MEATBALL SANDWICH* WITH EXTRA SAUCE AND ONIONS!
"I DON'T HAVE MUCH TIME. EVEN AS WE SPEAK, OUR *ENEMIES FROM THE FUTURE* ARE *SENDING* SOMEONE TO THE PAST TO *STOP* ME FROM *STOPPING YOU* FROM EATING THAT SANDWICH WITH EXTRA SAUCE AND ONIONS!

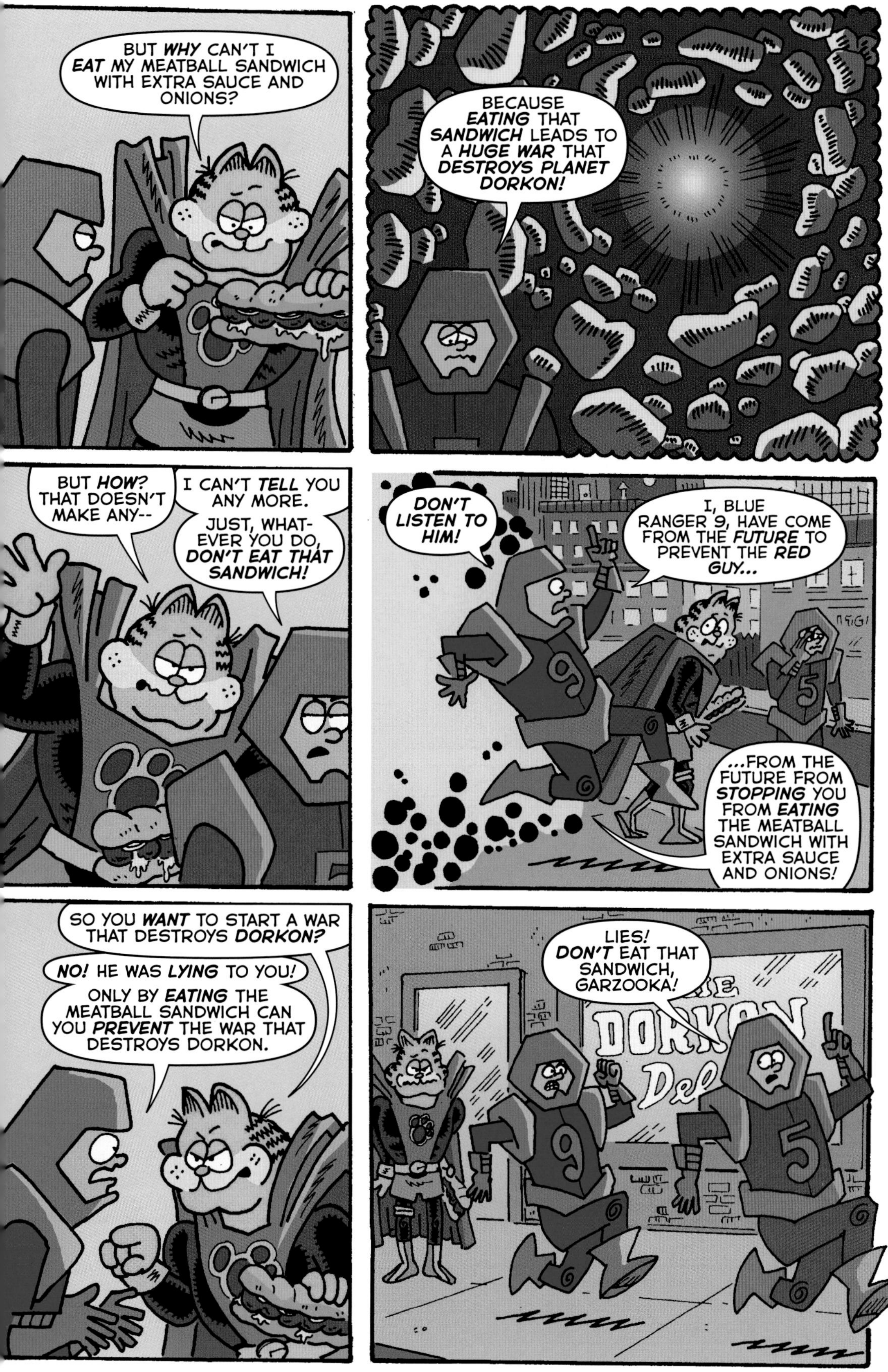

BUT *WHY* CAN'T I *EAT* MY MEATBALL SANDWICH WITH EXTRA SAUCE AND ONIONS?
BECAUSE *EATING* THAT *SANDWICH* LEADS TO A *HUGE WAR* THAT *DESTROYS PLANET DORKON!*
BUT *HOW?* THAT DOESN'T MAKE ANY--
I CAN'T *TELL* YOU ANY MORE.
JUST, WHAT-EVER YOU DO, *DON'T EAT THAT SANDWICH!*
DON'T LISTEN TO HIM!
I, BLUE RANGER 9, HAVE COME FROM THE *FUTURE* TO PREVENT THE *RED GUY...*
*...*FROM THE FUTURE FROM *STOPPING* YOU FROM *EATING* THE MEATBALL SANDWICH WITH EXTRA SAUCE AND ONIONS!
SO YOU *WANT* TO START A WAR THAT DESTROYS *DORKON?*
NO! HE WAS *LYING* TO YOU!
ONLY BY *EATING* THE MEATBALL SANDWICH CAN YOU *PREVENT* THE WAR THAT DESTROYS DORKON.
LIES! *DON'T* EAT THAT SANDWICH, GARZOOKA!
DORKON
Del

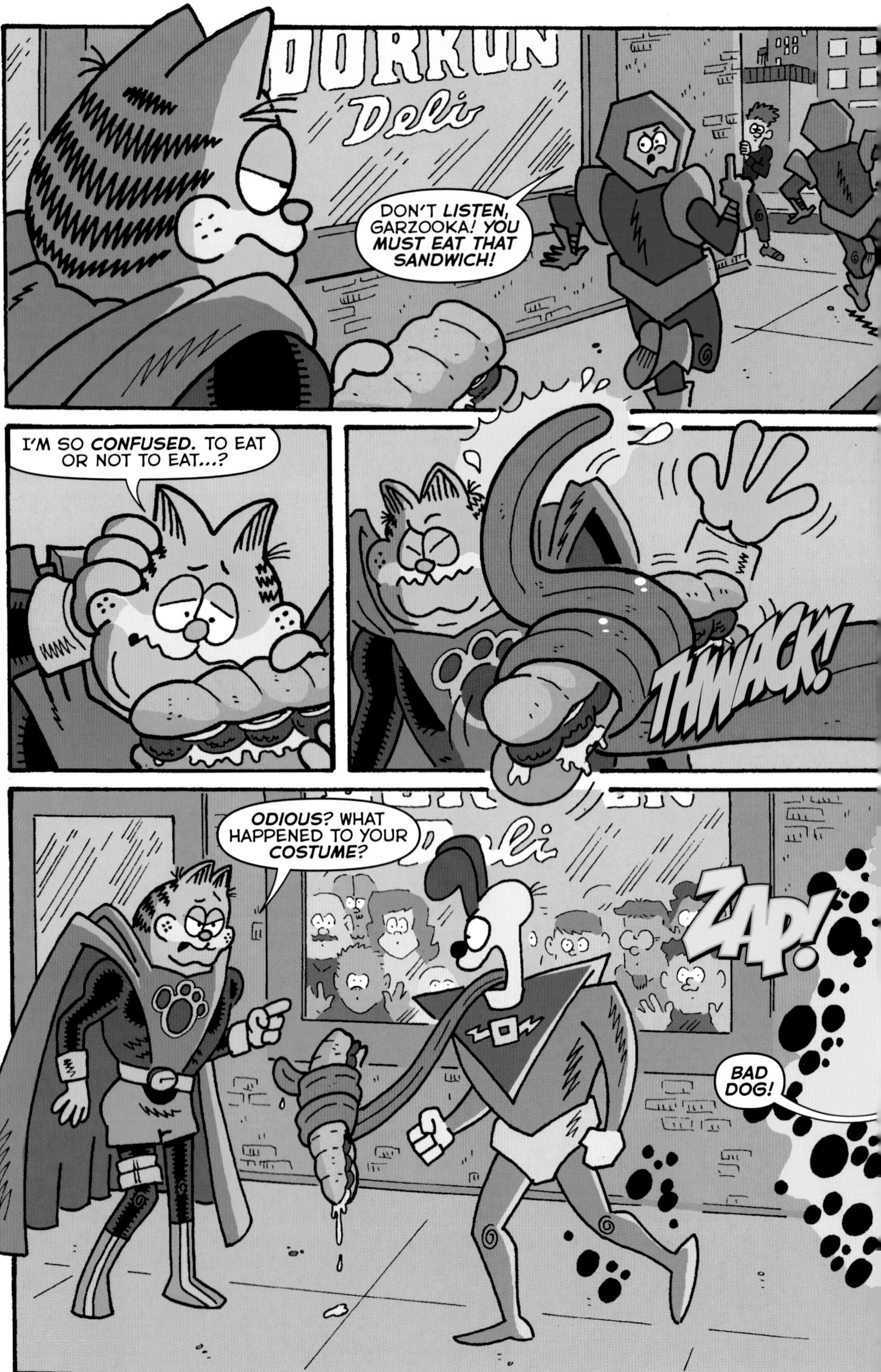
DORKUN
Deli
DON'T LISTEN, GARZOOKA! YOU MUST EAT THAT SANDWICH!
I'M SO CONFUSED. TO EAT OR NOT TO EAT...?
THWACK!
ODIOUS? WHAT HAPPENED TO YOUR COSTUME?
ZAP!
BAD DOG!

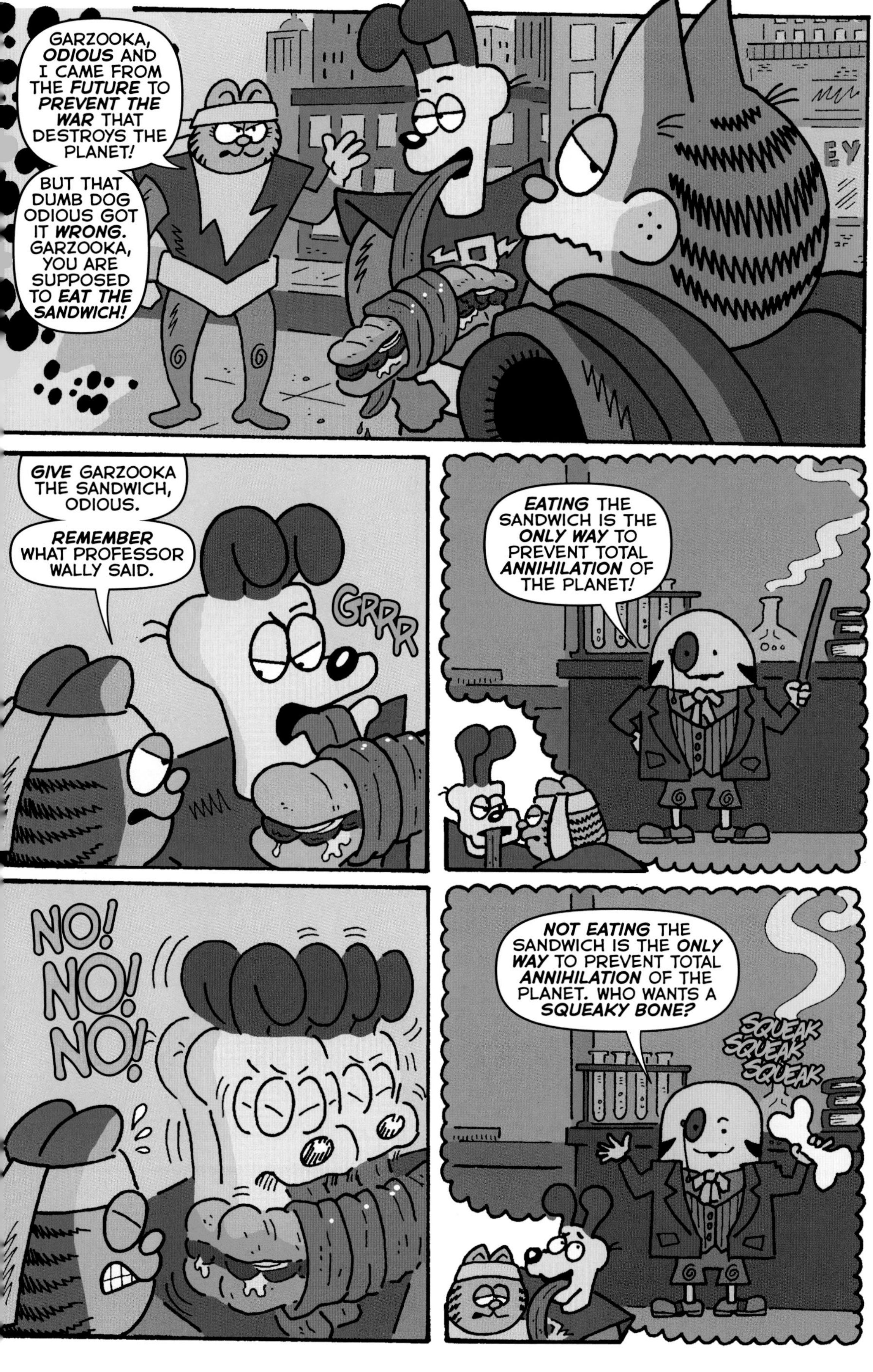

GARZOOKA, ODIOUS AND I CAME FROM THE FUTURE TO PREVENT THE WAR THAT DESTROYS THE PLANET!
BUT THAT DUMB DOG ODIOUS GOT IT WRONG. GARZOOKA, YOU ARE SUPPOSED TO EAT THE SANDWICH!
GIVE GARZOOKA THE SANDWICH, ODIOUS.
REMEMBER WHAT PROFESSOR WALLY SAID.
GRRR
EATING THE SANDWICH IS THE ONLY WAY TO PREVENT TOTAL ANNIHILATION OF THE PLANET!
NO! NO! NO!
NOT EATING THE SANDWICH IS THE ONLY WAY TO PREVENT TOTAL ANNIHILATION OF THE PLANET. WHO WANTS A SQUEAKY BONE?
SQUEAK SQUEAK SQUEAK

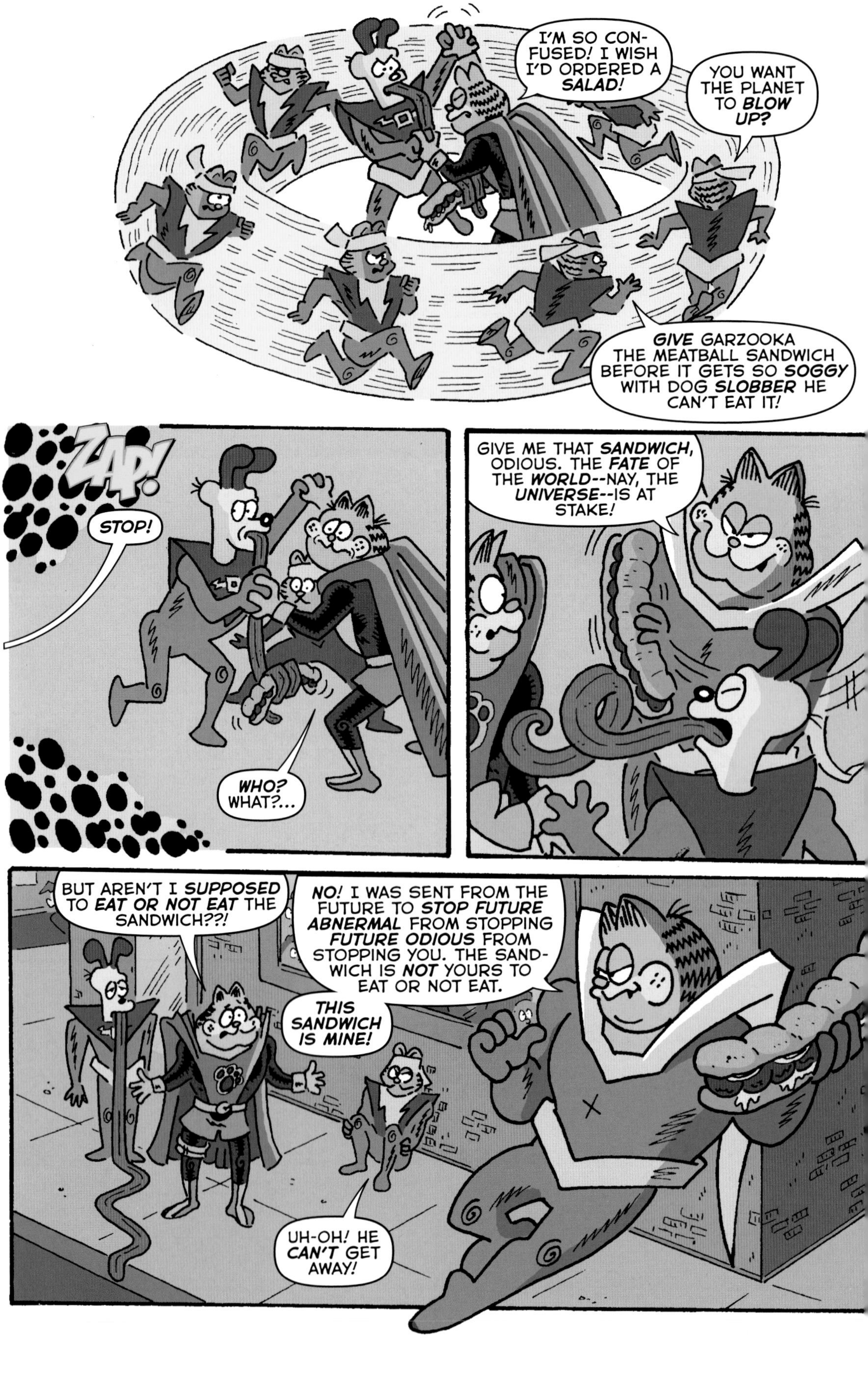
I'M SO CONFUSED! I WISH I'D ORDERED A SALAD!
YOU WANT THE PLANET TO BLOW UP?
GIVE GARZOOKA THE MEATBALL SANDWICH BEFORE IT GETS SO SOGGY WITH DOG SLOBBER HE CAN'T EAT IT!
ZAP!
STOP!
WHO? WHAT?...
GIVE ME THAT SANDWICH, ODIOUS. THE FATE OF THE WORLD--NAY, THE UNIVERSE--IS AT STAKE!
BUT AREN'T I SUPPOSED TO EAT OR NOT EAT THE SANDWICH??!
NO! I WAS SENT FROM THE FUTURE TO STOP FUTURE ABNERMAL FROM STOPPING FUTURE ODIOUS FROM STOPPING YOU. THE SANDWICH IS NOT YOURS TO EAT OR NOT EAT.
THIS SANDWICH IS MINE!
UH-OH! HE CAN'T GET AWAY!

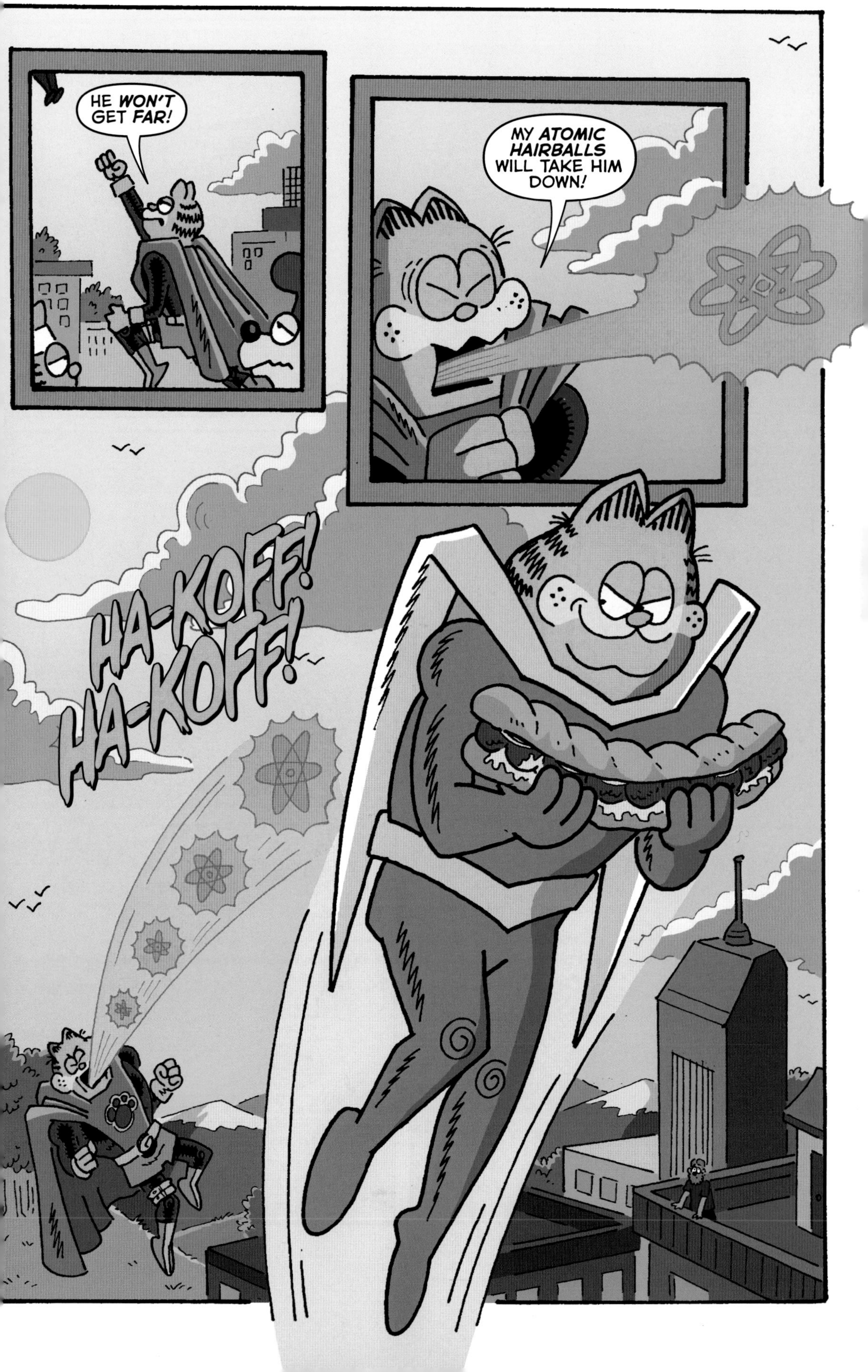
HE WON'T GET FAR!
MY ATOMIC HAIRBALLS WILL TAKE HIM DOWN!
HA-KOFF! HA-KOFF!

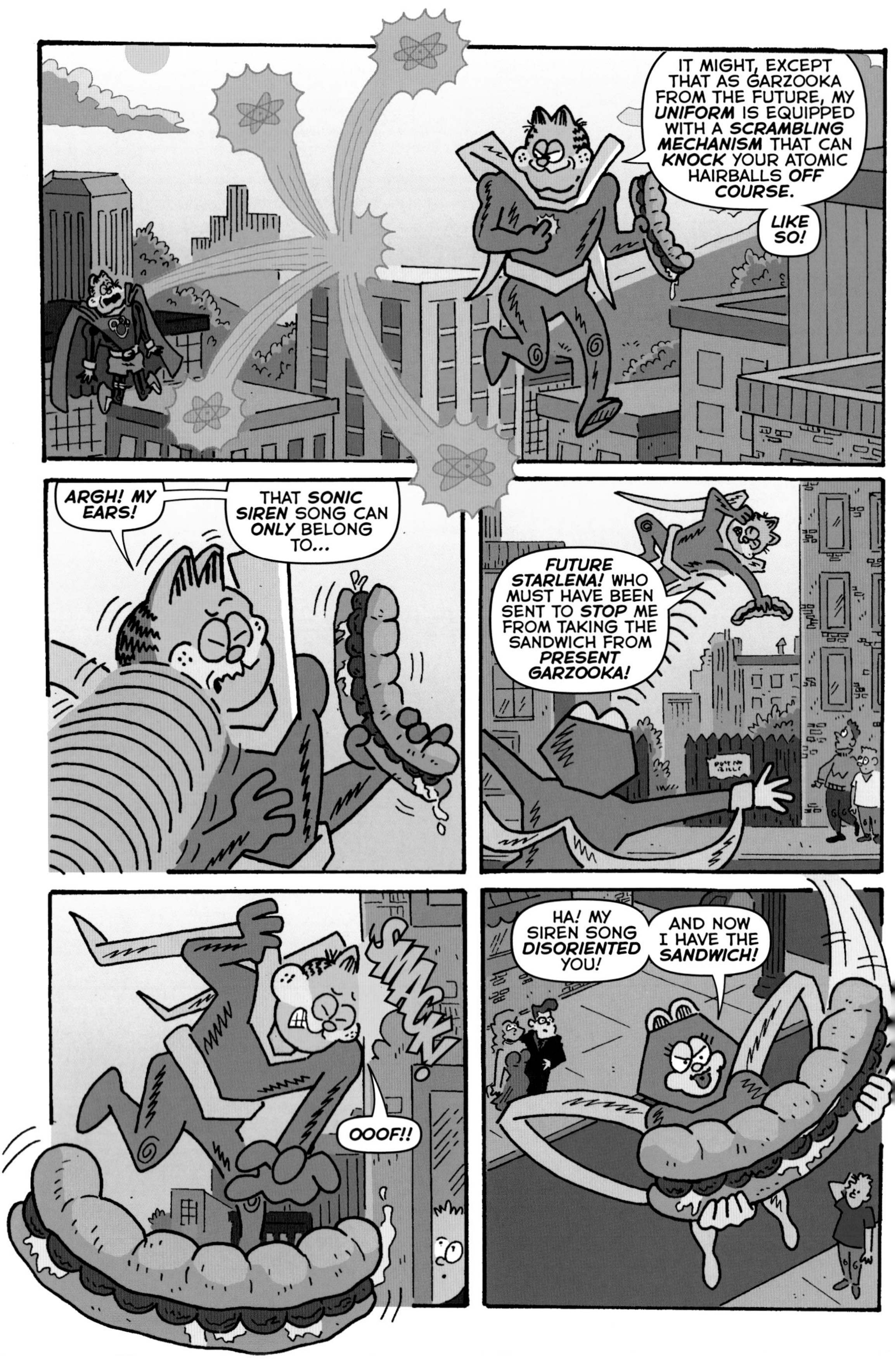
IT MIGHT, EXCEPT THAT AS GARZOOKA FROM THE FUTURE, MY UNIFORM IS EQUIPPED WITH A SCRAMBLING MECHANISM THAT CAN KNOCK YOUR ATOMIC HAIRBALLS OFF COURSE.
LIKE SO!
ARGH! MY EARS!
THAT SONIC SIREN SONG CAN ONLY BELONG TO...
FUTURE STARLENA! WHO MUST HAVE BEEN SENT TO STOP ME FROM TAKING THE SANDWICH FROM PRESENT GARZOOKA!
SMACK!
OOOF!!
HA! MY SIREN SONG DISORIENTED YOU!
AND NOW I HAVE THE SANDWICH!

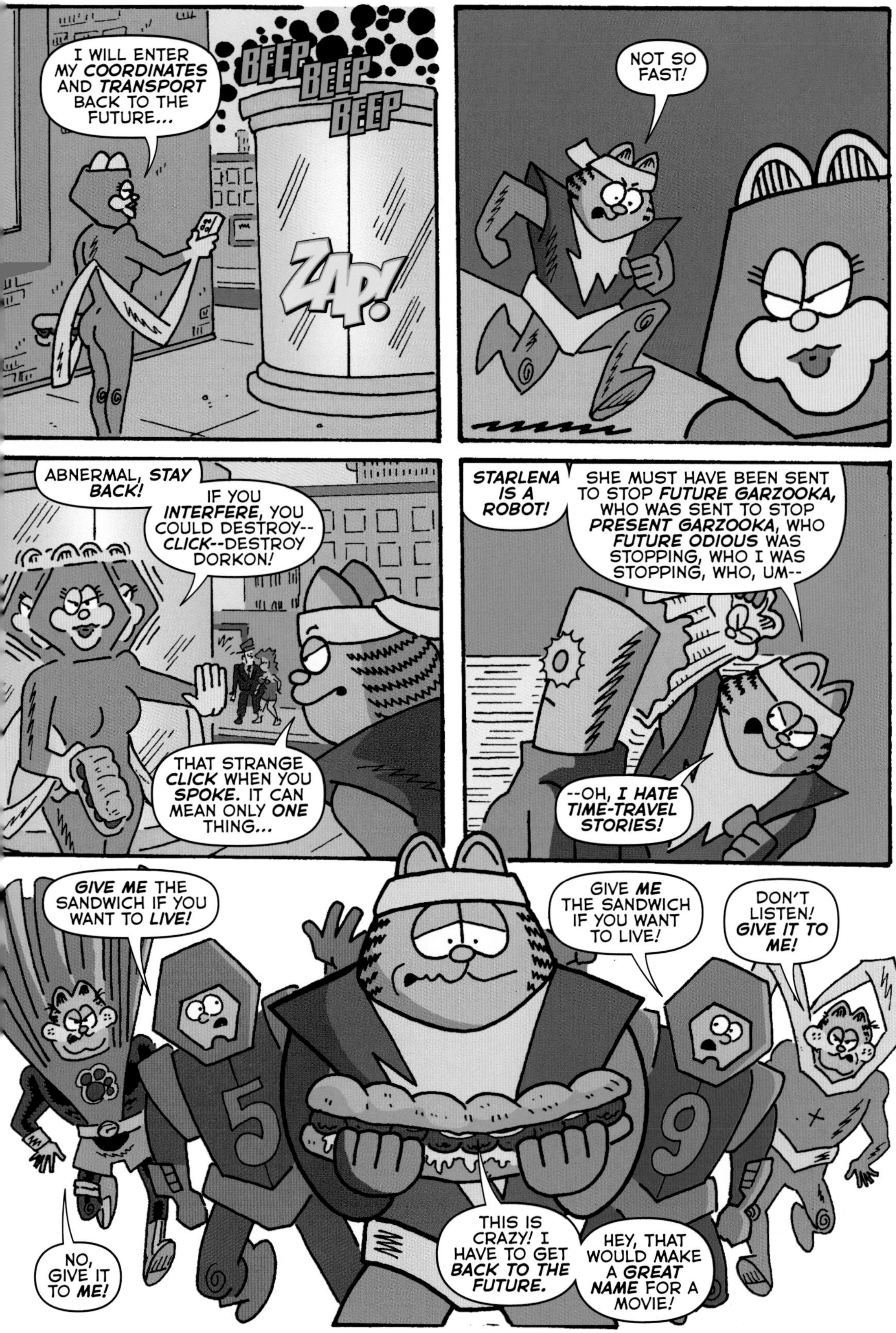
I WILL ENTER MY COORDINATES AND TRANSPORT BACK TO THE FUTURE...
BEEP BEEP BEEP
ZAP!
NOT SO FAST!
ABNERMAL, STAY BACK!
IF YOU INTERFERE, YOU COULD DESTROY-- CLICK--DESTROY DORKON!
THAT STRANGE CLICK WHEN YOU SPOKE. IT CAN MEAN ONLY ONE THING...
STARLENA IS A ROBOT!
SHE MUST HAVE BEEN SENT TO STOP FUTURE GARZOOKA, WHO WAS SENT TO STOP PRESENT GARZOOKA, WHO FUTURE ODIOUS WAS STOPPING, WHO I WAS STOPPING, WHO, UM--
--OH, I HATE TIME-TRAVEL STORIES!
GIVE ME THE SANDWICH IF YOU WANT TO LIVE!
GIVE ME THE SANDWICH IF YOU WANT TO LIVE!
DON'T LISTEN! GIVE IT TO ME!
NO, GIVE IT TO ME!
THIS IS CRAZY! I HAVE TO GET BACK TO THE FUTURE.
HEY, THAT WOULD MAKE A GREAT NAME FOR A MOVIE!

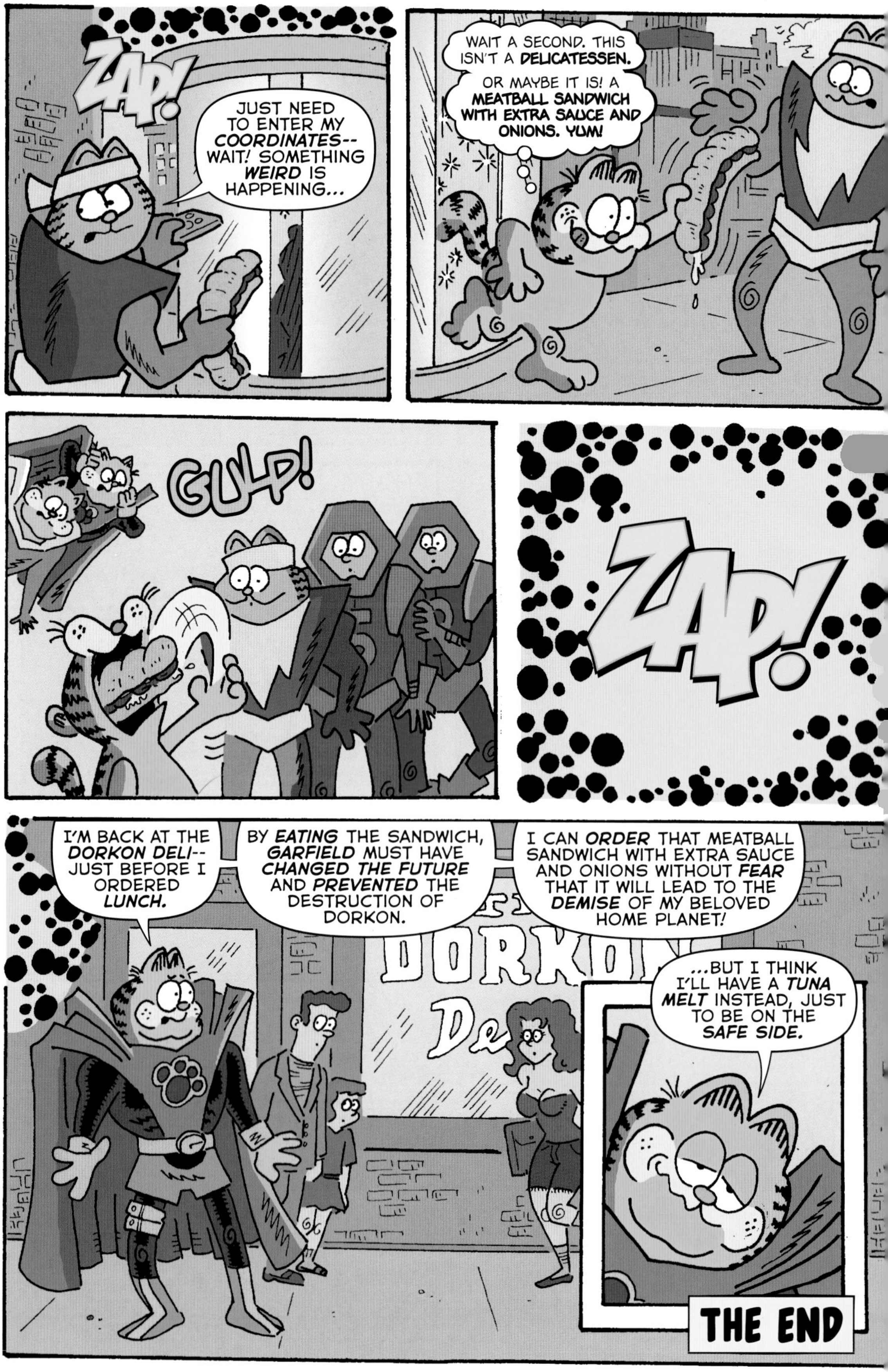
ZAP!
JUST NEED TO ENTER MY COORDINATES-- WAIT! SOMETHING WEIRD IS HAPPENING...
WAIT A SECOND. THIS ISN'T A DELICATESSEN.
OR MAYBE IT IS! A MEATBALL SANDWICH WITH EXTRA SAUCE AND ONIONS. YUM!
GULP!
ZAP!
I'M BACK AT THE DORKON DELI-- JUST BEFORE I ORDERED LUNCH.
BY EATING THE SANDWICH, GARFIELD MUST HAVE CHANGED THE FUTURE AND PREVENTED THE DESTRUCTION OF DORKON.
I CAN ORDER THAT MEATBALL SANDWICH WITH EXTRA SAUCE AND ONIONS WITHOUT FEAR THAT IT WILL LEAD TO THE DEMISE OF MY BELOVED HOME PLANET!
DORK
De
...BUT I THINK I'LL HAVE A TUNA MELT INSTEAD, JUST TO BE ON THE SAFE SIDE.
THE END

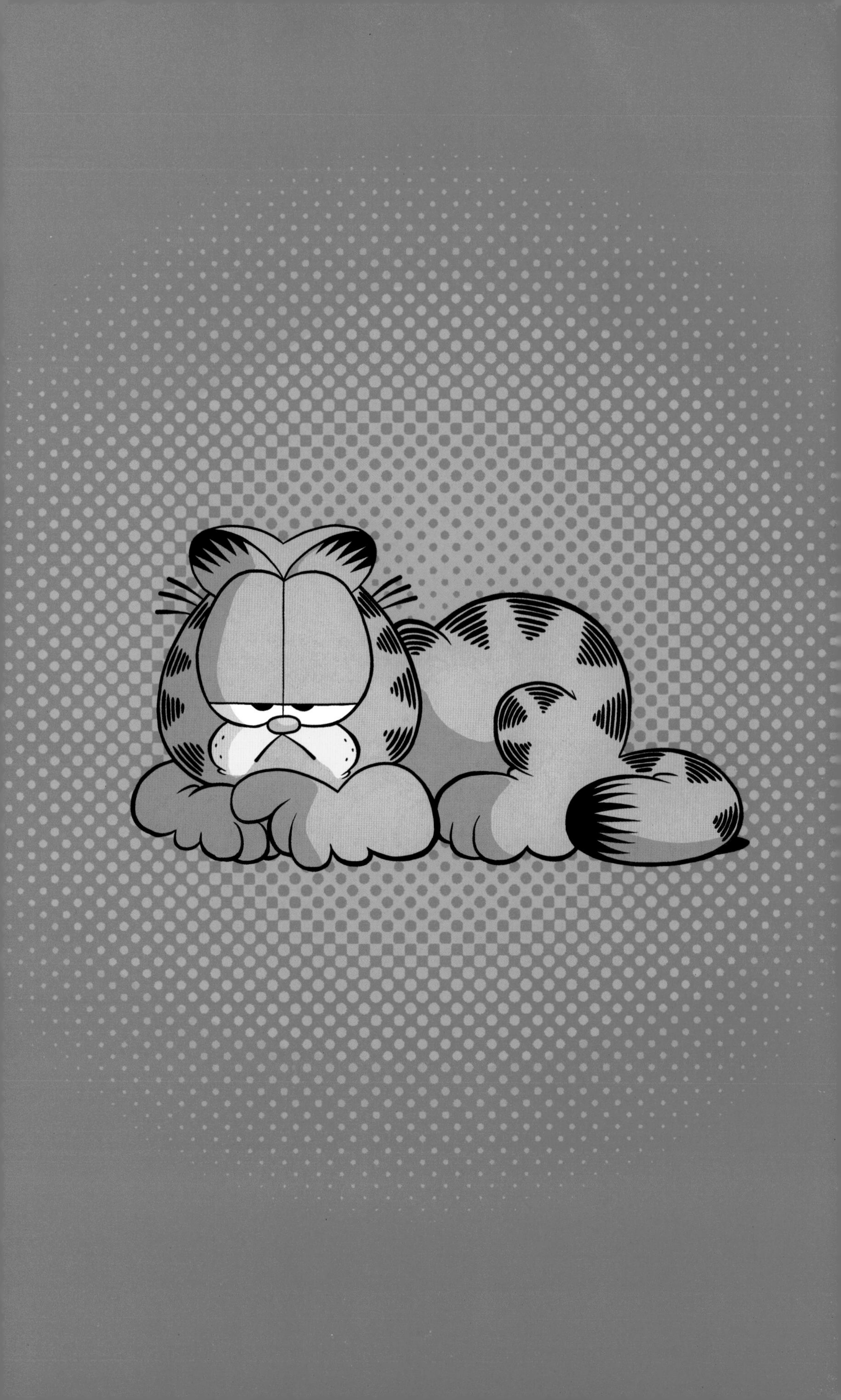

CHAPTER 4

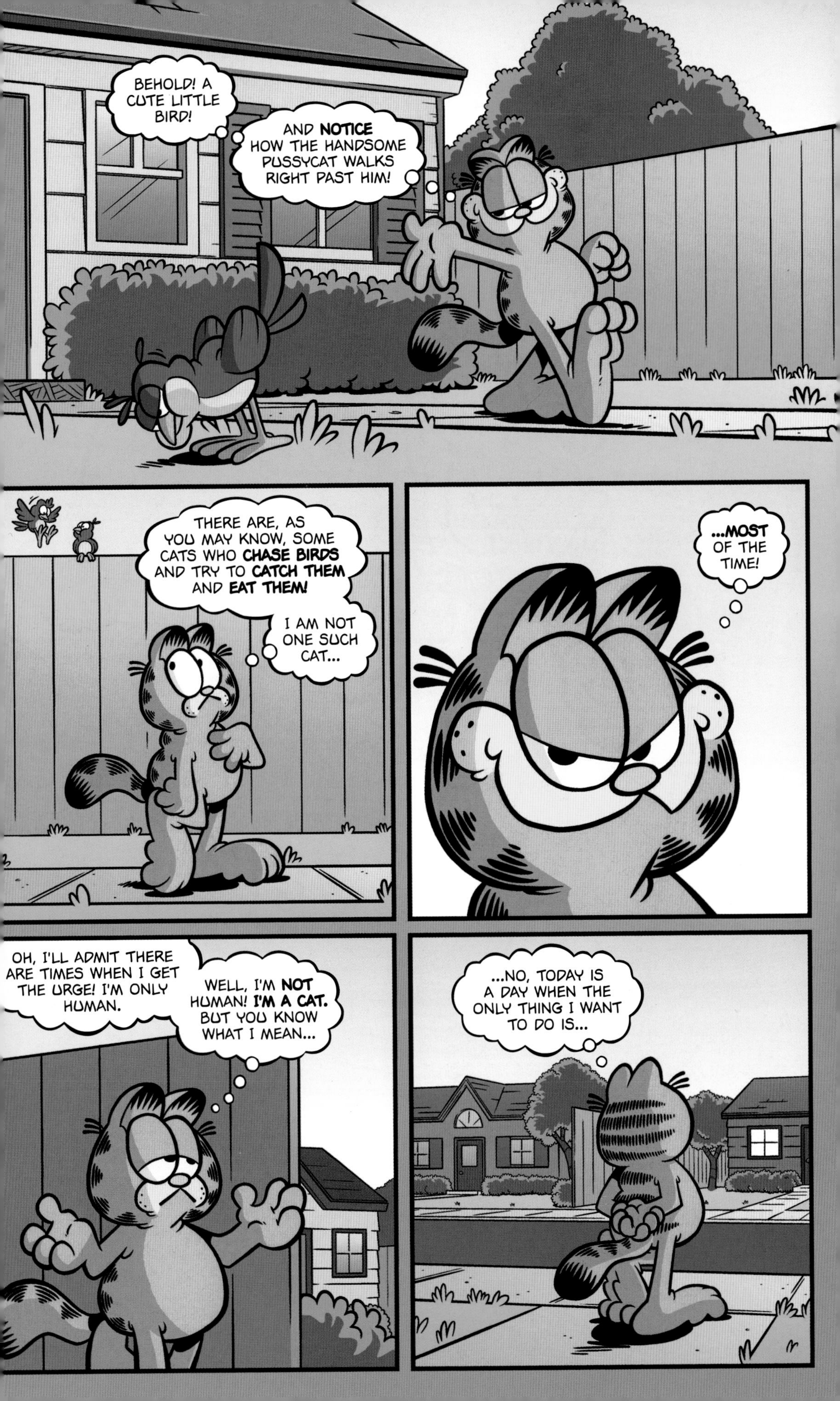
BEHOLD! A CUTE LITTLE BIRD!
AND NOTICE HOW THE HANDSOME PUSSYCAT WALKS RIGHT PAST HIM!
THERE ARE, AS YOU MAY KNOW, SOME CATS WHO CHASE BIRDS AND TRY TO CATCH THEM AND EAT THEM!
I AM NOT ONE SUCH CAT...
...MOST OF THE TIME!
OH, I'LL ADMIT THERE ARE TIMES WHEN I GET THE URGE! I'M ONLY HUMAN.
WELL, I'M NOT HUMAN! I'M A CAT. BUT YOU KNOW WHAT I MEAN...
...NO, TODAY IS A DAY WHEN THE ONLY THING I WANT TO DO IS...

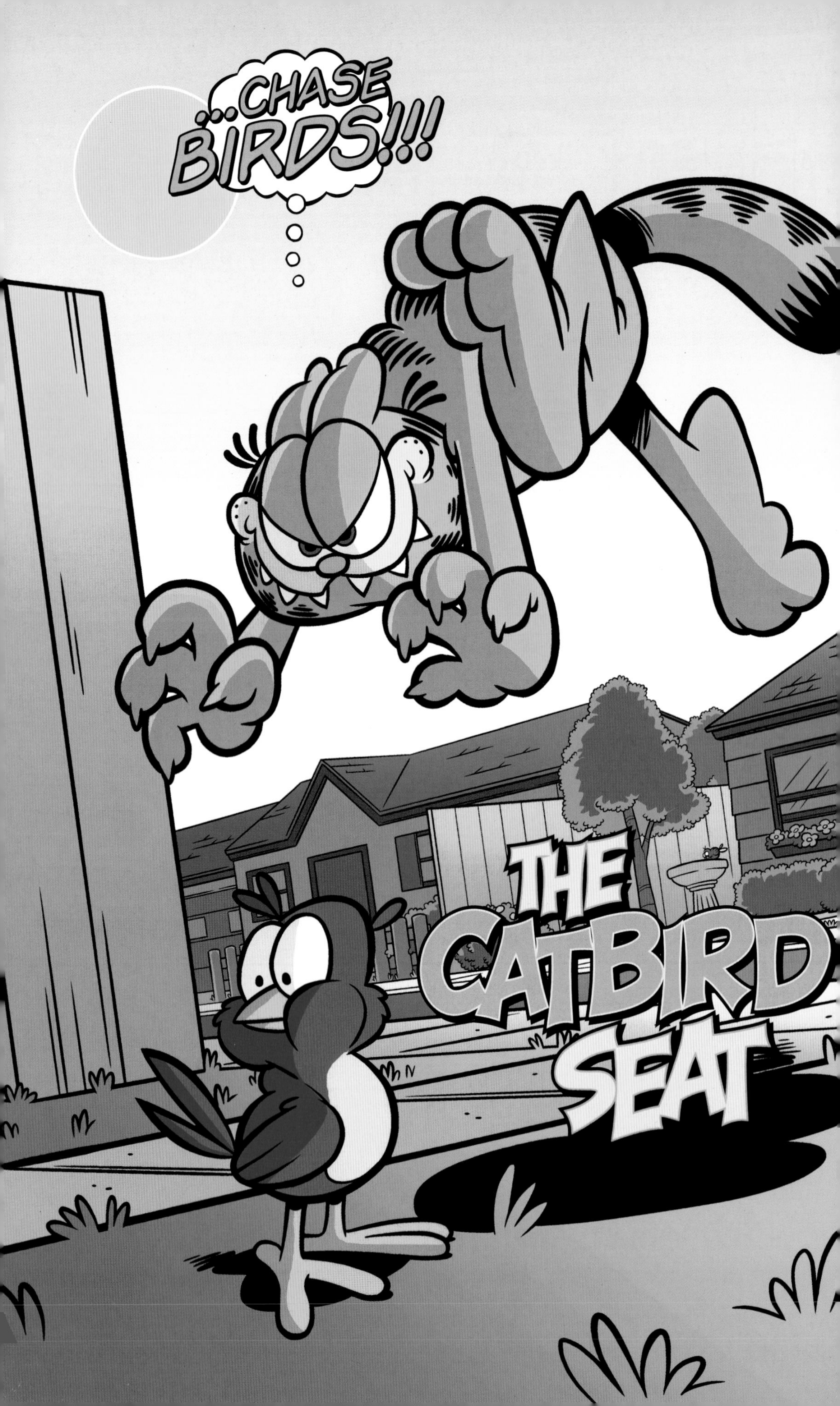
...CHASE BIRDS!!!
THE CATBIRD SEAT

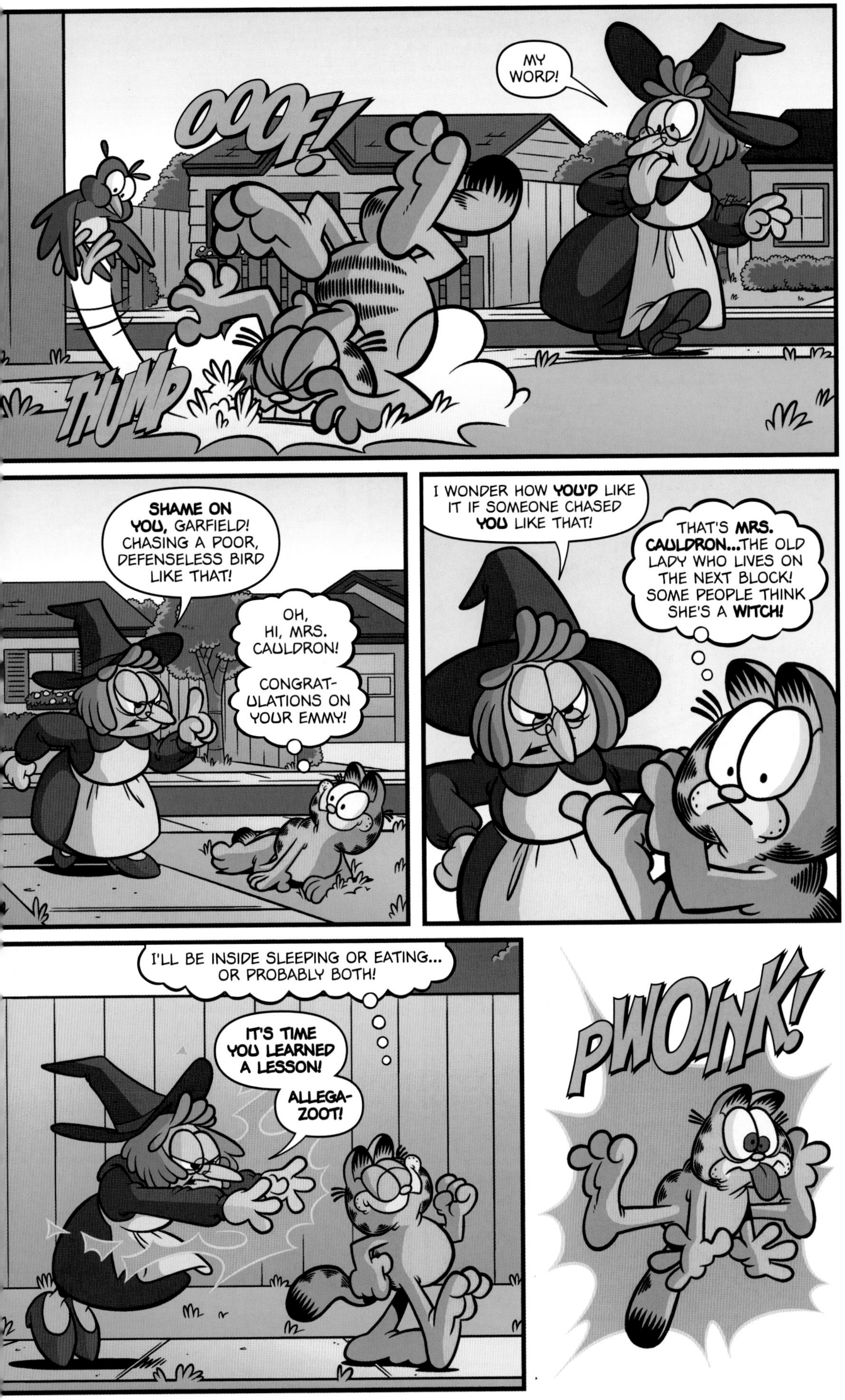

OOOF!
THUMP
MY WORD!
SHAME ON YOU, GARFIELD! CHASING A POOR, DEFENSELESS BIRD LIKE THAT!
OH, HI, MRS. CAULDRON!
CONGRAT-ULATIONS ON YOUR EMMY!
I WONDER HOW YOU'D LIKE IT IF SOMEONE CHASED YOU LIKE THAT!
THAT'S MRS. CAULDRON...THE OLD LADY WHO LIVES ON THE NEXT BLOCK! SOME PEOPLE THINK SHE'S A WITCH!
I'LL BE INSIDE SLEEPING OR EATING... OR PROBABLY BOTH!
IT'S TIME YOU LEARNED A LESSON!
ALLEGA-ZOOT!
PWOINK!

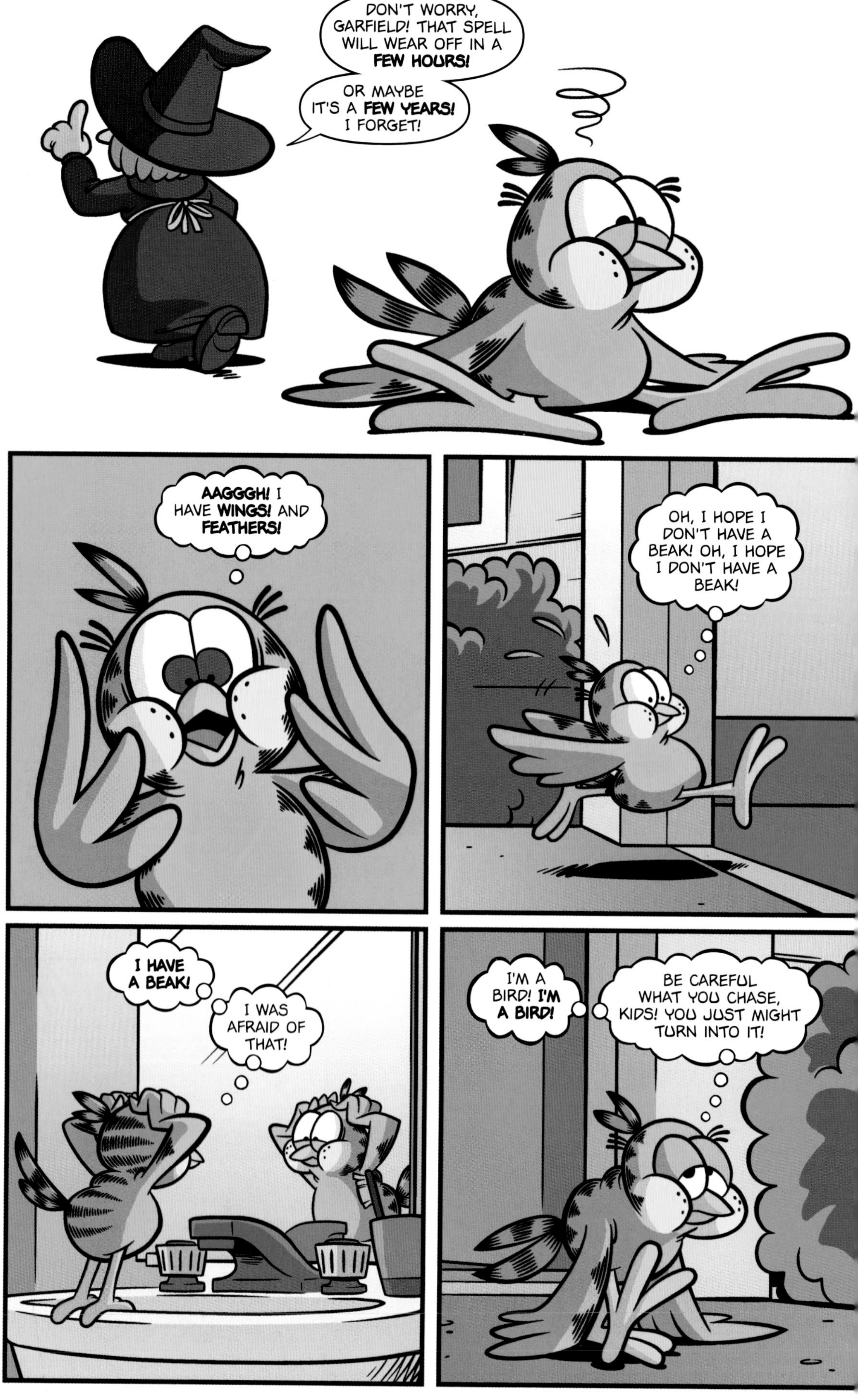

DON'T WORRY, GARFIELD! THAT SPELL WILL WEAR OFF IN A **FEW HOURS!**
OR MAYBE IT'S A **FEW YEARS!** I FORGET!
AAGGGH! I HAVE **WINGS!** AND **FEATHERS!**
OH, I HOPE I DON'T HAVE A BEAK! OH, I HOPE I DON'T HAVE A BEAK!
I HAVE A BEAK!
I WAS AFRAID OF THAT!
I'M A BIRD! **I'M A BIRD!**
BE CAREFUL WHAT YOU CHASE, KIDS! YOU JUST MIGHT TURN INTO IT!

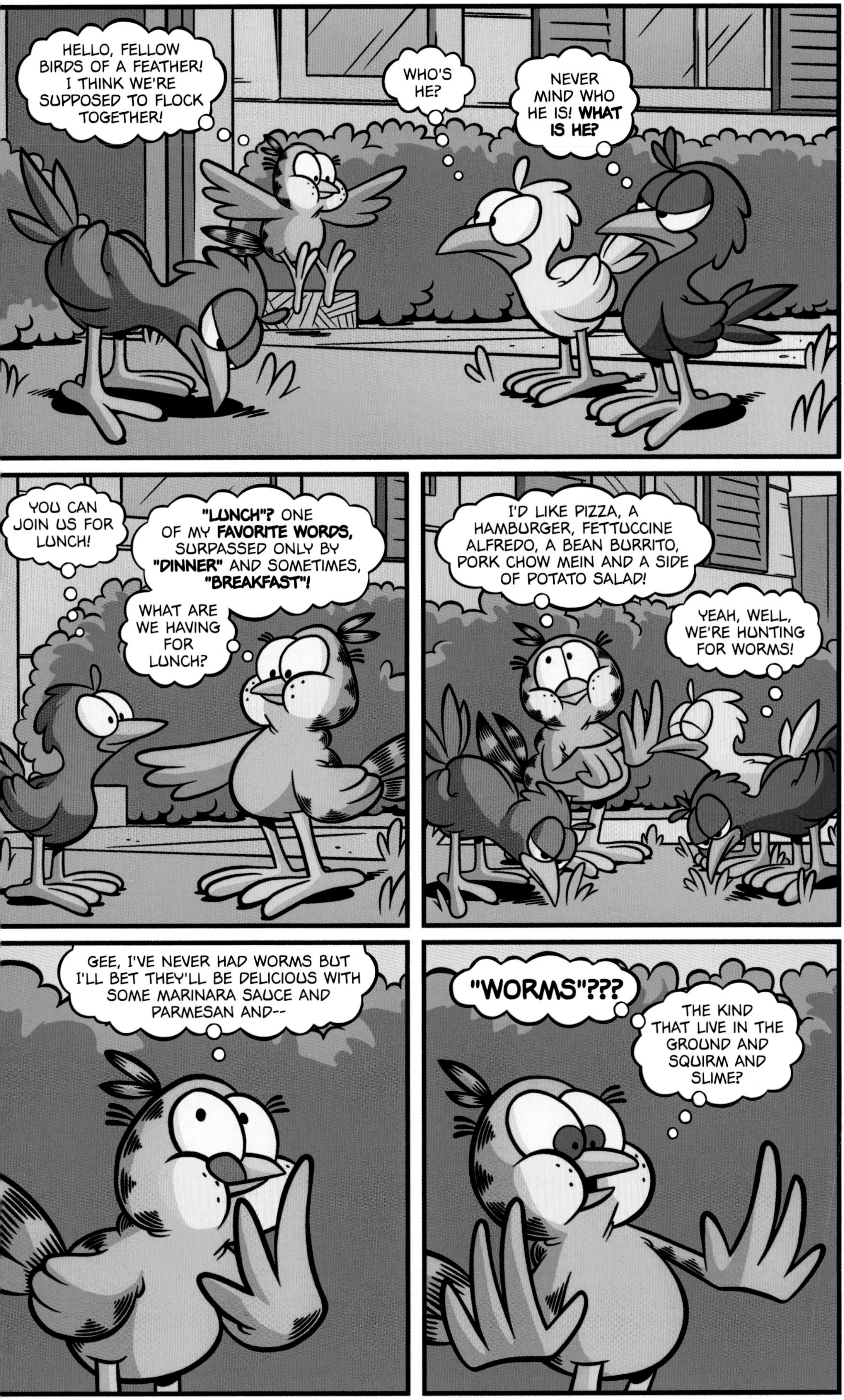
HELLO, FELLOW BIRDS OF A FEATHER! I THINK WE'RE SUPPOSED TO FLOCK TOGETHER!
WHO'S HE?
NEVER MIND WHO HE IS! **WHAT IS HE?**
YOU CAN JOIN US FOR LUNCH!
"LUNCH"? ONE OF MY **FAVORITE WORDS,** SURPASSED ONLY BY **"DINNER"** AND SOMETIMES, **"BREAKFAST"**!
WHAT ARE WE HAVING FOR LUNCH?
I'D LIKE PIZZA, A HAMBURGER, FETTUCCINE ALFREDO, A BEAN BURRITO, PORK CHOW MEIN AND A SIDE OF POTATO SALAD!
YEAH, WELL, WE'RE HUNTING FOR WORMS!
GEE, I'VE NEVER HAD WORMS BUT I'LL BET THEY'LL BE DELICIOUS WITH SOME MARINARA SAUCE AND PARMESAN AND--
"WORMS"???
THE KIND THAT LIVE IN THE GROUND AND SQUIRM AND SLIME?

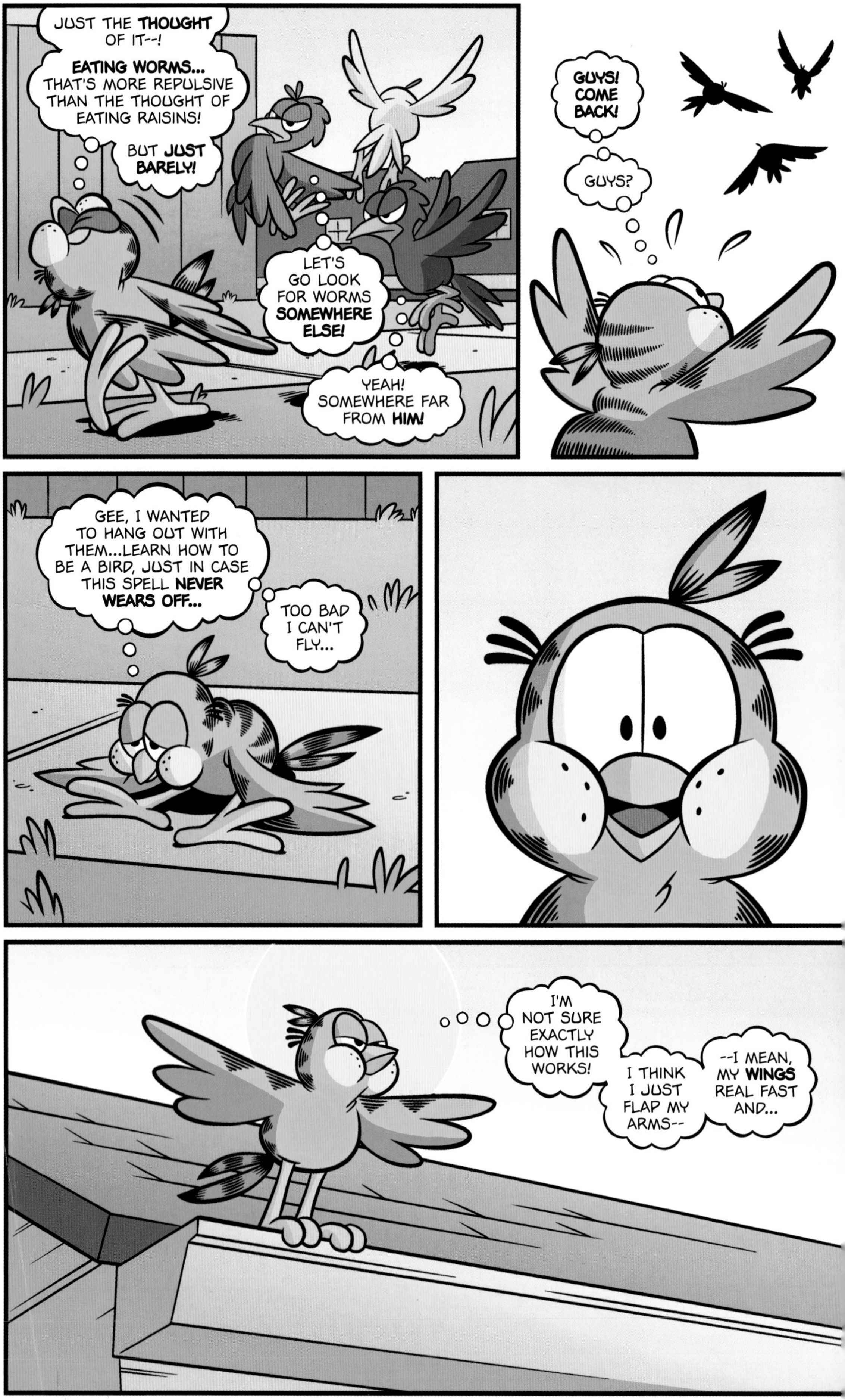
JUST THE **THOUGHT** OF IT--!
EATING WORMS... THAT'S MORE REPULSIVE THAN THE THOUGHT OF EATING RAISINS!
BUT **JUST BARELY!**
LET'S GO LOOK FOR WORMS **SOMEWHERE ELSE!**
YEAH! SOMEWHERE FAR FROM **HIM!**
GUYS! COME BACK!
GUYS?
GEE, I WANTED TO HANG OUT WITH THEM...LEARN HOW TO BE A BIRD, JUST IN CASE THIS SPELL **NEVER WEARS OFF...**
TOO BAD I CAN'T FLY...
I'M NOT SURE EXACTLY HOW THIS WORKS!
I THINK I JUST FLAP MY ARMS--
--I MEAN, MY **WINGS** REAL FAST AND...

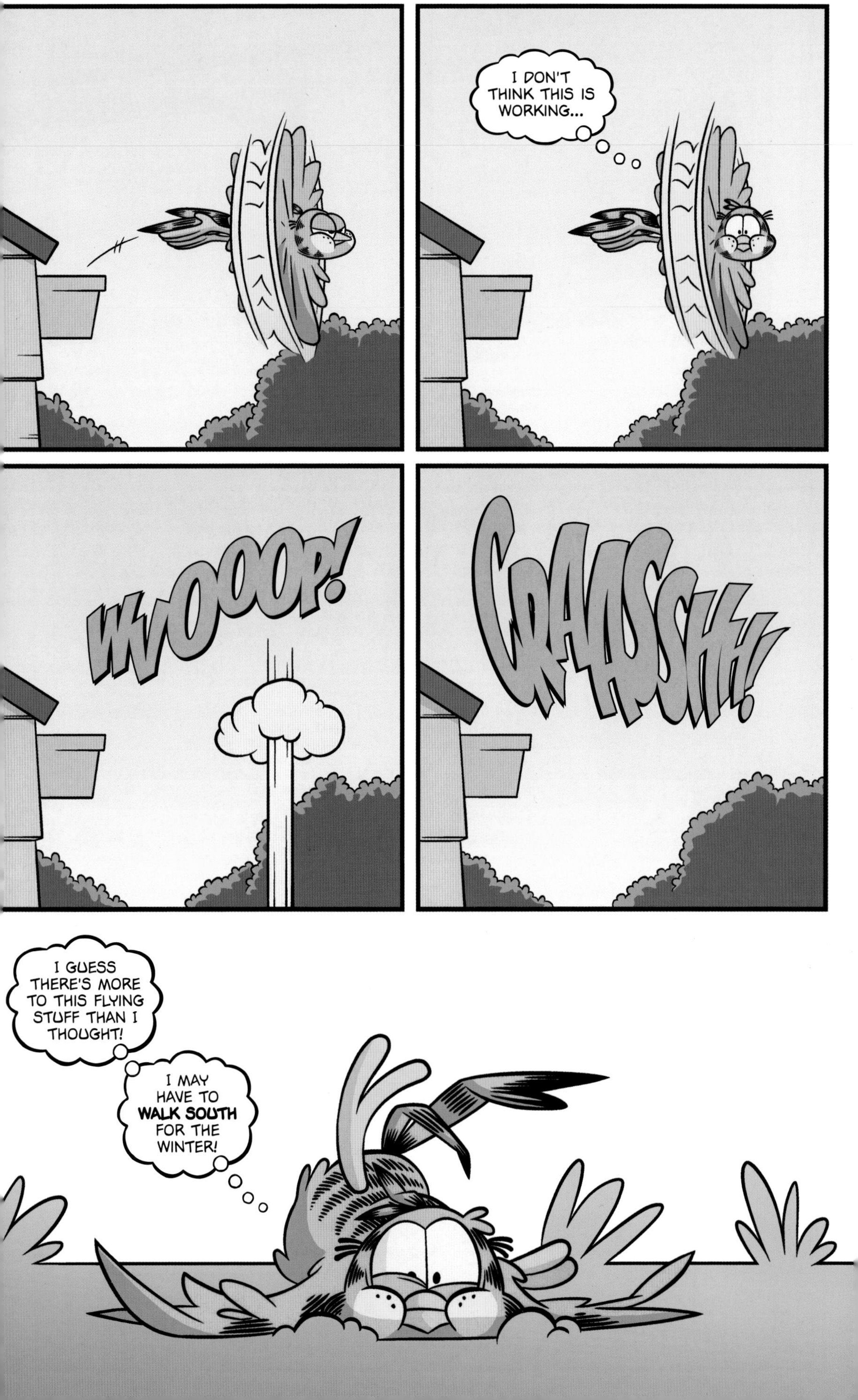
I DON'T THINK THIS IS WORKING...
WOOOP!
CRAASHH!
I GUESS THERE'S MORE TO THIS FLYING STUFF THAN I THOUGHT!
I MAY HAVE TO **WALK SOUTH** FOR THE WINTER!

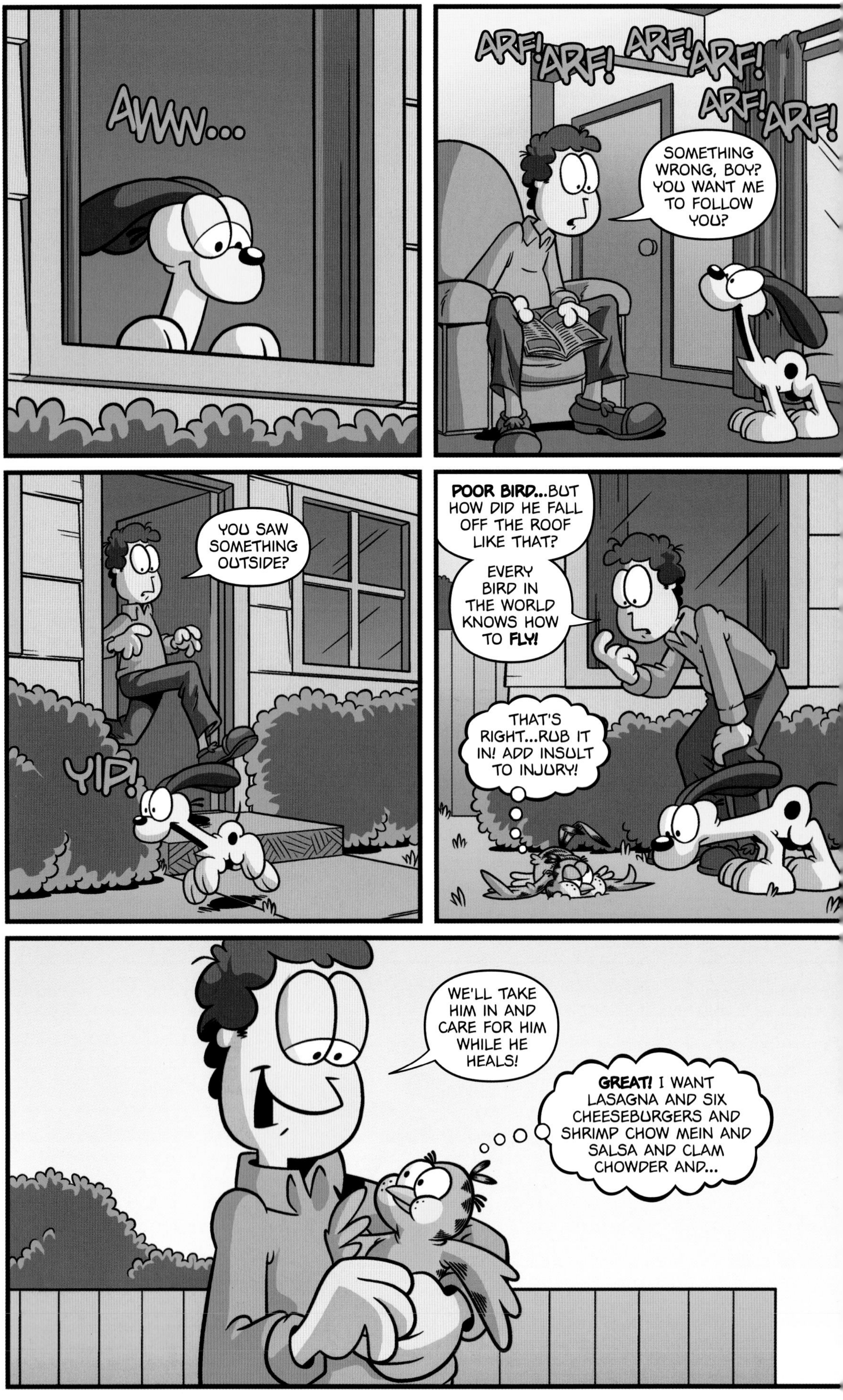
AWWW...
ARF! ARF! ARF! ARF! ARF! ARF!
SOMETHING WRONG, BOY? YOU WANT ME TO FOLLOW YOU?
YOU SAW SOMETHING OUTSIDE?
YIP!
POOR BIRD...BUT HOW DID HE FALL OFF THE ROOF LIKE THAT?
EVERY BIRD IN THE WORLD KNOWS HOW TO FLY!
THAT'S RIGHT...RUB IT IN! ADD INSULT TO INJURY!
WE'LL TAKE HIM IN AND CARE FOR HIM WHILE HE HEALS!
GREAT! I WANT LASAGNA AND SIX CHEESEBURGERS AND SHRIMP CHOW MEIN AND SALSA AND CLAM CHOWDER AND...

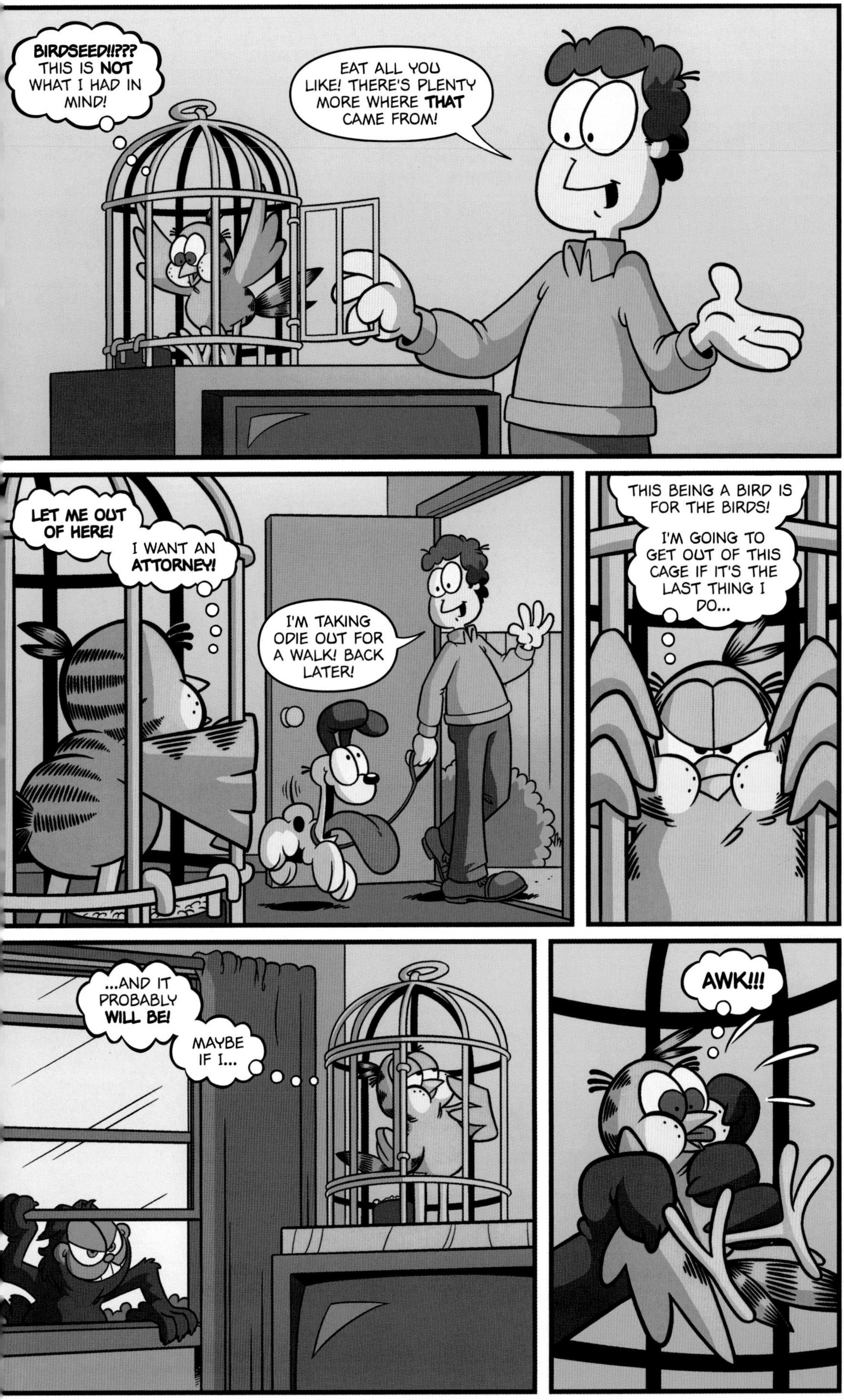
BIRDSEED!!??? THIS IS NOT WHAT I HAD IN MIND!
EAT ALL YOU LIKE! THERE'S PLENTY MORE WHERE THAT CAME FROM!
LET ME OUT OF HERE!
I WANT AN ATTORNEY!
I'M TAKING ODIE OUT FOR A WALK! BACK LATER!
THIS BEING A BIRD IS FOR THE BIRDS!
I'M GOING TO GET OUT OF THIS CAGE IF IT'S THE LAST THING I DO...
...AND IT PROBABLY WILL BE!
MAYBE IF I...
AWK!!!

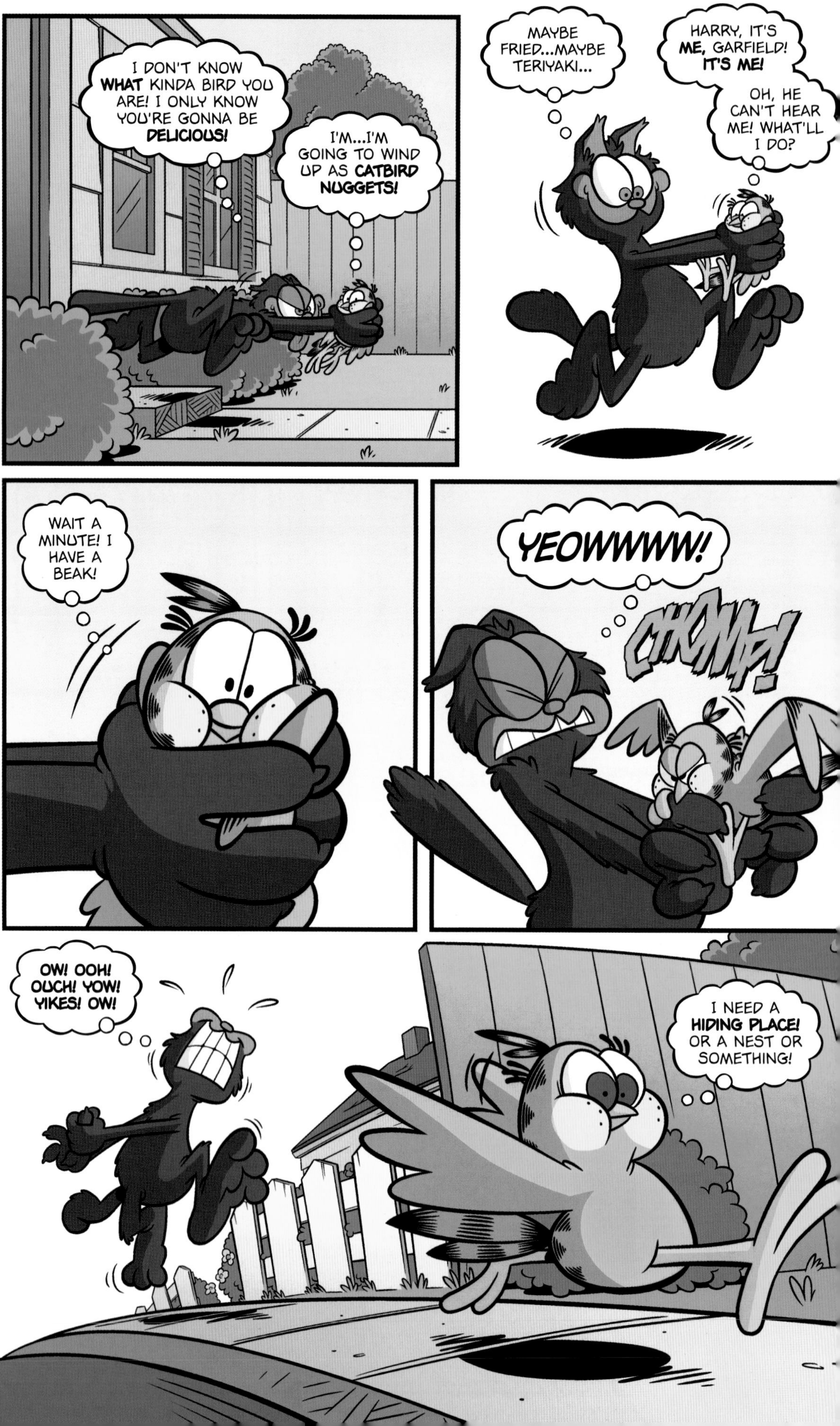
I DON'T KNOW **WHAT** KINDA BIRD YOU ARE! I ONLY KNOW YOU'RE GONNA BE **DELICIOUS!**
I'M...I'M GOING TO WIND UP AS **CATBIRD NUGGETS!**
MAYBE FRIED...MAYBE TERIYAKI...
HARRY, IT'S **ME,** GARFIELD! **IT'S ME!**
OH, HE CAN'T HEAR ME! WHAT'LL I DO?
WAIT A MINUTE! I HAVE A BEAK!
YEOWWWW!
CHOMP!
OW! OOH! OUCH! YOW! YIKES! OW!
I NEED A **HIDING PLACE!** OR A NEST OR SOMETHING!

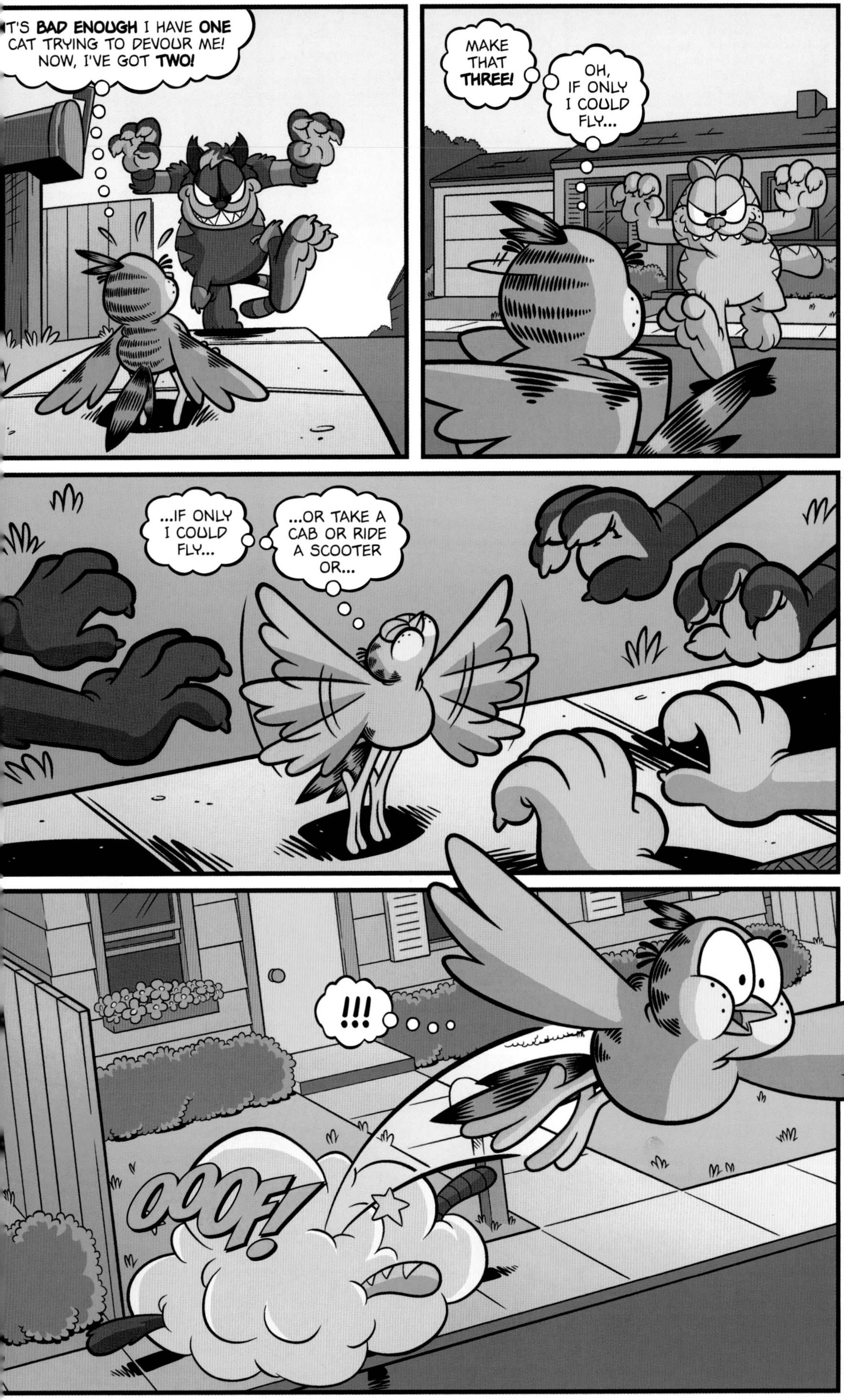
IT'S BAD ENOUGH I HAVE ONE CAT TRYING TO DEVOUR ME! NOW, I'VE GOT TWO!
MAKE THAT THREE!
OH, IF ONLY I COULD FLY...
...IF ONLY I COULD FLY...
...OR TAKE A CAB OR RIDE A SCOOTER OR...
!!!
OOOF!

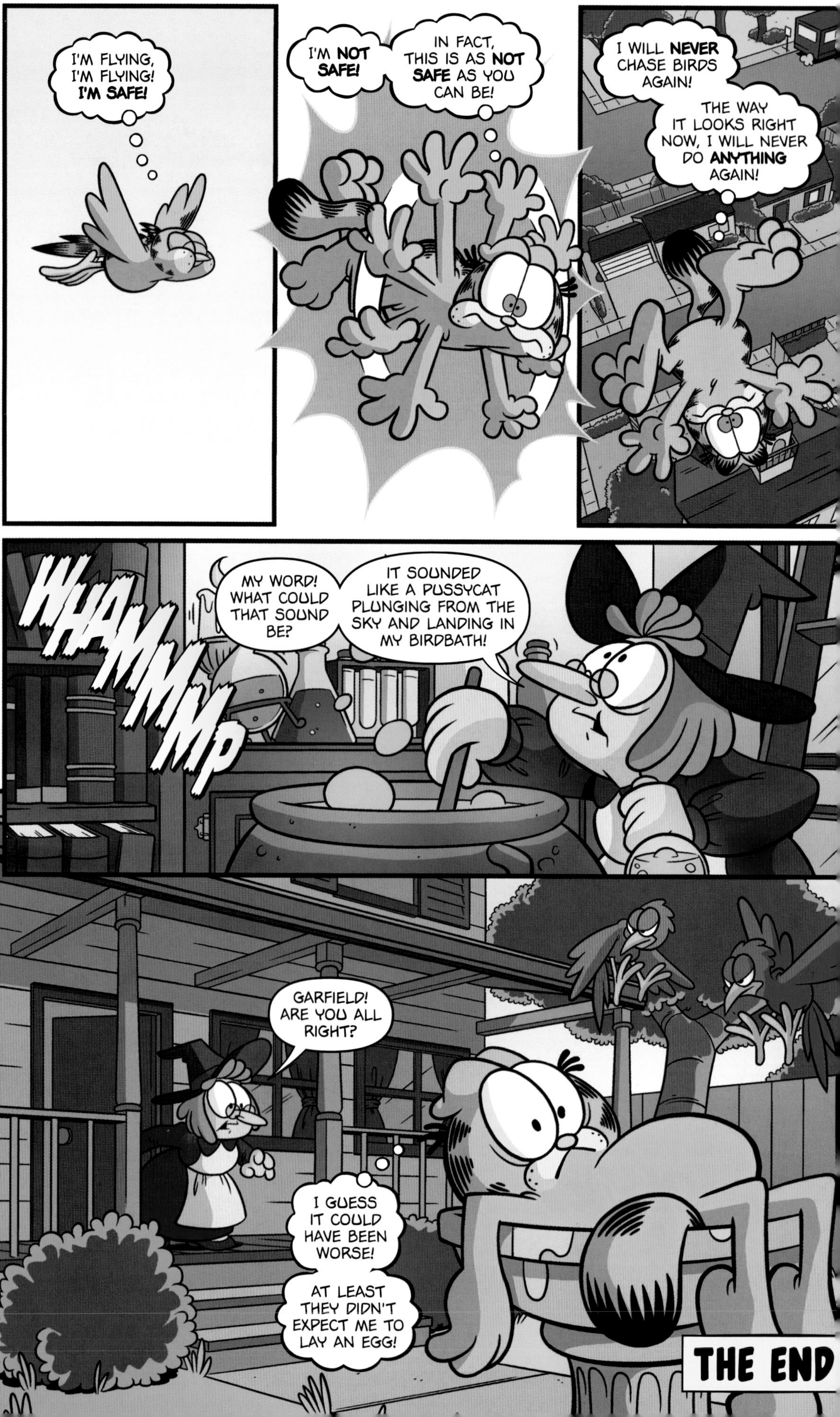

I'M FLYING, I'M FLYING! **I'M SAFE!**
I'M **NOT SAFE!**
IN FACT, THIS IS AS **NOT SAFE** AS YOU CAN BE!
I WILL **NEVER** CHASE BIRDS AGAIN!
THE WAY IT LOOKS RIGHT NOW, I WILL NEVER DO **ANYTHING** AGAIN!
WHAMMMMP
MY WORD! WHAT COULD THAT SOUND BE?
IT SOUNDED LIKE A PUSSYCAT PLUNGING FROM THE SKY AND LANDING IN MY BIRDBATH!
GARFIELD! ARE YOU ALL RIGHT?
I GUESS IT COULD HAVE BEEN WORSE!
AT LEAST THEY DIDN'T EXPECT ME TO LAY AN EGG!
THE END

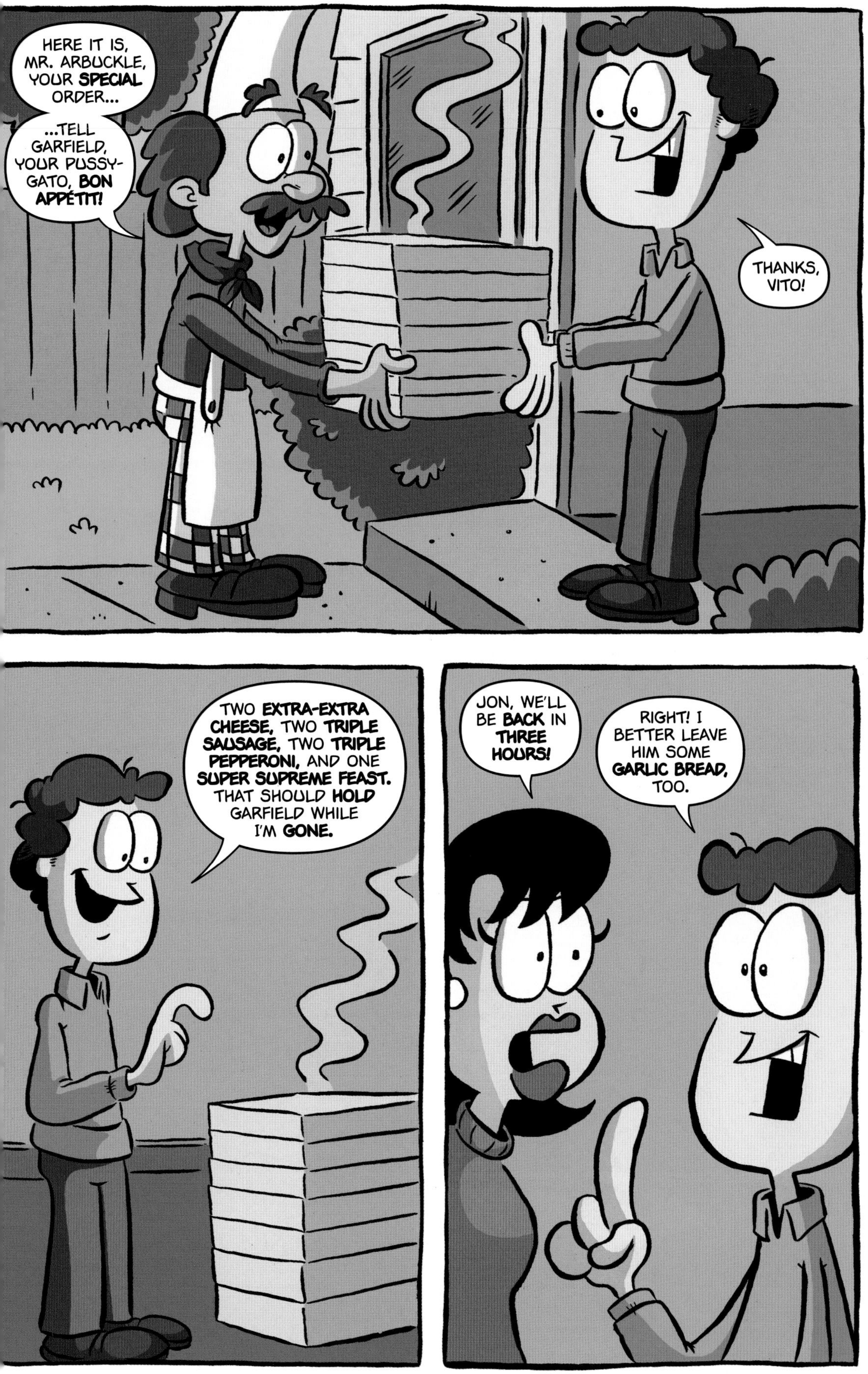
HERE IT IS, MR. ARBUCKLE, YOUR **SPECIAL** ORDER...
...TELL GARFIELD, YOUR PUSSY-GATO, **BON APPÉTIT!**
THANKS, VITO!
TWO **EXTRA-EXTRA CHEESE,** TWO **TRIPLE SAUSAGE,** TWO **TRIPLE PEPPERONI,** AND ONE **SUPER SUPREME FEAST.** THAT SHOULD **HOLD** GARFIELD WHILE I'M **GONE.**
JON, WE'LL BE **BACK** IN **THREE HOURS!**
RIGHT! I BETTER LEAVE HIM SOME **GARLIC BREAD,** TOO.

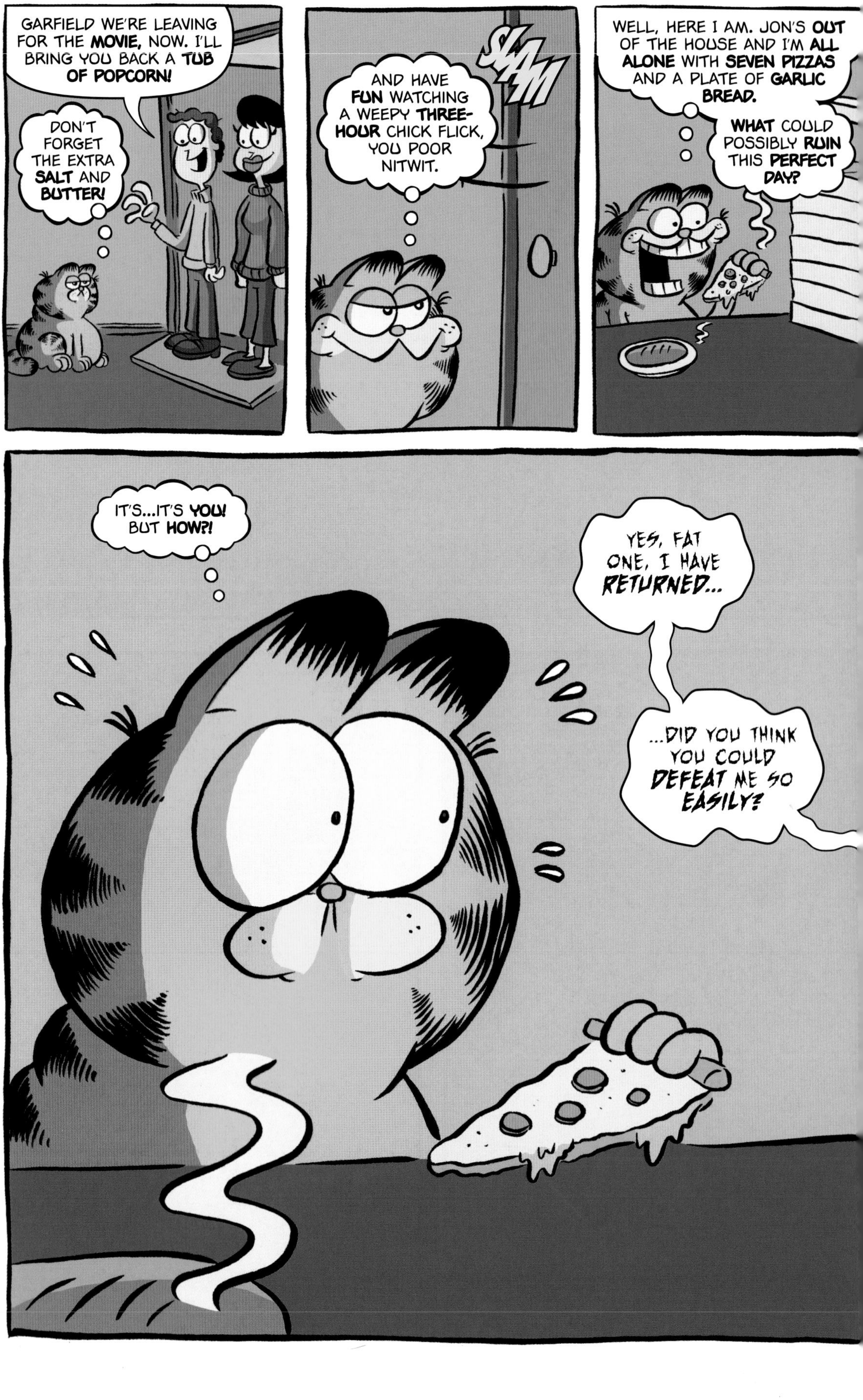
GARFIELD WE'RE LEAVING FOR THE MOVIE, NOW. I'LL BRING YOU BACK A TUB OF POPCORN!
DON'T FORGET THE EXTRA SALT AND BUTTER!
SLAM
AND HAVE FUN WATCHING A WEEPY THREE-HOUR CHICK FLICK, YOU POOR NITWIT.
WELL, HERE I AM. JON'S OUT OF THE HOUSE AND I'M ALL ALONE WITH SEVEN PIZZAS AND A PLATE OF GARLIC BREAD.
WHAT COULD POSSIBLY RUIN THIS PERFECT DAY?
IT'S...IT'S YOU! BUT HOW?!
YES, FAT ONE, I HAVE RETURNED...
...DID YOU THINK YOU COULD DEFEAT ME SO EASILY?

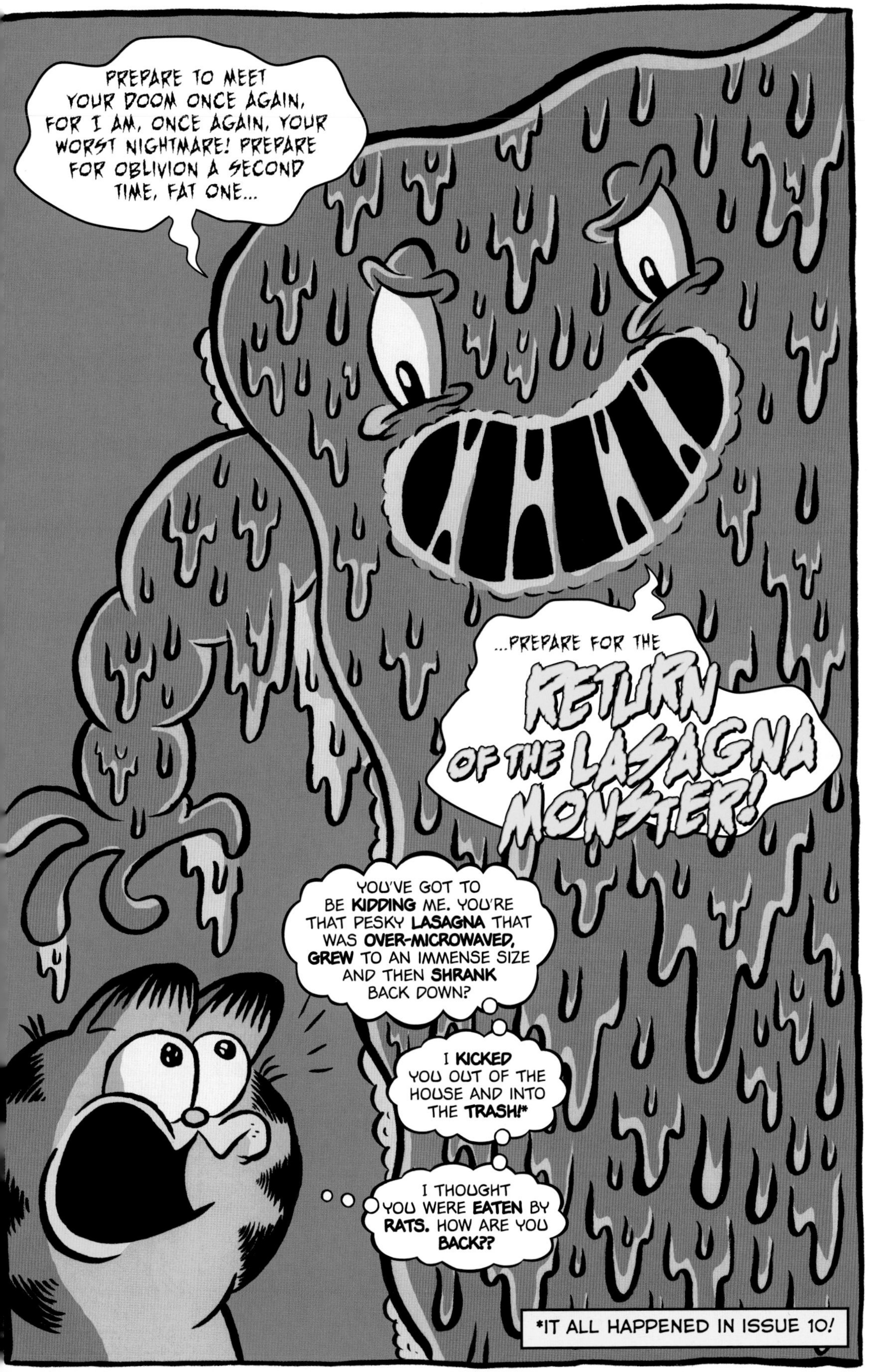
PREPARE TO MEET YOUR DOOM ONCE AGAIN, FOR I AM, ONCE AGAIN, YOUR WORST NIGHTMARE! PREPARE FOR OBLIVION A SECOND TIME, FAT ONE...
...PREPARE FOR THE RETURN OF THE LASAGNA MONSTER!
YOU'VE GOT TO BE KIDDING ME. YOU'RE THAT PESKY LASAGNA THAT WAS OVER-MICROWAVED, GREW TO AN IMMENSE SIZE AND THEN SHRANK BACK DOWN?
I KICKED YOU OUT OF THE HOUSE AND INTO THE TRASH!*
I THOUGHT YOU WERE EATEN BY RATS. HOW ARE YOU BACK??
*IT ALL HAPPENED IN ISSUE 10!

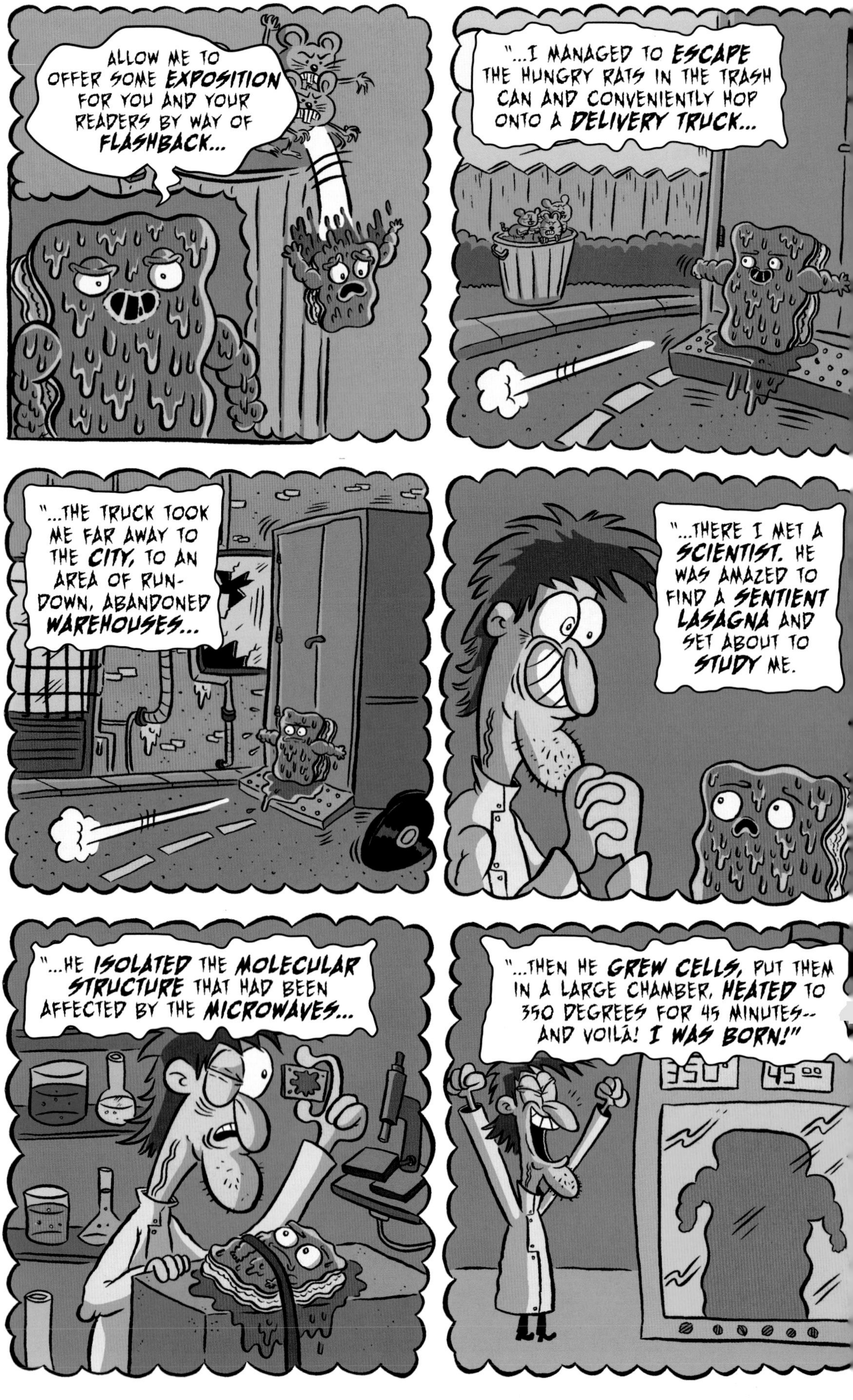
ALLOW ME TO OFFER SOME EXPOSITION FOR YOU AND YOUR READERS BY WAY OF FLASHBACK...
"...I MANAGED TO ESCAPE THE HUNGRY RATS IN THE TRASH CAN AND CONVENIENTLY HOP ONTO A DELIVERY TRUCK...
"...THE TRUCK TOOK ME FAR AWAY TO THE CITY, TO AN AREA OF RUN-DOWN, ABANDONED WAREHOUSES...
"...THERE I MET A SCIENTIST. HE WAS AMAZED TO FIND A SENTIENT LASAGNA AND SET ABOUT TO STUDY ME.
"...HE ISOLATED THE MOLECULAR STRUCTURE THAT HAD BEEN AFFECTED BY THE MICROWAVES...
"...THEN HE GREW CELLS, PUT THEM IN A LARGE CHAMBER, HEATED TO 350 DEGREES FOR 45 MINUTES-- AND VOILÀ! I WAS BORN!"
350°
45:00

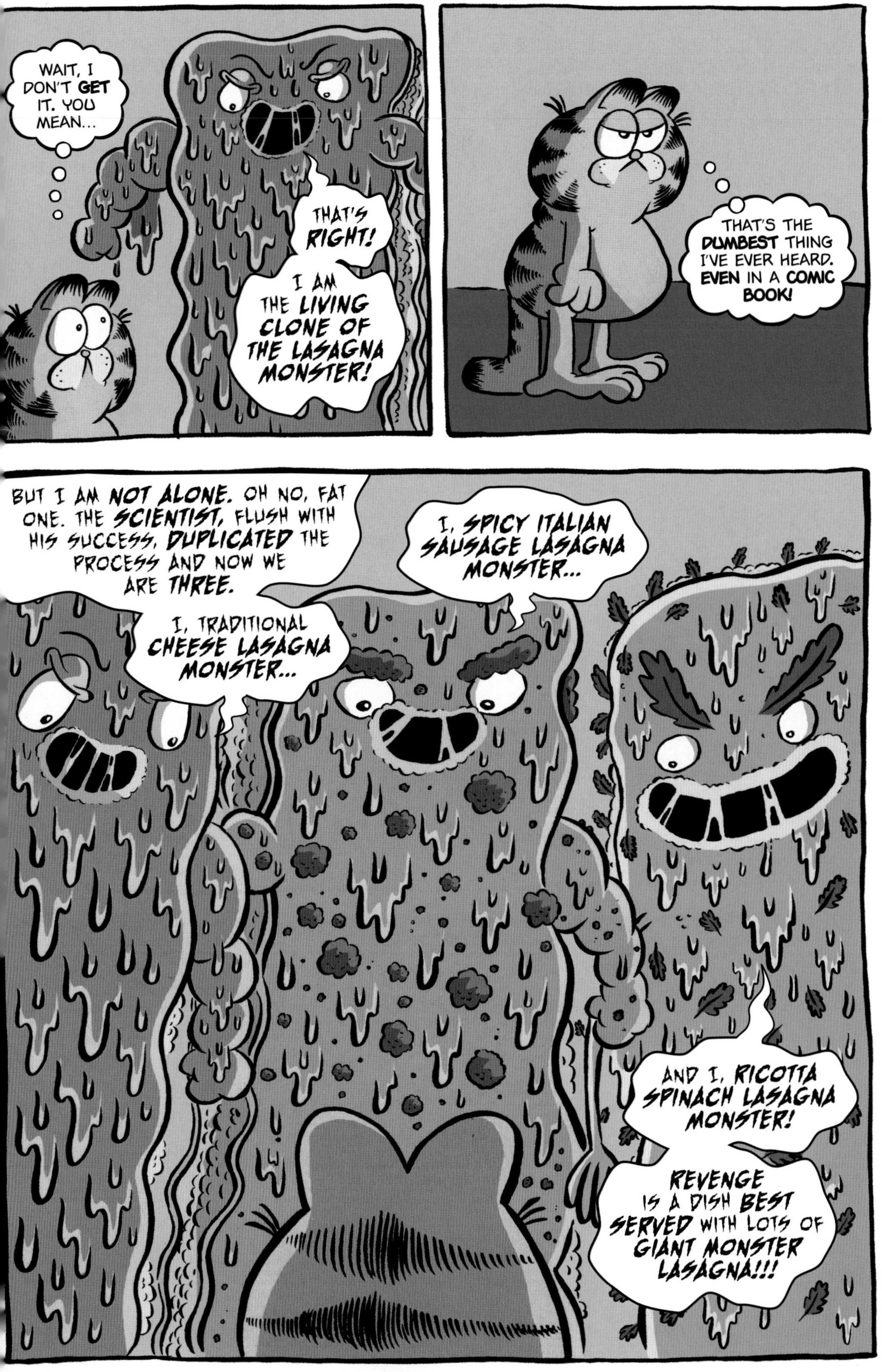
WAIT, I DON'T GET IT. YOU MEAN...
THAT'S RIGHT!
I AM THE LIVING CLONE OF THE LASAGNA MONSTER!
THAT'S THE DUMBEST THING I'VE EVER HEARD. EVEN IN A COMIC BOOK!
BUT I AM NOT ALONE. OH NO, FAT ONE. THE SCIENTIST, FLUSH WITH HIS SUCCESS, DUPLICATED THE PROCESS AND NOW WE ARE THREE.
I, TRADITIONAL CHEESE LASAGNA MONSTER...
I, SPICY ITALIAN SAUSAGE LASAGNA MONSTER...
AND I, RICOTTA SPINACH LASAGNA MONSTER!
REVENGE IS A DISH BEST SERVED WITH LOTS OF GIANT MONSTER LASAGNA!!!

HOW I'VE DREAMT OF THIS MOMENT...OR, MY CLONE DREAMT OF THIS, OR WE BOTH DID. OR...OH FORGET IT! TASTE THE DEADLY POWER OF MY MOLTEN CHEESY BLAST!
LUCKY I REMEMBERED TO GRAB THIS TRAY--JUST LIKE THE LAST TIME!
SPLUURRRTTT
THOSE SUCKERS LOOK HOT!
AND TASTE MY SUPER SPICY SAUSAGE SHOOTERS! BURN, BABY, BURN!
SPLORT! SPLORT!
SPLORT!
AND NOW, CAT, TASTE MY RAPID-FIRE RICOTTA ROCKETS!
ENOUGH! ENOUGH! ENOUGH! I'M NOT TASTING ANYTHING!
DUH-DUH-DUH-DUH!

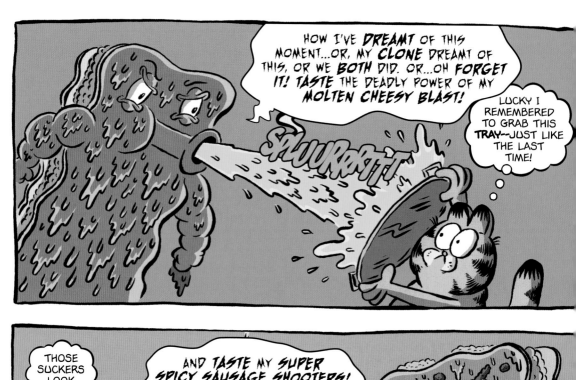

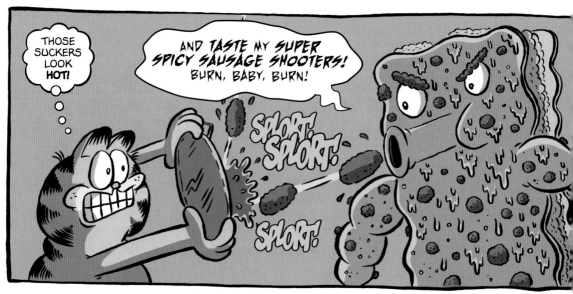

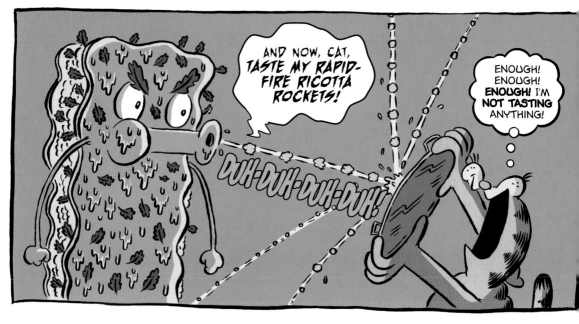

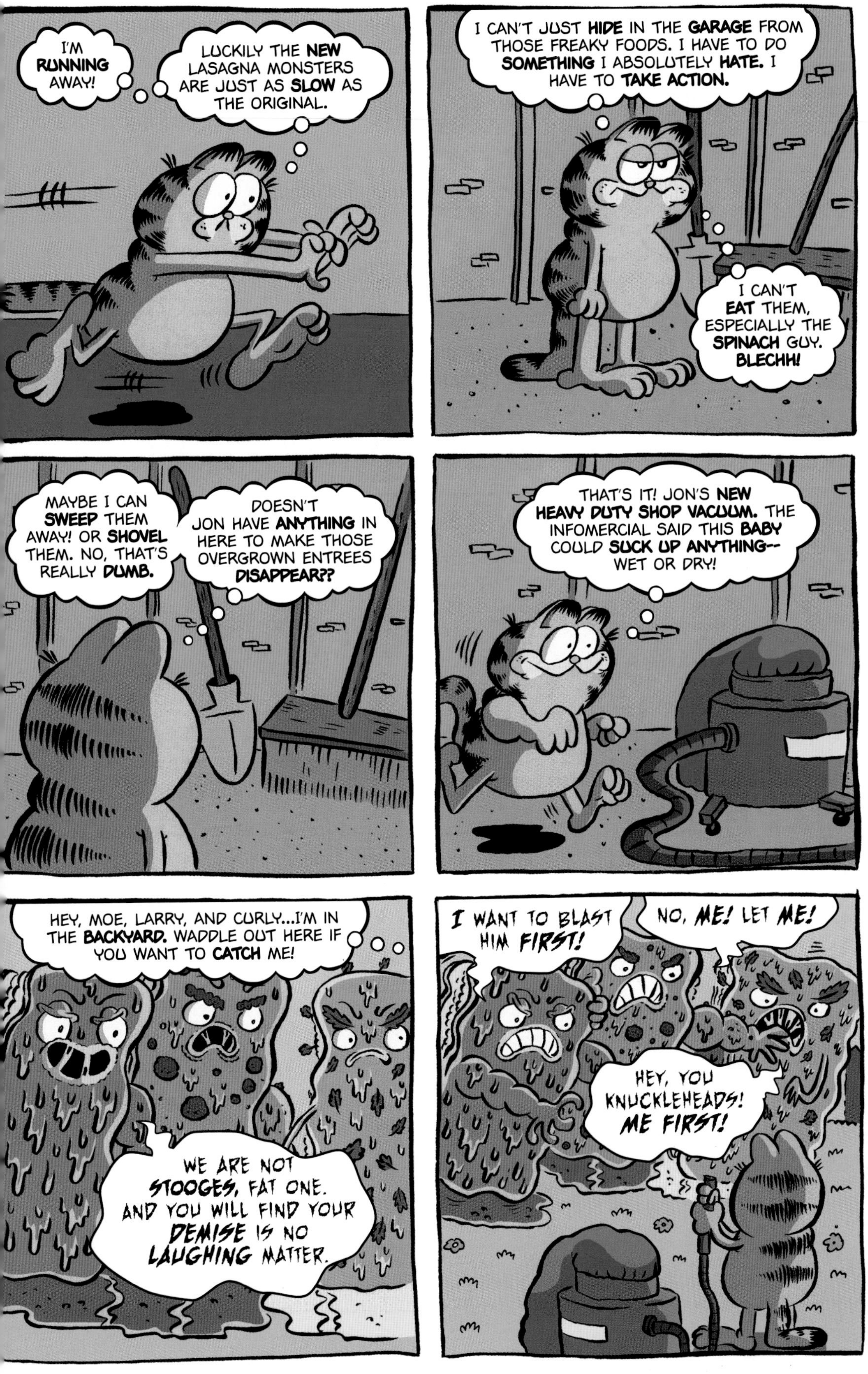
I'M **RUNNING** AWAY!
LUCKILY THE **NEW** LASAGNA MONSTERS ARE JUST AS **SLOW** AS THE ORIGINAL.
I CAN'T JUST **HIDE** IN THE **GARAGE** FROM THOSE FREAKY FOODS. I HAVE TO DO **SOMETHING** I ABSOLUTELY **HATE.** I HAVE TO **TAKE ACTION.**
I CAN'T **EAT** THEM, ESPECIALLY THE **SPINACH** GUY. **BLECHH!**
MAYBE I CAN **SWEEP** THEM AWAY! OR **SHOVEL** THEM. NO, THAT'S REALLY **DUMB.**
DOESN'T JON HAVE **ANYTHING** IN HERE TO MAKE THOSE OVERGROWN ENTREES **DISAPPEAR??**
THAT'S IT! JON'S **NEW HEAVY DUTY SHOP VACUUM.** THE INFOMERCIAL SAID THIS **BABY** COULD **SUCK UP ANYTHING--** WET OR DRY!
HEY, MOE, LARRY, AND CURLY...I'M IN THE **BACKYARD.** WADDLE OUT HERE IF YOU WANT TO **CATCH** ME!
WE ARE NOT **STOOGES,** FAT ONE. AND YOU WILL FIND YOUR **DEMISE** IS NO **LAUGHING** MATTER.
I WANT TO BLAST HIM **FIRST!**
NO, ***ME!*** LET ***ME!***
HEY, YOU KNUCKLEHEADS! ***ME FIRST!***

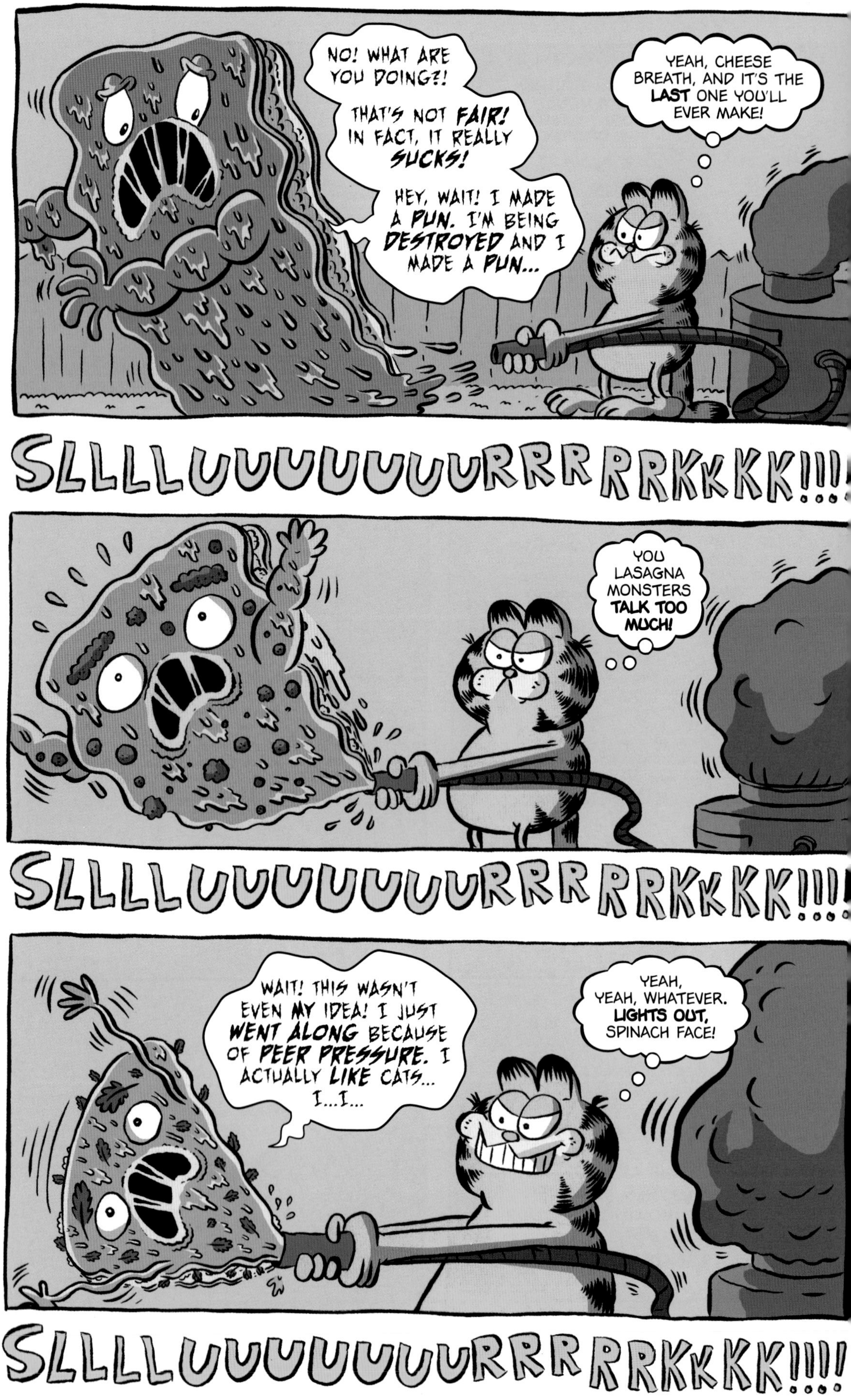
NO! WHAT ARE YOU DOING?!
THAT'S NOT FAIR! IN FACT, IT REALLY SUCKS!
HEY, WAIT! I MADE A PUN. I'M BEING DESTROYED AND I MADE A PUN...
YEAH, CHEESE BREATH, AND IT'S THE LAST ONE YOU'LL EVER MAKE!
SLLLLUUUUUUUURRRRRRKKKK!!!
YOU LASAGNA MONSTERS TALK TOO MUCH!
SLLLLUUUUUUUURRRRRRKKKK!!!
WAIT! THIS WASN'T EVEN MY IDEA! I JUST WENT ALONG BECAUSE OF PEER PRESSURE. I ACTUALLY LIKE CATS... I...I...
YEAH, YEAH, WHATEVER. LIGHTS OUT, SPINACH FACE!
SLLLLUUUUUUUURRRRRRKKKK!!!!

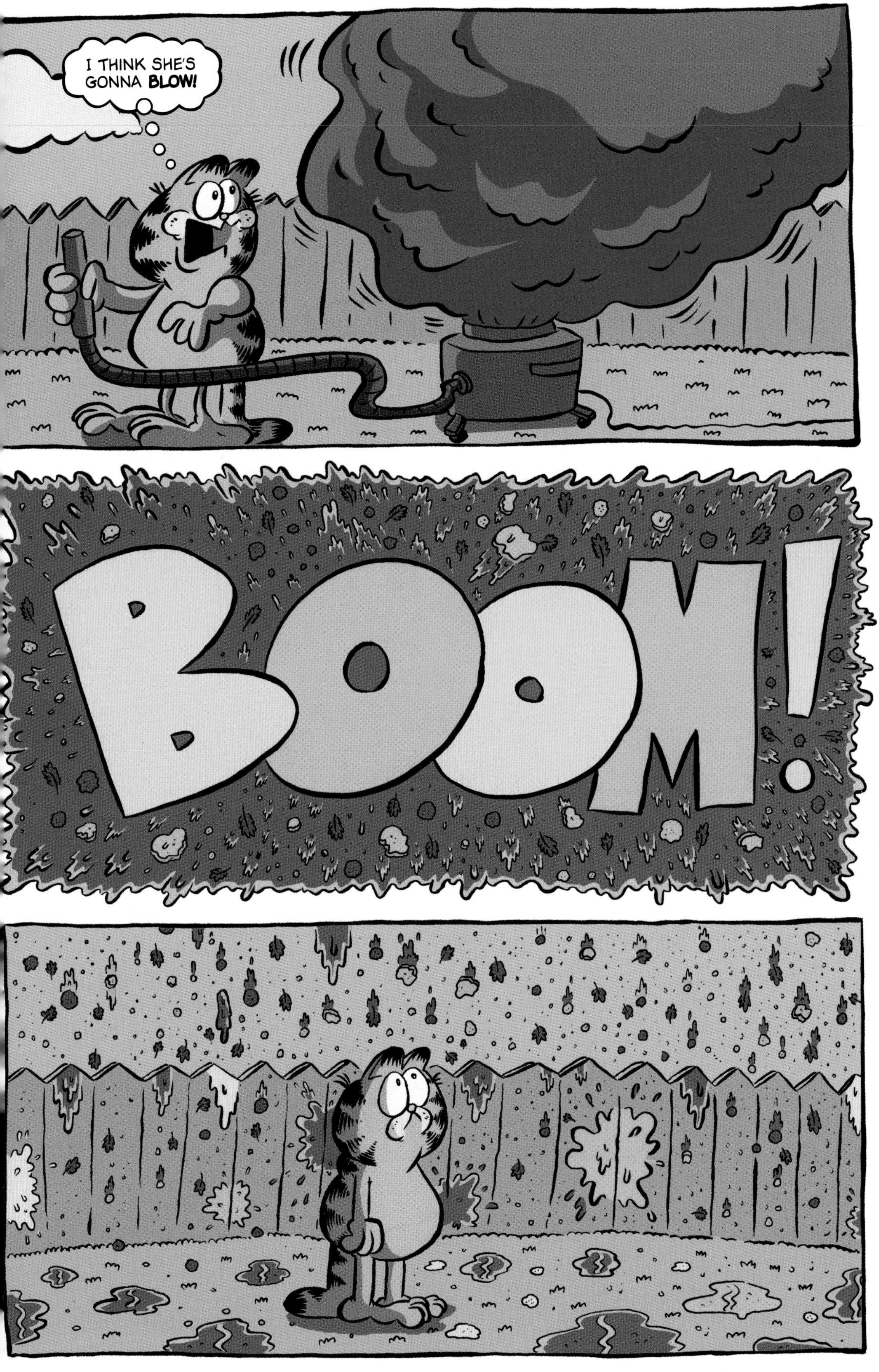
I THINK SHE'S GONNA **BLOW!**
BOOM!

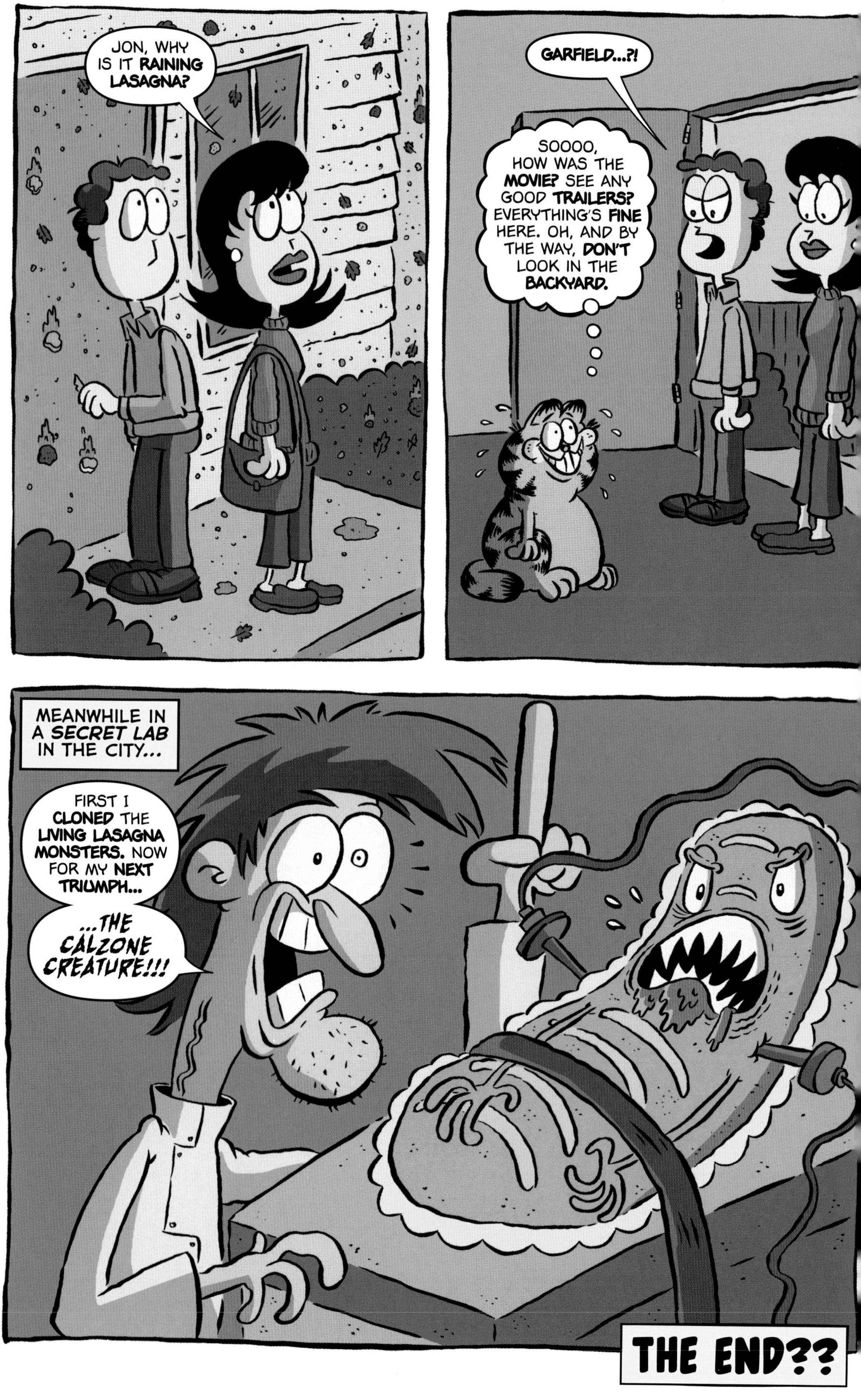
JON, WHY IS IT RAINING LASAGNA?
GARFIELD...?!
SOOOO, HOW WAS THE MOVIE? SEE ANY GOOD TRAILERS? EVERYTHING'S FINE HERE. OH, AND BY THE WAY, DON'T LOOK IN THE BACKYARD.
MEANWHILE IN A SECRET LAB IN THE CITY...
FIRST I CLONED THE LIVING LASAGNA MONSTERS. NOW FOR MY NEXT TRIUMPH...
...THE CALZONE CREATURE!!!
THE END??

COVER GALLERY

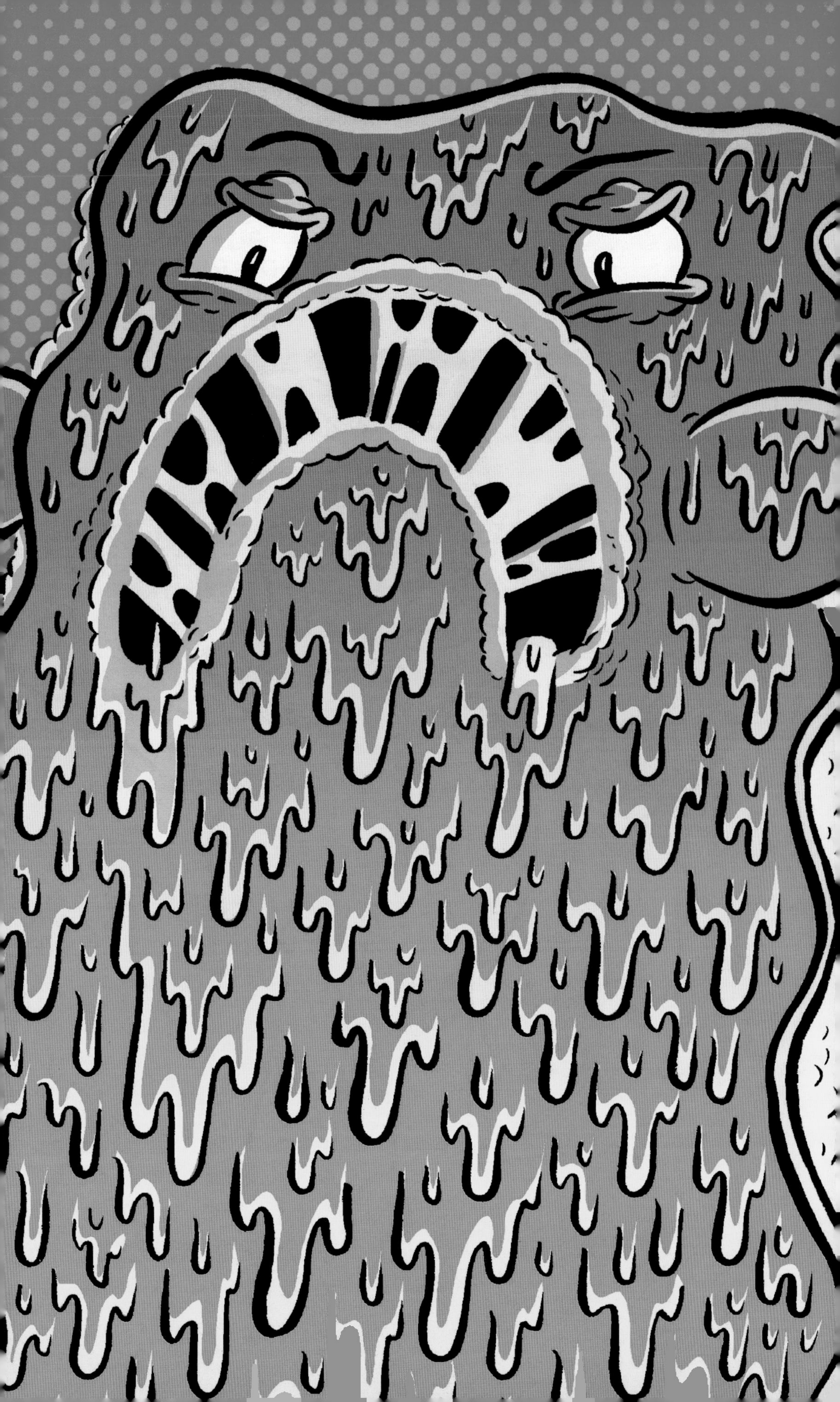

ISSUE 9A COVER BY
GARY BARKER & DAN DAVIS
COLORS BY **LISA MOORE**

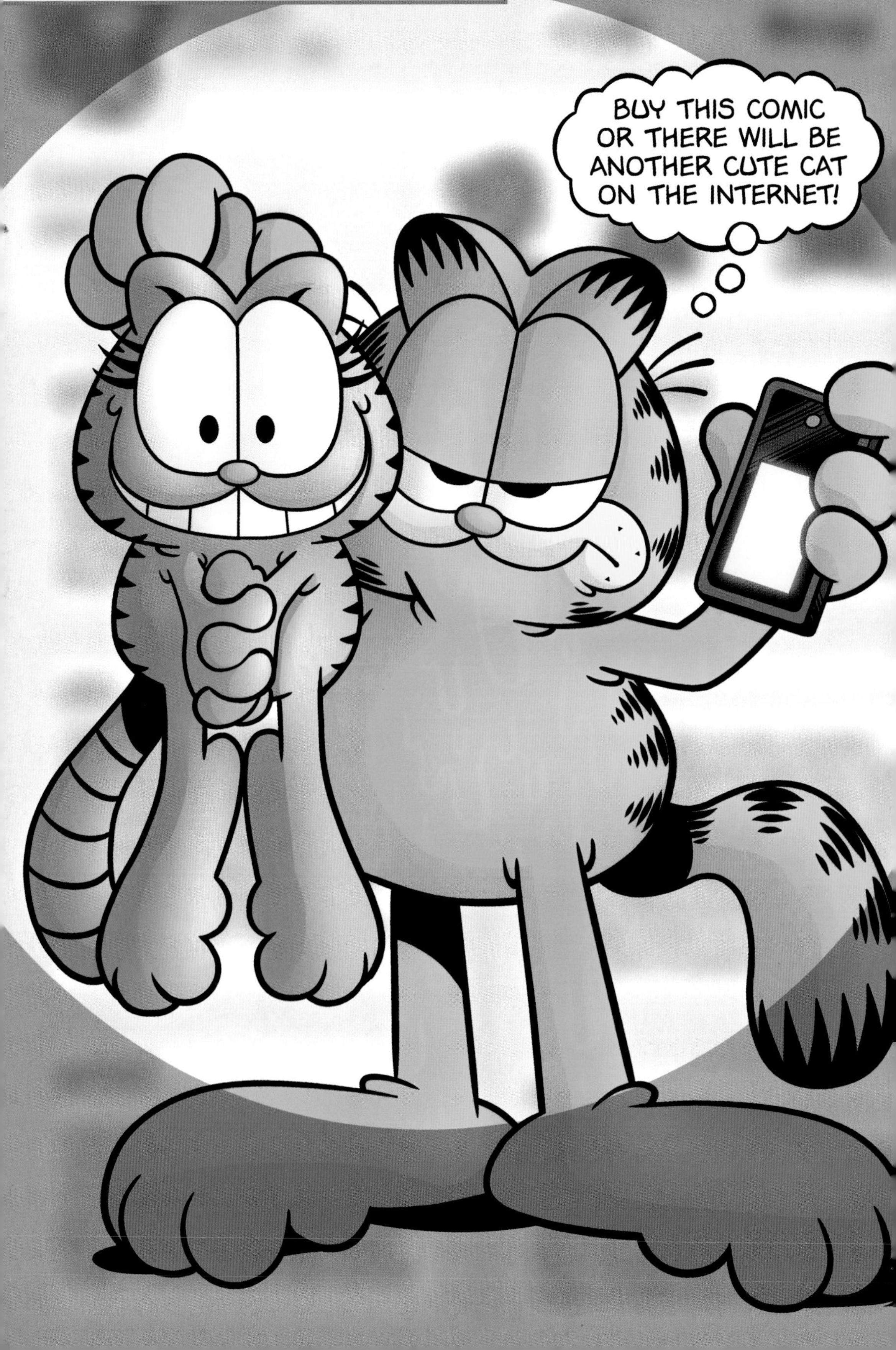
BUY THIS COMIC OR THERE WILL BE ANOTHER CUTE CAT ON THE INTERNET!

ISSUE 9B COVER BY
AL JAFFEE
COLORS BY **LISA MOORE**

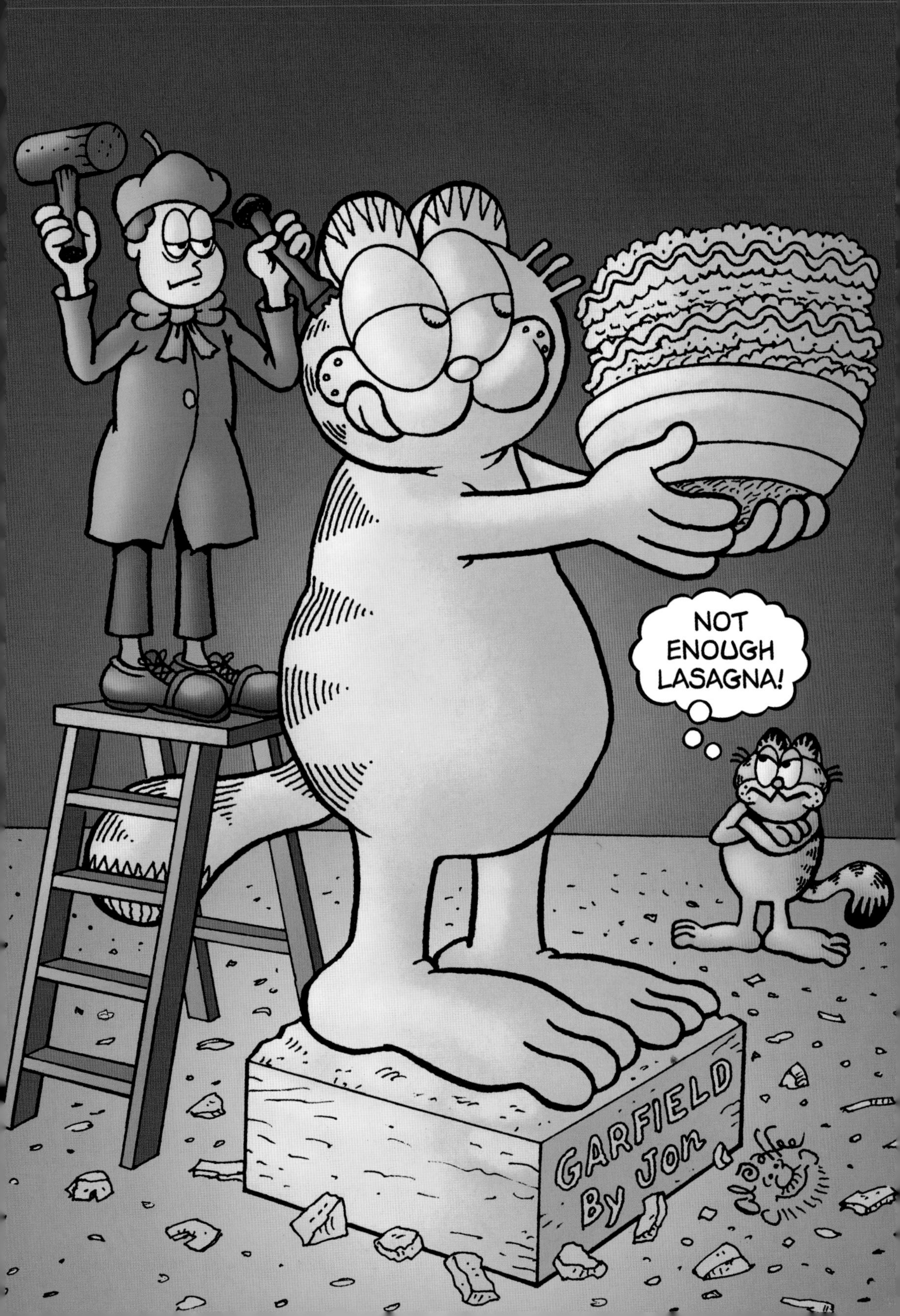
NOT ENOUGH LASAGNA!
GARFIELD By Jon
aljaffee

ISSUE 10A COVER BY
GARY BARKER & DAN DAVIS
COLORS BY **LISA MOORE**

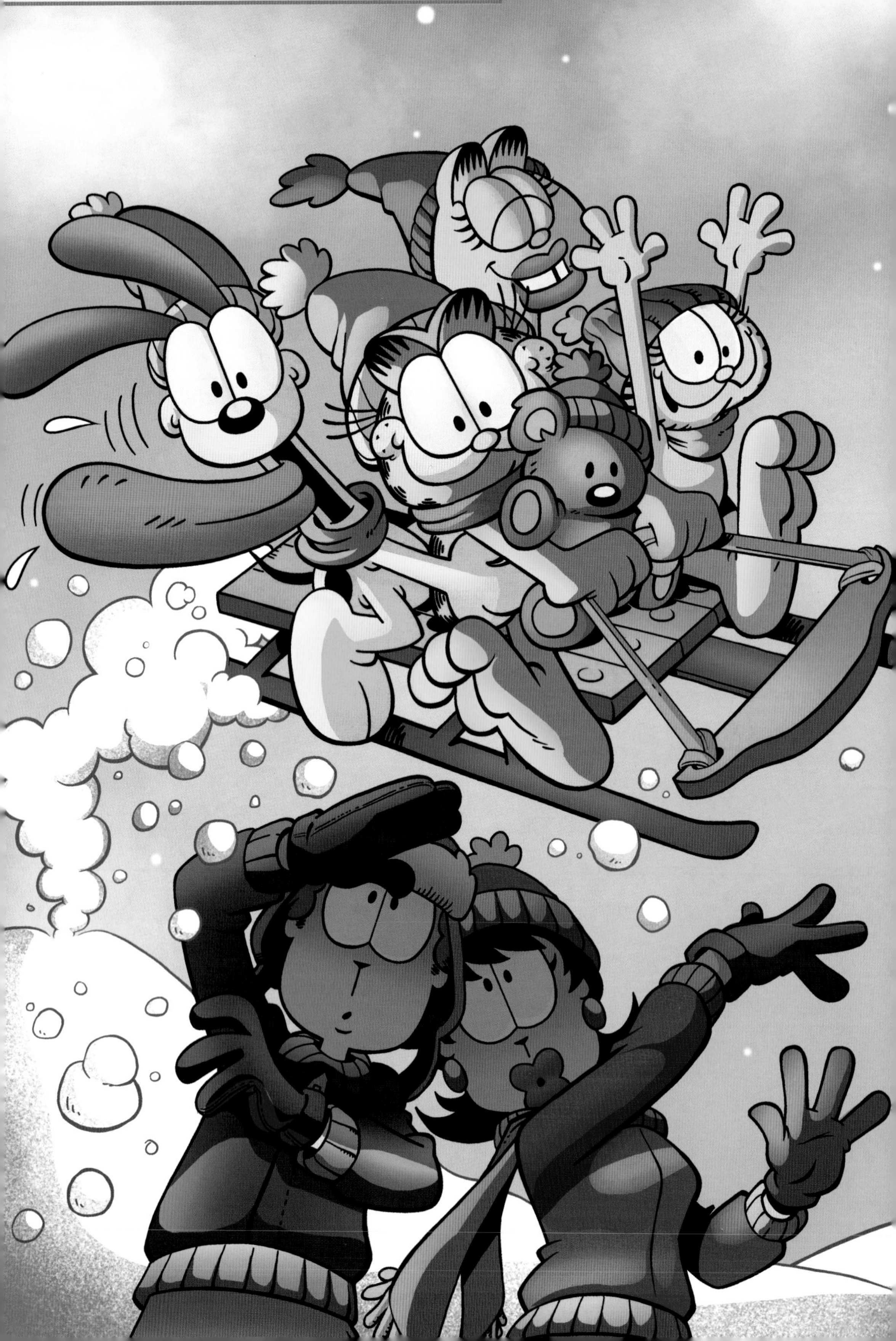

ISSUE 10B COVER BY
DAVID DEGRAND
COLORS BY LISA MOORE

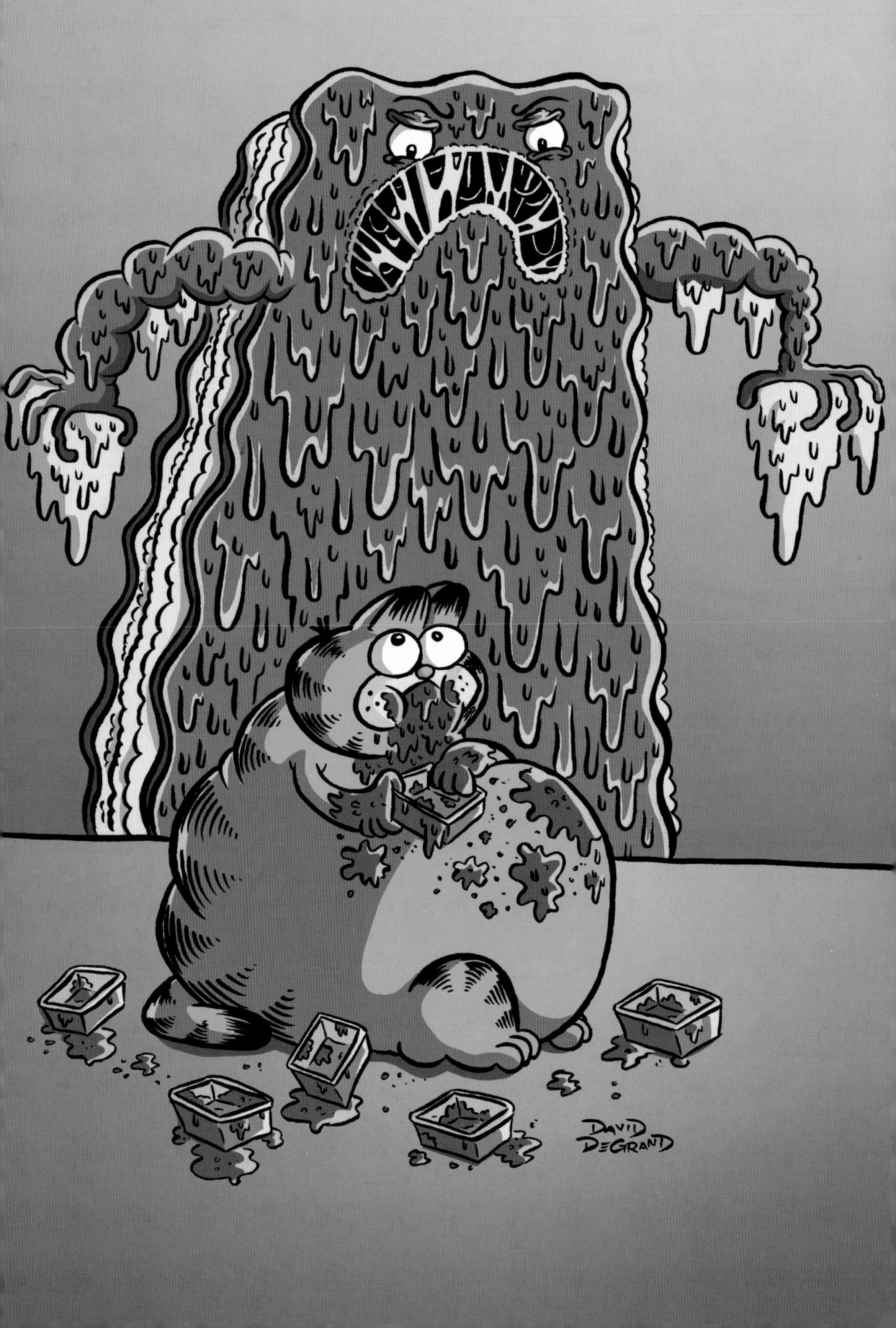
DAVID
DEGRAND

ISSUE 11A COVER BY
GARY BARKER & DAN DAVIS
COLORS BY **LISA MOORE**

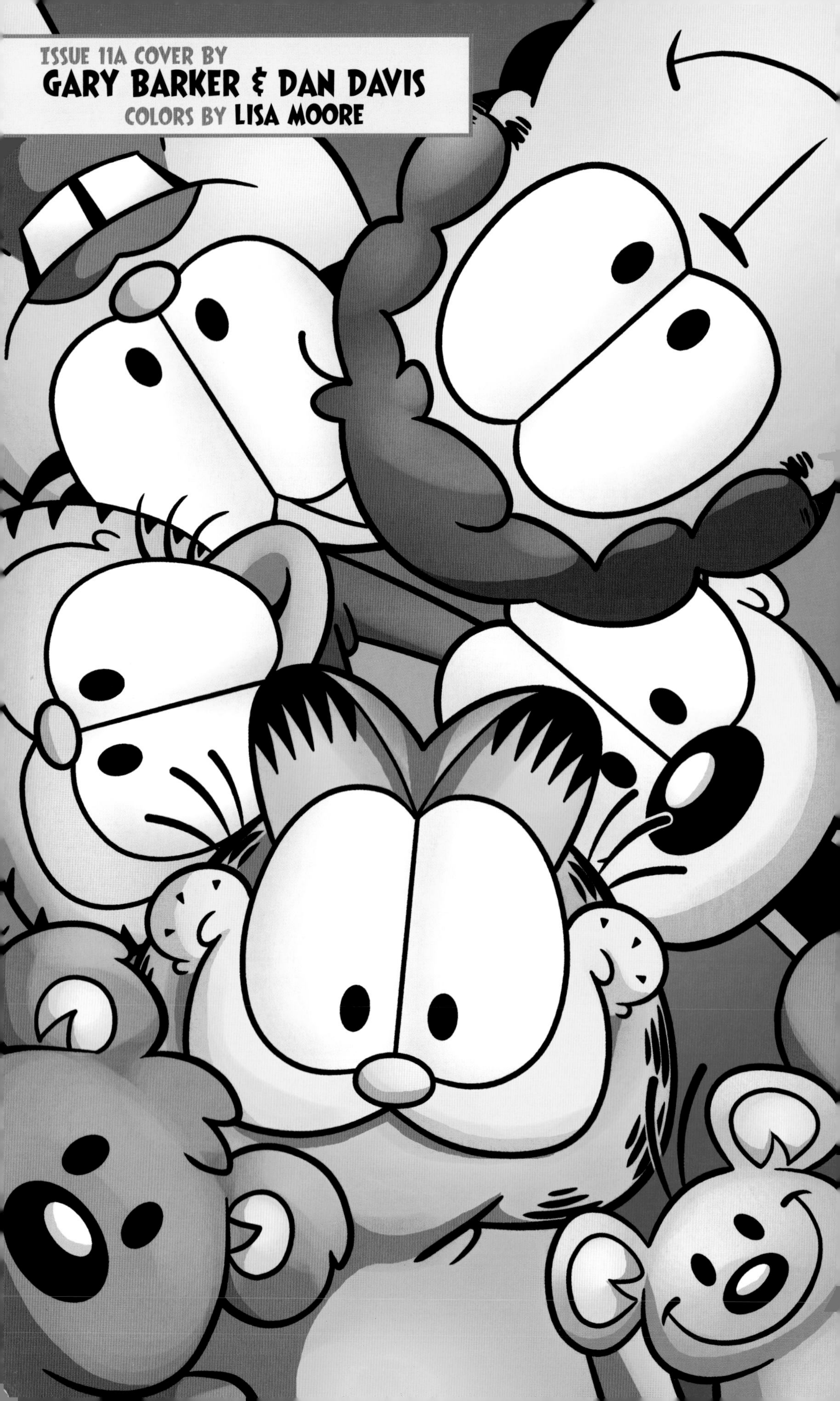

ISSUE 11B COVER BY
FRED HEMBECK
COLORS BY **LISA MOORE**

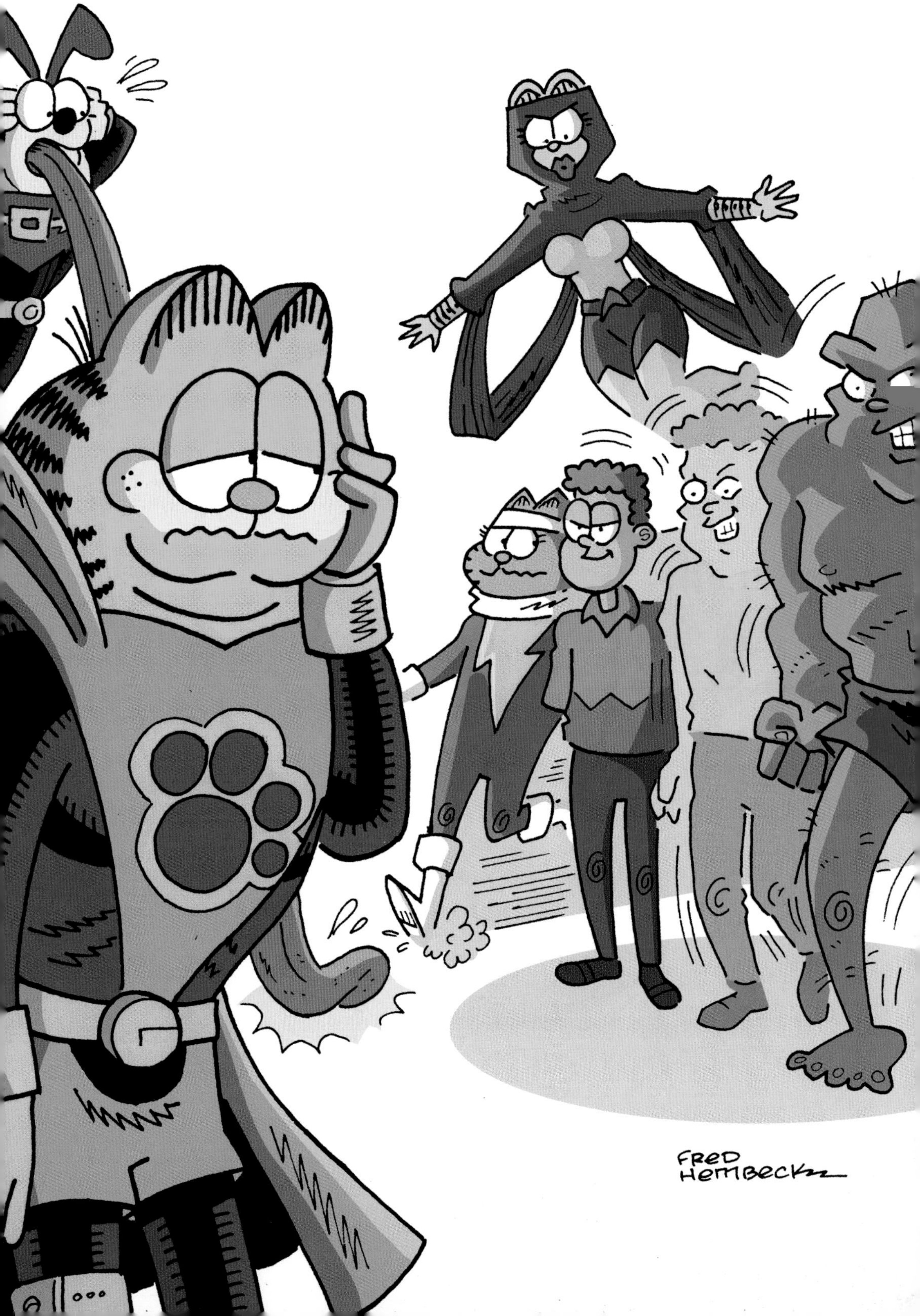
FRED
HEMBECK

ISSUE 12A COVER BY
GARY BARKER & DAN DAVIS
COLORS BY LISA MOORE

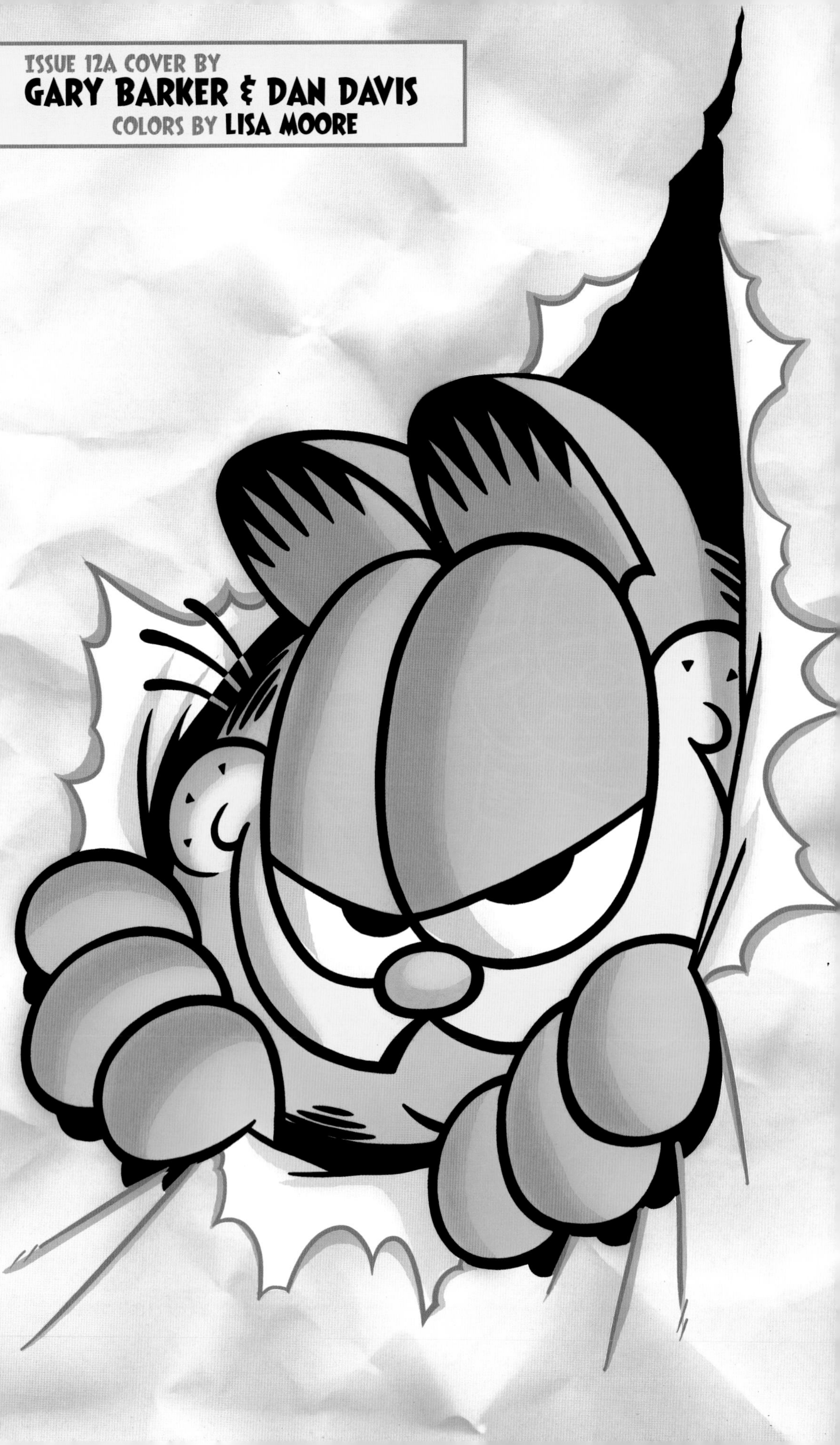

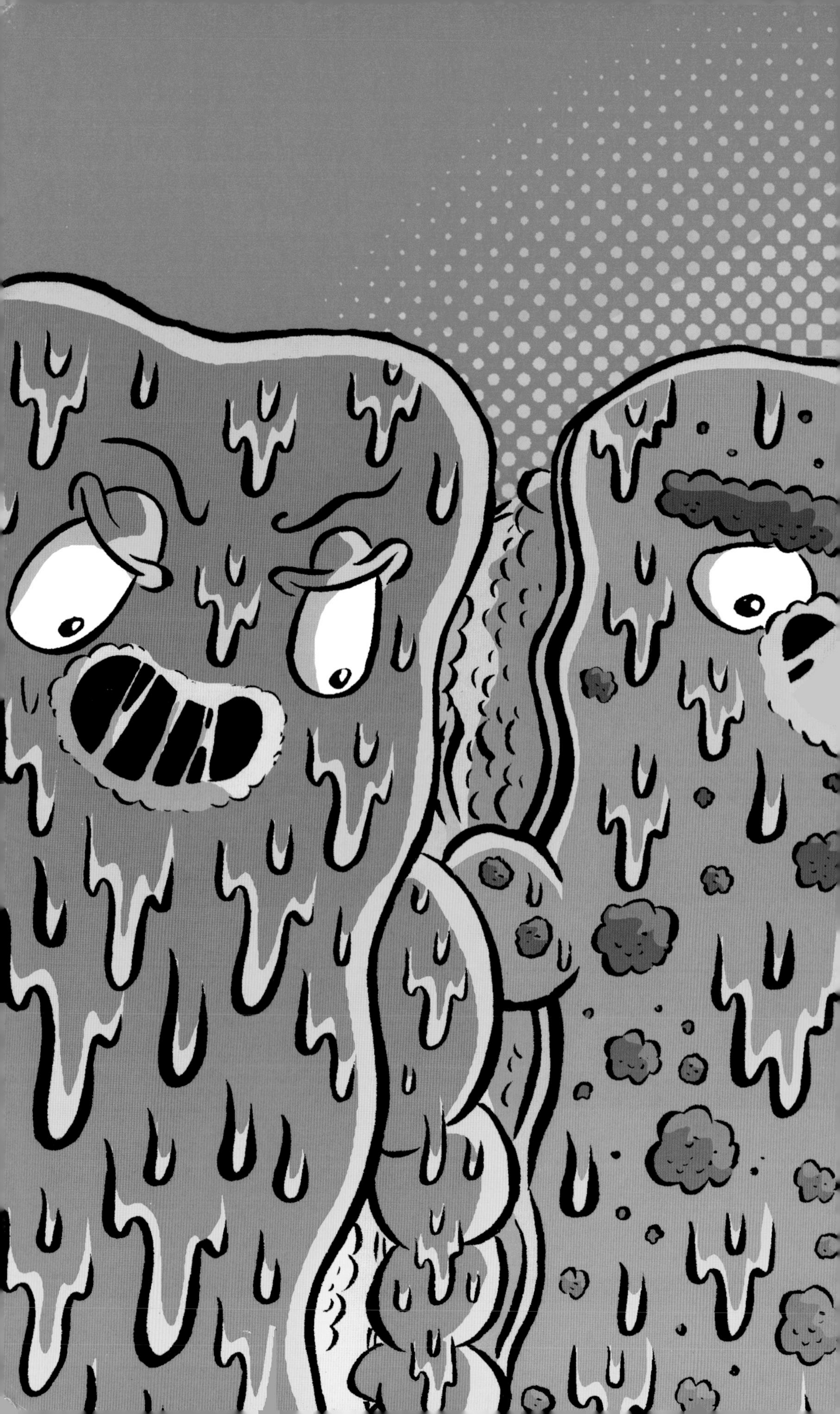

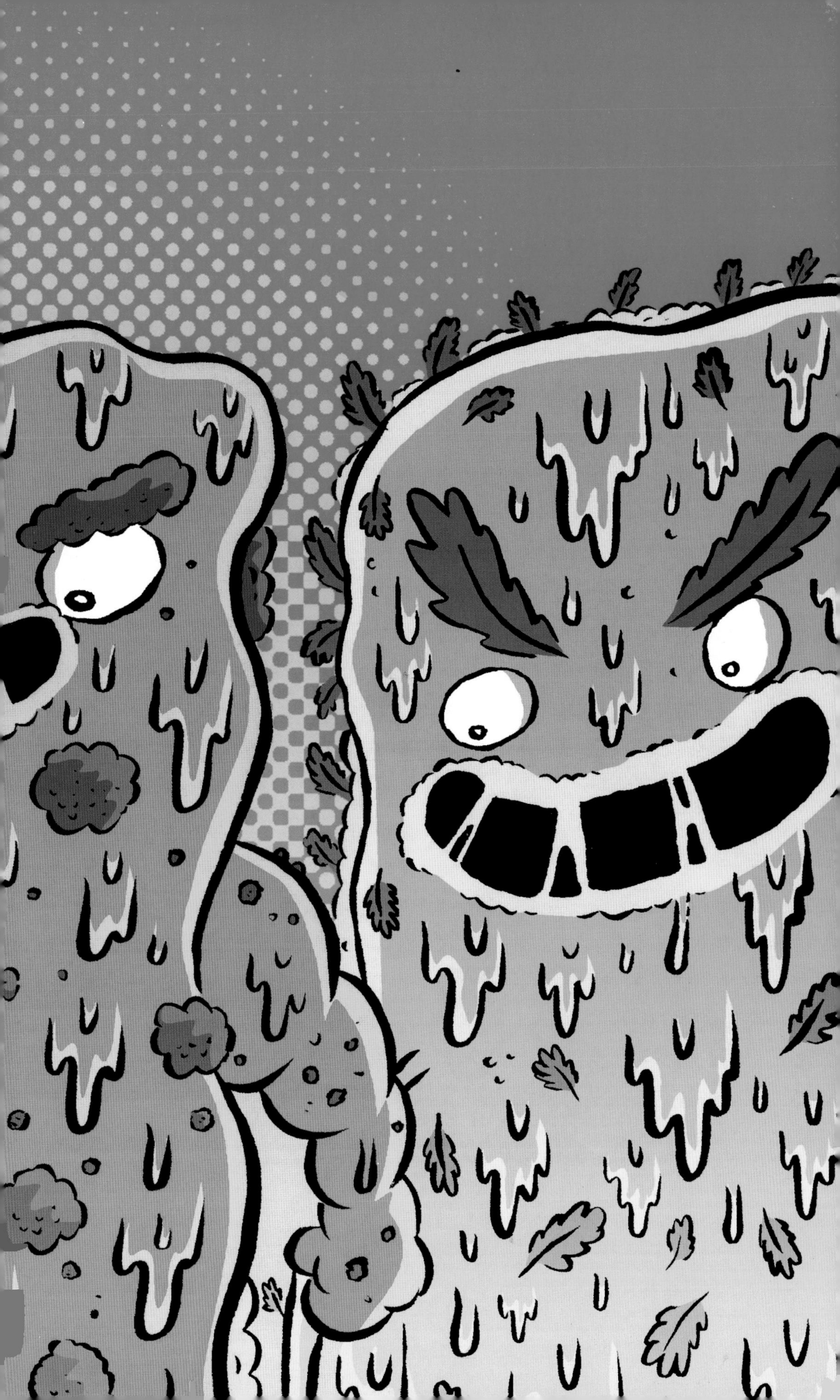